THE UNWELCOME WAGON

WAGON

Book & Mug Mysteries
Book 1

By Michelle L. Levigne

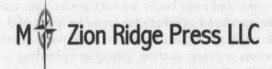

M ✦ Zion Ridge Press LLC

Mt Zion Ridge Press LLC
295 Gum Springs Rd, NW
Georgetown, TN 37366

https://www.mtzionridgepress.com

ISBN 13: 978-1-955838-18-4

Published in the United States of America
Publication Date: April 1, 2022

Copyright © 2022 Michelle L. Levigne

Editor-In-Chief: Michelle Levigne
Executive Editor: Tamera Lynn Kraft

Cover art design by Tamera Lynn Kraft
Cover Art Copyright by Mt Zion Ridge Press LLC © 2022

Chapter One

Wednesday, August 17

"What is that smell?"

Kai Shane inhaled again, despite the burn already settling into his sinuses, as he entered the office he shared with his cousins, Eden Cole and Troy Hunter. He looked around the wide-open room that took up half the second floor and found Eden, but not Troy. This early in the morning, he was probably working in the rooftop greenhouse.

The light next to the stairwell door that indicated if there was a client in the office had been off, otherwise Kai would have held his peace. Or maybe just turned around and headed back downstairs without entering. He winced in sympathy for Eden and whatever she had endured dealing with this latest visitor. He waved the cash bag with that morning's receipts for the coffee shop through the air. It didn't help dissipate the nearly visible cloud of stink.

"Did your last appointment leave that?" His throat tried to close up for a moment. "Whew!"

If anything, the smell got stronger as he approached her desk. Sort of fruity, but with a tang to it like a can of fermenting fruit cocktail had been opened just before it exploded. The burn hitting the back of his throat was just that. Something had burned. He looked around, expecting to see smoke in the air.

"I'm starting a new policy," Eden said, stepping away from the small vent she had just opened in the glass block front wall of the office.

It used to be a long panorama of wavy, antique glass from one corner to the other, looking down on Center Avenue, the heart of Cadburn Township. The cousins had removed it when they renovated the building. Eden had opened all four vents, six inches high and a foot wide, in the glass block wall.

"From now on, it isn't enough to ban smoking up here, I'm banning smokers. If they want to hire me, we meet in the park, or ..." She shrugged and dropped into her old-fashioned wooden swivel chair in front of her workspace. All three of her computers were audibly ticking, actively running programs and old-fashioned geometric screen savers.

"Some place where the smell won't offend our friends?" Kai guessed. "What does B.O. Plenty Junior want you to find for him?"

Eden grinned and leaned back, threatening the hinges and gears of the chair, and stretched her arms over her head. "Gonna get us all in trouble with the powers-that-wanna-be."

"Don't tell me. Another disgruntled citizen wants help declaring the last election null and void? Wouldn't it be easier, and faster, to just hire a hitman and take out that rotter?"

"According to the newest gossip, he has hitmen in his pocket." She dug her knuckles into her temples for a few seconds as Kai settled into his own chair at the workstation that sat between hers and Troy's. She finished by raking her fingers through her dark chocolate curls, dislodging the clip that held her mane off her neck.

"What does he need a hitman for when he's got Dudley Do-Wrong spying for him? The guy's got just enough brains to stop short of giving Sunderson reason to boot him off the force." He punctuated his complaint with a grin and the thud of his sandal-clad feet landing on the extension arm of his workstation. "Tell me, who's the hero of the month?"

"Nobody from the township, as far as I can tell. That's what makes it interesting."

"Better chance of unseating his royal lowness if he's out of arm's reach."

"Besides, you know I can't share details while the case is active." Eden wrinkled up her nose, turned to put her back to him, and tapped the keyboard of the middle monitor.

"Until you need some brainstorming help."

"I might at that. He's looking for books."

"The city accounting books? Or maybe historical records?" That got Kai's interest. According to his cousins, he would rouse from his death bed for an old or rare book.

"He's looking for family journals. And historical documents. He says - - *says*," she emphasized, and turned to face him again, "the truth has been covered over, or rewritten, or both, and if he finds the journals of Silas Cadburn and his sons, he could rewrite the history of the township. And undo a lot of legal action, a lot of title transfers and what-have-you, over the last fifteen, twenty years."

"Cadburn ... journals?" Kai held still, though his neck muscles ached from the urge to turn and look, up to the third floor. As if he could see through the ceiling/floor and walls. Specifically, to the hidden panel in the wall between his apartment and Troy's. "Interesting."

He didn't move. Years of surviving the foster care system had taught him the kind of poker face Bret, Bart and Beau Maverick would have envied. He could convince Torquemada he was innocent. Eden and Troy were the masters of investigation, but Kai was the perfect, believable wall of integrity and innocence that shielded their efforts to find out where they came from, what had happened to their parents, and who they really were.

Six years ago, the cousins had come to Cadburn Township on the trail of someone who might know their lost pasts and identities. They had come up against a dead end but had fallen in love with the town and decided to stay. Thanks to Troy's business acumen, they had the funds to buy the Aurora Building -- named for a Cadburn daughter. The Book & Mug coffee shop and bookstore, Kai's domain, took up the first floor. The second floor held Eden's apartment and the office for the three cousins, where Eden ran Finders as a private investigator. The third floor held Kai's apartment and Troy's. Most of Troy's apartment was kitchen, where he experimented with holistic medicines and herbals. The roof of the building held Troy's greenhouse and the cousins' patio for sunbathing and stargazing.

During the renovation of the Aurora Building, they had taken everything down to the studs and discovered a trove of old books, wrapped in multiple layers of cloth and plastic, inside the walls.

Roger Cadburn, descendant of Silas and head trustee, had set himself against them from the moment the cousins inquired about buying the building. He had been even nastier when they donated the first few books they found to the self-proclaimed Cadburn Historical Society instead of handing them over to him.

The cousins had debated whether that gesture of good will would be seen as wimping out or sucking up. Troy had wanted to keep the books for future ammunition in the war they had never declared. Eden wanted to donate the books to the Western Reserve Historical Society, totally bypassing all township politics. Kai, however, loved books enough to believe they belonged with their owner's descendants, no matter how nasty they might be. He had tried to discuss the books, to determine if Roger was interested. The prickly trustee was just contrary enough to have a snit fit if they didn't turn over the books to the "proper authorities." That was one of his catchphrases during township business meetings.

Roger had cut him off the two times he tried to approach him about the books, in public, with witnesses. He had been so nasty, Kai felt no guilt turning to the local historical society. He and his cousins had decided to say nothing about the second and third caches of books they'd discovered. When the people of Cadburn Township finally got fed up and voted Roger out of office, then they would quietly turn the books over to proper authorities. For now, Kai thought of the books as an insurance policy.

Maybe it was immature and mean-spirited to withhold the old books that probably could be traced to the Cadburn family -- but then, Roger was even more so. Maybe the cousins had given up too soon, trying to make peace, but there were some people who were better off left behind a wall of silent animosity.

Kai determined early on that the glares and snide, double-edged comments from Roger and his supporters were actually good for business. People supported Book & Mug to irritate Roger's sycophants, who in turn refused to darken the door of the bookstore and coffee shop. It was a win-win.

3

Eden didn't much care about the opinion of politicians in her line of work. The good will of Captain Sunderson and the Cadburn Township police department was more important.

Troy focused on his herbal research, ignoring the sniping on both sides. He found some amusement in imagining the shock and chagrin, and resultant bootlicking, if anyone ever learned how vast his investments were, and the extent of his financial wizardry. He could buy half the township at a moment's notice if he wanted. If necessary, to rescue their friends and supporters from Roger and his bullies. For now, he kept that weapon hidden. Surprise was the most potent weapon of all.

As much as they could, the cousins ignored the wall Roger Cadburn and his social-climber wife kept reinforcing, seeing slights and insults at every turn. They avoided the power couple to protect each other and let the Cadburns smack their heads against the wall whenever possible.

"Yeah," Eden said, and for a moment they shared wry matching smiles that emphasized their family resemblance. "First step is determining if this client has any claim. I don't take anyone's word for it when it comes to the history of this town. We finally found a place to put down roots, and we're going to protect it. Even from a client who paid up front." She sighed, leaned back a little, and rubbed her eyes. "In cash."

"Uh huh." Kai felt sorry for Eden. Not that she would ever let herself be cheated by a client no matter how sad or believable their story or circumstances might be. He pitied her when she had to deal with people who lied to the person they were turning to for help to find justice, or resolution, or closure.

"I'm heading out soon to the bank." She arched her back, generating one loud crack of releasing tension. "Make sure that stack of hundreds is legit."

"Guy must be desperate. Or have a lot to hide." He snorted and thought about adding that anyone having to deal with the Cadburn family probably was desperate, and afraid of something. He didn't say it though. He had lived in Cadburn long enough, and learned enough of the history, to have some respect for the founding father and his family. Too bad the current heir of the name and legacy did nothing to earn respect. Every action indicated Roger believed the universe, not just the people of Cadburn, owed him. Everything.

Eden's co-conspirator and hardware specialist, Rufus Lucciola, arrived with a *clang-bang* of the old brass elevator as Kai was putting the cash bag in the floor safe. He called out a greeting as the young man wheeled his chair into the office and headed through the storage room to the stairwell. The aroma trail of fruity-bitter smoke from Eden's client had cleared from the stairwell. Why did that strike him as odd? He paused on the landing between first and second floor, and in the quiet, he heard a car driving past.

He shouldn't have heard any sounds from the street. The building renovations had included heavy fire and security doors. Kai turned left at the bottom of the stairs, instead of right, and checked the door leading out to the street. It was ajar, maybe less than a quarter inch. Enough to hear street sounds. He tugged on the handle without turning the knob. The door came open. A blob of what looked like poster putty blocked the hole for the heavy bolt.

Behind him, the door into the stairwell from the coffee shop opened. Kai didn't bother looking. Only two other people had the key to get to the stairwell from inside Book & Mug, and Eden was still upstairs. That left their cousin Troy, now stepping into the stairwell. He focused on digging out the putty.

"Okay, that's interesting," Troy said, looking over Kai's shoulder. He brought with him a green scent, and the bitter aroma of fertilizer, meaning he had just come back from ransacking a local garden supply store. "Who did we let in this far, who wants to get back in without our permission?"

"More important question. What'll it take to change the security system to warn us when somebody pulls a trick like this again? Maybe on both doors?" Kai finally had all the putty in a ball in his fist.

"I just love how E manages to find the most interesting clients." Troy reached past him and tested the door. It didn't open until he turned the knob. They headed up the stairs together.

Eden wasn't in her office, but her apartment door was open. Troy sat down at his workstation and opened the program running the security cameras for the building. He had just reached the screen that let them choose a time and camera to play back when she came out with her purse over one shoulder and taking a few hopping steps as she put on her shoes.

Kai explained to her what had happened while Troy cued the playback. The smelly client was clever enough not to stand there in the open doorway and visibly block the door bolt. They had to rewind the video several times to catch the moment when he paused and opened the door just a little, giving enough room to insert the putty. The smoothness of his motions, the certainty of his aim, indicated this was something he was good at, maybe practiced often.

The security video wasn't much help, because the man kept his head turned, indicating he knew the camera was there. What he couldn't know, hopefully, was that Eden recorded every visit with clients from several angles, for security purposes and to protect herself from malpractice claims.

She had learned the hard way with a problem client near the beginning of her business. He insisted she had verbally promised something that was impossible to deliver. He had demanded his money back when Eden's investigation didn't give the results he wanted. Fortunately, she was good enough to find proof that was his standard practice with everyone. Even more fortunately, the man was paranoid about social media and hadn't done anything to trash her reputation before she'd gained enough leverage to stop him in his tracks. She also included acknowledgement in the client contract that all meetings were recorded.

Kai headed downstairs to attend to business while Eden got to work harvesting images from the security system. He was gone nearly an hour, going through a crate of books that his buyer, Devona Lucciola, had just brought in. When he returned to the office, Eden was still working on that task, with Troy sitting nearby, offering suggestions.

"Problem." Eden frowned and gestured at the multiple images on one computer screen. "I think the guy was wearing a very good wig and maybe even makeup."

Kai wondered if the client hadn't really been interested in hiring Eden's investigative services, because he hadn't signed the contract before he left. He had promised to come back in a week, when he would give Eden more details of what he wanted her to find. What did he really want that he would lie to get into the building and prepare a way to get back in without the cousins knowing? What did he think he could find or accomplish by sneaking into the building?

Images of the client from different angles filled all three of her monitors. Jacob Styles, if that was his real name, was just shy of looking so average he would blend into a crowd. There was something about him that struck Kai as familiar. When he mentioned that, both his cousins agreed. Styles looked like someone they all knew, but the resemblance was too slight for them to agree on who that might be, after nearly twenty minutes of thinking, making suggestions, and turning them down.

Glasses with slightly blue-tinted lenses blurred the color of his eyes.

"They could be brown," Eden said. "No way of telling."

"And do we really want to get close enough to him and that stink to find out?" Kai muttered.

She jabbed backward with her elbow, getting him in the hip. Kai and Troy both stood behind her, looking over her shoulders. Styles had a receding hairline and his medium brown hair was trimmed short and neat. Just like his beard.

"The hair could be fake too," Troy pointed out.

Eden agreed and mentioned several instances where men she had been hired to find were too easy to identify because they got sloppy about beards and hair styles. They thought shaving would render them just as unrecognizable as Superman putting on Clark Kent's glasses.

Styles wore a sport jacket despite the August warmth, pale blue, with a darker blue polo-style shirt underneath, new-looking jeans, and conspicuously clean black sneakers. Other than the impression that all his clothes were new, his only distinctive feature was the smell.

After some discussion, they agreed with Eden's impression: a fruity, cheap cigar made to imitate something expensive and imported.

"Almost wish you hadn't taken that gunk out of the door," Troy said.

"We could just set a trap for the guy, wait until he comes back, then find out what he's after."

"And if he comes with a gun?" Eden said. "This is one of those times that make me seriously consider changing my policy on no guns. He specifically mentioned looking for historic books and documents. Journals. Maybe this was a feint, to see what we know."

"We don't know anything. Yet." Kai took a few steps backward toward the door to the storeroom that opened onto the stairwell. He did have a business to run, and firmly believed the owner should work just as hard as the employees. "The thing is, he'll know that we know or at least suspect something, when he comes back and can't get in."

"Cover our backsides," Eden said. "I have to go check on that money. While I'm out, I'll stop in and talk with Sunderson, ask her to keep it quiet, but ask the foot patrol cops to keep their eyes open. Just in case."

"Wish there was more we could do," Troy muttered, still leaning over her shoulder to study the multiple images of Styles. "I can order more gear to beef up the security, but ..." He shook his head and stepped away to go to his computer.

Kai headed back downstairs to the coffee shop. He needed to attend to his business. He trusted his employees, but he wasn't the type to leave everything in their hands for long stretches of time. Besides, time away from the puzzle, focused on other things, could lead to unexpected brainstorms.

Chapter Two

Thursday, August 18

Saundra Bailey waited a full thirty seconds after her apartment door closed behind the movers. Then she hurried to the door, tugged it open an inch, and listened for the telltale *cling-clank* of the old-fashioned brass cage elevator opening. Three sets of footsteps, and the rattle of the furniture dolly, then the *clank-cling-click* of the elevator door closing. She shut the door, thick enough to block the groan of the elevator descending. Another thing she loved about her new apartment.

She leaned back against the door and slid down a few inches and just luxuriated in the newness of everything.

New apartment. New town. New job. Out from under the eagle eye of her Mulcahy relatives, who kept watching her even though she had been ostracized. She had hoped changing her name to her mother's maiden name would be the last straw. The Mulcahy clan should have washed their hands of her at long last.

They hadn't. When Aunt Cleo found her the children's librarian position in Cadburn, Saundra had gladly jumped on it. She could always trust Cleo's judgment and promises. After all, they were all the family each other had, with all the acceptance and shelter and support the word implied.

Thinking of Aunt Cleo ...

Saundra pushed off the door and headed for the kitchen. Her three-bedroom apartment on the corner of the lovely old-fashioned building had two balconies. One off the living room, the other off the kitchen. Some previous tenant had left behind a little greenhouse that took up the kitchen balcony. Saundra suspected the family friends who had told Cleo about the job had chosen this apartment for her specifically because of the greenhouse. The movers had deposited the pots of plants and trays of seedlings and racks of glass bottles full of cuttings in nutrient solution in the greenhouse and kitchen. Time to arrange everything.

She took two steps to the kitchen balcony door, when the apartment door thudded softly, and the doorknob clicked. Saundra froze, half-expecting her noxious relatives to come barging through the door. Mulcahy money usually persuaded landlords to hand over keys, even when it was against policy and security standards. Saundra had lost count of the times she had come home to find Bridget or Edmund snooping or poised to deliver another lecture and list of ultimatums from their disapproving elders. Each time, she had the gnawing certainty they had searched her home before she arrived. Whatever they were searching for, they never found, because as far as she could tell, nothing ever went missing. She knew better than to trust to luck for that to endure for much longer. If moving five hours away didn't guarantee her some privacy and security at long last, she didn't know what she would do.

The door rattled. Louder. Like the person on the other side couldn't believe the door was locked.

Saundra had sworn after her mother died that she wouldn't let her father's family bully her any longer. Pulling her shoulders back and taking a deep breath, she crossed the living room and reached for the doorknob. Again, the door rattled. A burst of rare fury gave her speed. She twisted the knob and yanked the door open.

A yelp and a cloud of fruity cigar smoke struck her before she saw the man who was bent over, holding onto the key he had been trying to insert in the lock. He straightened and took a step forward. For a second, she thought he might stab her with the key.

"Can I help you with something?" She wanted to growl, but she did need to be careful of first impressions. She was the new children's librarian. The last thing she needed was to hack off a local who would turn out to be someone important.

He glared at her, then went up on his toes to look over her and past her.

"You have the wrong apartment." She gripped the door frame with her left hand and tightened her grip on the doorknob with her right. Just in case he tried to bully his way inside.

Lines deepened around his eyes and mouth and for a second, she was sure he would burst out with something angry and filthy. Instead, the stranger stumbled backward, into a strong beam of sunlight from the window at the end of the hall, then turned, aiming for the elevator. Saundra cataloged his features as Aunt Cleo had taught her. Receding, greasy, gray-streaked mousy brown hair. Razor-burn on his face. Ratty black T-shirt, sagging jeans held up with a rivet-studded belt that belonged in the 70s. Pot belly, narrow hips, acne-scarred complexion. Furious brown eyes that compelled her attention, so she noticed the green ring around the iris. That fruity-rancid cigar aroma.

He looked back once as he went around the corner and Saundra shivered at the threat in those eyes. She could only hope he was a local lunatic everybody ignored. A visitor, and not a resident of this building. She didn't need to get the evil eye from him every time they met up in the hall or the laundry room. Her work as a librarian had exposed her to too many people who felt entitled to punish others when they themselves were in the wrong.

10

"It's not going to be like this," she murmured as she closed the door and checked the security chain. Should she take it as a good sign that there was only one chain, not three, and only one rather than two deadbolts like she had needed in her last apartment? "Cleo promised Cadburn is nice, safe, and quiet."

Saundra slid the chain into place and took a deep breath. Forget the weird incident. Get back on track. Where?

Right. The greenhouse on the balcony. Aunt Cleo's collection of rare herbs and miniature trees with aromatic bark entrusted to Saundra's care had top priority.

The movers had finished hauling in her belongings at 10am. One of the benefits of a relatively spartan existence other than the embarrassment of riches in plants and books. By 11:30, Saundra was done in the greenhouse. A few spots in the plastic panels of the walls and roof had thin cracks and would have to be replaced before winter struck Ohio. Saundra had also identified places where the caulking needed to be refreshed, but otherwise she was pleased. The heater and watering system were dusty enough to indicate the last tenant hadn't used them, but other than that they were practically new.

Unpack two dozen paper ream boxes of books now, or venture out to see what the little township of Cadburn offered in restaurants? Be virtuous and walk the five blocks to the center of town, or drive? Detour to the Cadburn Township Library? Introduce herself to Mrs. Tinderbeck, her new boss, even though she wasn't supposed to report for work until Monday?

A knock on the door startled a little yelp out of her. Saundra took a step back and held her breath. Then a moment later let it out with another gush. What was she afraid of? Other than Stinky Cigar Man having got up his courage to try again.

Saundra raked her fingers through her hair as she headed for the door. She rubbed at her face just in case she had been careless and got soil or green fertilizer solution on her face. This morning, in the hotel in Strongsville, she had resolved she would make a fresh start and treat everyone as if they wanted to be her friends. Other than Stinky Cigar Man, of course. Her hand still shook a little as she pulled the door open.

"Saundra." The woman's freckled face showed few lines despite the silver streaks in her short-bobbed cinnamon hair. The man standing behind her, holding a paper ream box without a lid, had a smile as wide as his face, and a deeply receding gray hairline. "There you are, darling! Welcome to Cadburn."

Patty Hill and her brother, Roy Fitz, old family friends, had passed along news of the librarian position and found the apartment for her.

They exchanged hugs despite full arms. Patty had a heavy cotton shopping bag that Saundra estimated had to weigh at least ten pounds when she handed it over. Roy chuckled and tipped his head to touch

Saundra's forehead when she hugged him, then headed for the kitchen with the box.

She smelled chili and what she hoped was apple pie as he passed her. A moment later, her stomach rumbled.

Patty laughed. "Good timing? I hope you don't mind us barging in like this. I remember what it was like when I moved to town to look after Roy two years ago, and I had a furnished house to move into."

Roy was the pastor of Cadburn Bible Chapel. Patty had come to town to act as secretary and general organizer, keep the ministries untangled, and make sure he ate decently and wore clean clothes, in Roy's words.

The bag Patty handed over was from the Welcome Wagon, full of flyers and coupons from every business in Cadburn, and samples of products. Cookies from Sugarbush Bakery. Grapes and a wedge of cheese from Green's Grocery. A magnetic notepad and attached pen from The Office. An assortment of two-pill packets of pain relievers and antacids from Corner Drug. Roy pointed out the coupon from Book & Mug, a coffee shop and bookstore, offering a dollar off a book and a free large specialty drink of the day.

The siblings helped her organize her kitchen and living room before they sat down to devour the chili that was Roy's specialty, and half the apple pie. All the boxes were emptied and crushed and tossed down the garbage chute. Saundra learned more details about the town, especially what booths to visit first for that weekend's street festival. Cadburn regularly closed off Center Avenue, in the heart of the business district, and set up booths. The themes and activities and items for sale depended on the season, the weather, and the upcoming holidays. This weekend was the Back-to-School Festival, the transition from summer to fall. It offered goodies for students heading off to college and everything the local children could want to decorate their desks and lockers at school and start the new school year.

Roy and Patty offered advice on which businesses to visit first, to finish making her apartment home. The Welcome Wagon bag had a map of the center of town, which held most of the businesses and the municipal buildings, with the town park at the eastern end. Saundra wasn't surprised at all when they only discussed the businesses and owners they liked. No negative words from these people who were the next best thing to family for her and Cleo.

Saundra made note, however, of the places and people they *didn't* mention. There were very few of them. Patty teased Roy about focusing on Book & Mug.

"The girl needs to start meeting people right away. Why not start with someone who loves books as much as she does? You'll like the Musketeers," Roy said.

Anybody he recommended could be trusted, Saundra knew. Besides, someone who paired a used bookstore with a coffee shop was someone she would enjoy getting to know.

"Musketeers?" she asked.

"Kai Shane, Troy Hunter, and Eden Cole own the building. They live there. Cousins. Close as shadows. Troy's into investments and runs the Heart of Health -- that's a nutrition store. Eden does investigations, and Kai runs Book & Mug. You can't miss the building. There's three of them exactly alike on Center. Three stories, dark red brick, with the name in pink granite across the top front face. For the Cadburn daughters. Book & Mug is in Aurora, but everybody calls it the Mug Building now." He chuckled. "Rankles Roger to no end."

"Roy," Patty murmured, and made as if she would slap his hand. He chuckled louder.

"Don't get me started on small-town politics. Anyway, even if you don't see the name, you'll know the building. The only one in town with a greenhouse on the roof."

"With all Cleo's plants you're growing," Patty added with a chuckle, "Roy should have just mentioned the greenhouse and left out the rest."

When Roy opened the door to leave, Saundra thought she glimpsed a black T-shirt. She hurried to the door to look out into the hall, but no sign of Stinky Cigar.

"Something wrong?" Roy exchanged that crinkled forehead look with Patty that Saundra hated. It always meant someone was keeping a secret from her to protect her. She was twenty-six years old, for heaven's sake -- she didn't need protecting anymore.

With a quiet sigh, Saundra organized her thoughts and explained as simply as she could, just to get it over with.

"What does this fellow look like?" Roy asked. Something in his tone, a new intensity, made her wonder if this had happened to other people, and Stinky Cigar Man had a reputation.

She described the man. "Do you know him?"

"He doesn't sound familiar," Patty said slowly. "Which means he could be a stranger. You said he was trying to use a key to get in?"

"That's what it looked like to me. But the key was dark bronze, from that little glimpse I had, and our keys are silver."

"Makes sense," Roy said with a grunt. "They renovated this building about ten, fifteen years ago. The owners got caught up in a big urban renewal project. Sank a lot of money into refurbishing a bunch of buildings. Then the economy tanked, and some employee embezzled millions and ran. Businesses were closing. They had to sell a handful of properties to stay afloat. Kind of sad."

Saundra wondered what the chances were that the man who had been at her door was a former tenant from that long ago and had held onto his key when he moved out. Maybe he had been evicted?

She shook off her questions as she and Patty and Roy made their goodbyes. Just to prove she wasn't spooked, she left her door open and walked with them to the elevator. Her apartment was at the end of the hall. Anyone who wanted to get to her apartment would have to go past her in the elevator lobby.

The elevator binged, then click-creaked and the door folded back to reveal two women. *Overdressed* was the first word that came to Saundra's mind. They looked like they were going to a garden party, with flowered sundresses and purses and sandals and jewelry all coordinated -- one in lavender and the other in coral. The big-brimmed sun hats really were too much.

The platinum blonde held a Welcome Wagon bag, just like the one Patty had given Saundra three hours ago.

"Oh ... Patty. What a coincidence running into you." Her pale blue gaze slid over Roy like he wasn't even there, then landed on Saundra. "Or maybe not?"

"Well, there was so much chatter at the meeting, I guess you didn't hear when I said three times I would be handling this Wagon visit." Patty wore that cool smile that held no malice, yet warned she wouldn't let the nastiness or stupidity of others ruin her day.

"And I guess you didn't hear --" She let out a sharp-edged sigh when her companion touched her with a glossy manicured fingertip that matched her coral outfit. "Well, this isn't a very nice welcome to the neighborhood, is it?"

"On the contrary," Saundra said, repressing a shudder. This was starting to sound too much like a power play, put-her-in-her-place lecture she had heard too many times growing up. "Patty and Pastor Roy are old family friends, and I can't think of any nicer way to be welcomed to my new home."

"Old friends," the other woman murmured. "You know, Ashley ... Patty did say that. And the by-laws do say --"

"I know what they say," Ashley snapped. Her gaze went up and down Saundra, measuring her. "Well ..." Her sigh clearly indicated she felt somewhat abused. She held out the loaded Welcome Wagon bag. "If you're Sandy Bailey, then welcome to Cadburn Township."

"Uh ... thanks." Saundra mustered a smile -- her practiced one, for dealing with entitlement-attitude parents who wanted to tailor the library reading program to suit their child, and only their child, ignoring all the other children's needs and interests and educational levels. "I'm looking forward to learning more about the area."

She took the bag. It didn't feel as full as the one Patty had given her. A pause, to let them say more. But they didn't. Both turned as if on cue to look at her open apartment door. A flicker of irritation had her tip her head back a little. If they wanted her to invite them in, they were going to have to ask. She was done with being intimidated into being the civil one all the time.

14

"And you are?" she said, after a few more seconds of ringing silence.

"Ye gads," the coral-clad woman said with a chuckle that made her seem much warmer and more welcoming than Ashley. "How could we forget that?" Her gaze darted to Patty, who just stood there with her cool smile, silently letting the two of them do their own damage and damage-control. "Colette Daily. This is Ashley Cadburn. She's president of the Welcome Wagon."

"I'm honored. Thanks so much."

This time only Ashley glanced again at her open door. Silently, Saundra ordered them to leave. Before the situation got even more awkward than it already was.

"You're not going to invite us in, are you?" Ashley said.

"You haven't even stepped out of the elevator and onto the floor, ladies," Roy pointed out with a warm chuckle. That got a grin and a bit of a blush from Colette, but Ashley's eyes went frosty.

"Already turning her against us? Not even giving us a chance to get to know her?" She turned to Patty.

"I haven't said a word about anyone in Welcome Wagon," Patty said, raising her hands in a gesture of innocence.

"Patty and Roy have only had good things to tell me about the township and the people who live here," Saundra offered. She would have preferred to point out how anti-welcoming these Welcome Wagon officials were right now. She knew better, though.

"How nice of them," Ashley said.

"So, Saundra, what brings you to Cadburn?" Colette said.

"We should get going," Patty said. "Breakfast, Sunday?"

"Wouldn't miss it." Saundra almost asked where they were going, when Patty and Roy headed down the hall, but she saw the neat little brass sign pointing the way to the stairs. She was only on the second floor, so it wasn't a hardship to have them walk. Besides, Ashley and Colette were still standing in the elevator. She turned back to face them. "You were saying? What brings me here? I'm the new children's librarian."

"Librarian. So you're the one ..." Ashley let out a sigh and her expression seemed to warm a little. Not enough to give Saundra any hope this encounter could be salvaged.

"One what?"

Ashley shrugged, her smile turning brittle. Saundra knew that expression from too many unpleasant situations, where someone saw herself as being magnanimous in the face of some unwarranted insult or attack. Then she muffled a little gasp and hoped her expression stayed neutral, when she remembered something Mrs. Tinderbeck had told her. Many community groups met at the library, including the Welcome Wagon. She wasn't going to be able to avoid these women, was she? How long before they forgot this awkward first meeting?

15

"Well, we should probably get going, too," Colette said. "You probably have gobs of unpacking to do."

"One of the downsides of moving." Saundra knew better than to offer the information that Roy and Patty had helped her.

"Well, we'll see you Saturday at the booth, at least," the other woman continued. "You do know about the street festival?"

"Oh, yes. Looking forward to it. Patty and Pastor Roy have had nothing but good to say about town since he first moved here. I'm so glad to be living here now."

Please, please, end this misery and just leave?

Finally, they did, with Ashley still smiling her brittle smile. Saundra sagged in relief when the elevator doors closed and she heard it descend. She didn't feel completely alone in the hallway, though. She tried not to run the dozen or so feet to her apartment door. Just in case someone was watching. Her heart beat a little faster for a few moments after she locked the door behind her.

~~~~~

By the end of the long, achy-tired day, Saundra had worked out of her spooked feelings. She loved the old-fashioned apartment with all the lovely little details, like deep windows that would double as seats when she had bought some good thick cushions. The high ceilings. The wooden floors with borders in geometric patterns in different shades of wood. Built-in cabinets on either side of the gas fireplace. A clawfoot tub long enough to stretch out and soak. She decided she had earned a little indulgence.

First, though, she made good use of the hidden compartment in one of the window seats, to put away important documents and Cleo's strongbox. Roy had been good friends with a previous tenant, so he knew to tell Saundra about two secure hiding places in the apartment. She was quite pleased to have difficulty finding the right place to press down and unsettle the wooden panel before she could lift the lid. That would make it all the harder for intruders and snoops and thieves to discover. Once she had the window seats covered with thick cushions, no one would ever suspect anything was hidden inside.

With that final task accomplished, she could relax. Tonight, she ordered Chinese food delivered from the Celestial Dragon and ate while watching *Galaxy Quest* for at least the twentieth time. Grocery shopping was on the list for tomorrow. She ended moving day with a long hot soak in that glorious tub, with lemon-scented bath salts.

~~~~~

Curtis Bridgewater came to the Guzzlers meeting at Book & Mug that evening with a black eye. The Tweed cousins, Cilla and Melba, fussed over him. Kai fought not to smile as the big, shuffling man visibly wobbled back and forth between feeling foolish and lapping up the cooing attention like a puppy.

That pretty much described Curtis, one of the town's characters. An earlier era, less politically correct, would have kindly labeled him "slow." The mockery and people taking advantage of him would have been much more open, even encouraged in some circles. Kai had decided Cadburn was just the sort of town he wanted to live in when he had met Curtis on that first visit and saw how the "challenged" people were treated. What a lot of people didn't realize, and Eden had discovered first, was that Curtis knew everything about everyone. Especially the history of the township, going back several generations. Maybe further. Curtis, his father, grandmother, and her siblings, had been something like family retainers for the Cadburn family. That translated into them handling maintenance and managing the three Cadburn buildings on Center Avenue, and various other properties once owned by the family. Including the grand old apartment complex where a woman who called herself Sybil Orwell had lived. That was the last of many names Eden had been able to uncover for the woman who might have tossed the cousins into the foster care system and then figuratively threw away the key. As far as their investigations had revealed, Sybil -- if that was her real name -- had trashed every bit of documentation that would reveal their identities and help them find their real families.

Curtis remembered Sybil. He remembered everyone who had lived in the apartment building. He remembered incredible things, funny stories and tragic. The problem, in Kai's estimation, was that Curtis was an incredibly polite man. Or perhaps *inhibited* was the more accurate word. He didn't share his stories until he was asked. Many people held the general opinion that Curtis wasn't just slow, he was stupid, and had very little worthwhile to offer the world. So they never asked, and never learned all the things he could teach them about their own hometown.

Kai believed differently. He and his cousins took Curtis under their wings when they settled in town, and he had rewarded them with an almost embarrassing intensity of loyalty. That hadn't earned him any points with the bullies and politicians like Cadburn and his sidekicks. Chances were good that Roger was behind this latest assault on Curtis to get back at the cousins or someone else who valued the big, elderly man. Not that Trustee Cadburn would ever soil his hands with violence, but he would be behind it.

The worst part in all this? Kai couldn't ask Curtis which Cadburn minion had hit him. Curtis had an unbreakable, aggravating sense of loyalty to the Cadburn family. He wouldn't say anything mean about any of them. Even if it was true. Even if his testimony would help to convince people that all Roger's skills in running the township so efficiently didn't make up for what a rotter he was and a miserable excuse for a pseudo-human being.

So tonight, Kai silently apologized to Curtis for anything he might have done lately to rile Roger, by whipping up the most incredible frozen coffee confection extravaganza to cheer the big, friendly, bashful old man.

That was the official reason for the meeting after all. The Guzzlers met every third Thursday to help Kai come up with new coffee or tea or frozen drinks for Book & Mug, or find names for the ones he had invented since the last meeting.

Most of the meeting was spent just talking and catching up on each other's lives. There were fourteen official Guzzlers, but only five met tonight. The others were busy with last-minute chores for the street festival. Set-up would commence tomorrow, starting with the official placement of the barricades along Center Avenue. Kai anticipated extra business in the coffee shop from the workers setting up the booths, and then the people who would be occupying those booths, when they took breaks from the August sun and heat. He already had dozens of water bottles jammed in all the refrigerators getting cold. The water would be free, as a good will gesture. And not just because he knew those who came in for water would be tempted by the pastries and sandwiches and candy he offered, or browse in the bookstore side of the shop. When he was feeling especially crabby, he was willing to admit that the good will gesture irritated Cadburn and his group of cynics and sourpusses. Knowing that was reward enough.

Even though he thought it might turn out disgusting, Kai whipped up a concoction of frozen crème de menthe, swirled into the glass with chocolate and peppermint syrups, with chocolate whipped cream on top, and sprinkled with crushed peppermint sticks. He hoped no one would ask how old the peppermint sticks were. They had actually been on a shelf in the back room, waiting to be tossed. Olivia, his chief barista, had found them during the regular ridding of the storage room. He had saved them just because he knew Curtis liked anything peppermint, especially if they were green-and-white striped. The timing was perfect.

His choice was also perfect. The syrups didn't melt together into a disgusting brownish-reddish-greenish mess when he put them into the glass.

Curtis' eyes got wide and his mouth dropped open like a little kid. He even bounced in the booth seat a few times when Kai put the glass in front of him.

"You're a good boy," Cilla told Kai later, when he walked her and her cousin to the door. They were the last to leave when the group dispersed for the night. She tugged him down by his collar so she could plant a kiss on his forehead, then chuckled and rubbed her lavender lipstick off with the ball of her thumb. She ended on a sigh. "I don't know why some smart, lucky girl hasn't snatched you up already."

"Because the girls around here are too smart?" he quipped.

"Not smart enough." Melba shook her head. "All three of you need someone wonderful in your lives. Start another dynasty to run this town before that young snot runs it into the ground."

"Might want to be careful how loud you say that," Kai offered. He glanced up and down the street.

There were still a few cars in parking slots in front of the various restaurants and shops that were open late. He flinched when he saw a Cadburn black-and-white, then he recognized the dent in the bumper. That was Officer Shrieve's vehicle. Of course. Shrieve was a distant cousin of the Tweeds, and he always showed up to escort them home on Guzzler meeting night. The Tweeds refused to drive in nice weather, even though they lived four long blocks away. They were eighty-plus years old and insisted they had gotten to that age because "we don't coddle ourselves." He would drive a hundred yards behind them during the entire walk to their duplex, with his lights off, and they would pretend they didn't see him. Then on Sunday they would have some incredible bakery to give him on their way to church.

Kai loved the people of Cadburn. Most of them, anyway.

"Let him try something," Melba said, punctuated with a snort. She winked at him. "He used to be bearable. When that sweet Deirdre was still alive. We always hoped she'd make a decent human being out of him. Ever since that Ashley came into his life ... Well, they're perfect for each other. One of these days, he's going to finally go too far, and he'll be too proud to admit he was wrong. Then he'll be gone."

"Big arrogant booby of a bully," Cilla added.

"Uh, do you know ...?" Kai touched two fingers to his eye, then his lip.

The elderly cousins shrugged. They hadn't heard what had brought on Curtis' latest injury. That just meant whatever it was had happened quickly and recently. Sooner or later, the reason for the beating would make the rounds of the wagging tongues of Cadburn, and Kai would hear it. Too late to retaliate. Again.

Someday, he would be able to retaliate against Cadburn, and not just make it stick, but ensure Curtis was safe once and for all.

He was still thinking about that when he finished closing up the coffee shop and turned out the lights in the bookstore, lowered all the blinds, turned on the alarm system, and went upstairs. Eden had already gone to bed, and the office was dark when he peeked in. Kai went up the stairs to the third floor. Troy was at work with the door of his apartment open, meaning he wanted Kai to stop in. Something was steeping in the two-cup French press. It smelled spicy and looked purplish, with dark bits swirling around in the hot water. When Troy asked how the meeting had gone, Kai reported on Curtis' latest injury, and his need to retaliate.

"I bet Eden could dig up something strong enough to send the creep running. Get him ridden out of town on a rail." Troy tapped the glass side of the container, his gaze focused on the slowing swirl of the contents. "The problem is that he has connections, and they'll know the minute she starts digging. They're probably waiting for us to give them an excuse to strike. We ignore them, and they waste a lot of time and energy waiting for us to fight back. They do all our work for us, punishing themselves."

"Burning out a few dozen brain cells, too, hopefully," Kai offered. That got a snort from Troy.

"Wish I could figure out why he has to pick on Curtis."

"Do jerks like him need a reason or an excuse?"

Chapter Three

Friday, August 19

Saundra was up at 7 that morning, and out the door before 8. She drove, anticipating heavy shopping, and hit Green's Grocery and Seevers' Cleaver, the butcher shop and self-proclaimed source of the "best ribs on the North Coast." She oriented herself on the short drive, locating the important buildings: township hall, police station, parks office, fire department, and the long stretch of property that held all the Cadburn Township schools and the library.

The business district straddled Center Avenue, dead-ending on the east end at the park, with a basketball court, baseball diamond, soccer field, and fully equipped playground. To complete the quaint smalltown picture, it had a gazebo, a fountain, and wading pool. The south side of Center Avenue bumped up against a long, relatively straight section of Cadburn Creek which was wide enough to be considered a river. Many businesses on that side of the street had porches or decks that hung out over the water. The south side of the river looked to be a good ten feet higher than the north side, making Saundra imagine some tectonic shift in the far distant past of Northeast Ohio, with the river following the fault line where the land had parted. She remembered some mention in her research into Cadburn of the river here serving as a corridor for the Underground Railroad when it was much shallower and less treacherous to cross. There were tales of hidden tunnels from the river to the cellars of houses sheltering fugitive slaves.

The black lampposts lining the street looked old-fashioned, the street signs had old-style writing, and hanging pots of flowers hung from every other lamppost. Pairs of park benches painted dark green dotted the sidewalk, maybe ten feet apart. The benches were set up back-to-back, one facing the street and the other facing the storefronts. Saundra thought that was a logical arrangement. Most of the pairs sat near signs for the local bus route.

Not that buses were running today on Center Avenue. City services workers were putting up barricades on the streets that intersected with Center Avenue to allow for the booths to be set up for the street festival. Fortunately, there was plenty of municipal parking on lots a block away from Center. She had an easy time walking to the different shops she needed to visit. She finished her shopping with a quick stop at Book & Mug, just to get some fancy coffee to celebrate move-in day.

She stepped into the shady sanctuary of the coffee shop/bookstore and caught her breath. It was like stepping into a long-cherished daydream of what she would do when or if she ever retired from the library. The shop took up the entire width of the building, cool and welcoming, done all in dark wood. It was divided neatly in half, front to back, with coffee shop on the right and bookstore on the left. Booths lined the walls of the coffee shop, with four-seater tables in the open area between them. The right wall was cinderblock, painted to look like the street stretching out to the east toward the park. The divider wall separating bookstore from coffee shop was glass block, shoulder-height. On the other side were shoulder-height shelves full of books. The glass block wall made a corner about halfway back to the counter, extending the seating area of the coffee shop.

Saundra mentally planned her route to work to detour to the coffee shop. The library and schools were a straight shot down Longview Road from her apartment building. She could walk south on Willow to Center, down to Book & Mug, then north on Apple, to get to the library. If she walked, she could justify a cup every day. It was a decent trade-off, wasn't it? The exercise against the gas money saved against the cost of the coffee. And maybe if she read on her lunch break to reduce her to-be-read pile a little faster, she could regularly check all those bookshelves. Couldn't she?

For now, though, she restrained herself by only getting a half-pound of rum raisin coffee. Just to celebrate moving to a lovely new town that already felt like home. The barista, Olivia, was friendly and offered the news that a new shipment of books from an estate sale had been loaded on the shelves last night. When she called, a young woman she introduced as Devona stepped over from the bookstore side to give Saundra an idea of what types of books predominated among the new books. Devona's moon face lit up with the true delight of a booklover as she spoke.

Saundra yielded to temptation. She had to celebrate moving to Cadburn, after all. She bought three books, all the second books in series from three different authors. The symmetry of it amused her, so she was smiling when she stepped out of Book & Mug and headed east down Center.

At Willow, she would have to make a left turn to get to the municipal parking lot. She approached the corner. Someone had already set up a barricade, blocking car access to Center from Willow. Behind her, a child burst out in tears. She turned to look. A little girl with long ponytails, wearing pink shorts and T-shirt, came pelting down the sidewalk toward her. She dashed past Saundra and stumbled going down the curb. A man called out from the left coming up the intersecting street.

Saundra heard the car. The humming engine. The little girl went to her knees in the street. No sound of brakes.

That idiot driver didn't see the barricade, did he?

Before Saundra could think what to do, a big man stumbled past her, into the street, and scooped up the little girl. The driver of the car shouted, cursing, and brakes squealed. The big man fell forward, wrapping himself around the little girl.

Saundra dropped her shopping bag on the curb and went to her knees, reaching for the child. The man slowly uncurled, eyes wide with surprise, gasping a little. The driver jumped out of the car and ran around to the front.

"Curtis, you big dummy!" the driver shrieked, and drew back his foot to kick the man who was still lying on the pavement.

"Don't you dare!" Saundra snapped and vaulted to her feet.

"Hey, lady, you're not from around here. This is the town dummy. We can kick him around if we feel like it," he said with a sneer. Then he took a step back and looked her over and got that look she always hated. The one that Edmund's friends always used on her, meaning she was pretty enough for them to be nice, but they didn't think she had a brain in her head.

"You kick heroes?" She bent down and picked up the little girl, who wailed and clung to her and hid her face in the front of Saundra's shirt.

The man's mouth dropped open. He actually looked about twenty IQ points smarter with that expression.

"He saved her life. You didn't see her in the street, did you?" She stomped forward. He took a step back. "You didn't see the barricade either, did you?" Another step forward. Another step backward from him.

"Wonder who you'd be blaming if you scraped up that new paint job," a man said from behind Saundra.

She turned. He was the tallest, widest, reddest police officer she had ever seen. This late in the summer, shouldn't he be tanned the color of mahogany instead of looking like a late May burn?

"What idiot put that there?" The man gestured at the barricade.

"You okay, Curtis?" the officer said, going down on one knee and holding out a hand to the big man.

Saundra wondered, because he just lay there, on his back now, his gaze tracking the conversation. He didn't look like he was in any pain, but he did look a little stunned.

"Daphne okay?" he said, after a few more seconds. Like he had to think what he was going to say.

"Is your name Daphne?" Saundra asked, and gently nudged the child back so she could look down into the big, teary hazel eyes. "She fell, and then the car --" She gestured at the spot in the street under the bumper of the car.

"Yeah, I saw." The officer glanced over his shoulder in the direction the child had come from. "Your daddy's kind of tied up right now. How about I find Ashley?" He held out his arms. Daphne nodded and let him take her from Saundra.

During the exchange, the driver had jumped in his car and backed up. Scowling into his rearview mirror, he made a three-point turn, going up on the curb on the opposite side of the street, before heading back down the way he had come.

"He actually thinks he's not gonna get a slap for this," the officer said. He summoned up a smile. "Thanks for your help, ma'am. Too bad strangers have to step in and ..." He shrugged. "In case anyone asks, mind if I get your contact info?"

"Oh -- well -- I'm Saundra Bailey. You can find me at the library, starting Monday. I'm the new children's librarian."

"Are you?" His smile looked more natural now. "Daphne loves books, don't you, honey?" He jiggled the little girl. "My cousin Deirdre's little girl. I'm Ted Shrieve, by the way."

"Nice to meet you. Both of you. Will I see you at story time, Daphne?" The child nodded and managed a smile for her.

Saundra shuddered a little, when Officer Shrieve hurried down the sidewalk with Daphne riding his shoulders. Curtis was sitting up now. What was wrong with them, herself included, that they didn't pay any attention to him? He was a hero, after all. Daphne could have been seriously hurt if that driver had struck her. Saundra had a horrid mental image of that car striking Daphne and then smashing her into the barricade. That driver obviously hadn't seen it any more than he had seen her.

"Are you sure you're all right?" She went down on one knee and gripped Curtis' shoulder. He offered her a crooked shrug and an even more crooked grin. He had a black eye and slightly swollen lip. Both injuries looked half-healed, meaning he had gotten them before today. Not that she was an expert on injuries. Maybe Curtis made a habit of getting hurt rescuing people?

"I'm okay." His voice sounded a little congested.

"You're sure?"

"You dropped your stuff." He groaned a little as he rolled forward onto his knees.

"Maybe you should stay there until I get a doctor or somebody." Saundra stepped back to scoop up her shopping bag. She didn't know why, but she was certain he was going to try to pick up the bag and carry it for her.

"Nah. I'm okay." He pulled himself upright and spread his arms, as if to demonstrate.

"Hey, Curtis?" Olivia leaned out the door of Book & Mug. "Are you okay? Somebody said that idiot Clint tried to run you down."

"He snatched a little girl out of the street before she got hit," Saundra said. "He says he's okay, but could somebody look at him? The bumper hit his hip."

"Curtis is tough." She held out a hand. "Come on, big guy. Let's put some ice on that, okay?"

"Okay." He sighed and turned, shuffling sideways. "I didn't scare you, did I?" He gestured at Saundra. "She's nice. Her name is Saundra. She yelled at Clint real good."

"Yeah, Saundra's a nice lady. She works at the library. I bet she can help you find some really good books."

"Yeah?" His face lit up, and he nearly ran into the side of the door as he grinned back at Saundra. "Will you?"

"Sure, Curtis," Saundra said, trying to smile and hold back a sudden, ridiculous need for tears. "I'll see you on Monday, okay?"

He nodded, bobbing his head like a little boy, and disappeared into the coffee shop.

"Don't worry, I'll get someone to check him out," Olivia said, and retreated back inside

Saundra heaved a sigh. She wished her car didn't seem so far away. It was barely 9:30. What an introduction to her new home.

The aromas coming from Sugarbush Bakery made her steps slow. She paused too long to look in the big, deep display window. Long enough for the different scents coming through the open door to make her mouth water. Blueberry scones and apricot danish. How could she choose between them? She bought two of each, big enough to have half for a decent breakfast. Next stop: pop into the office supply store next door, appropriately called The Office, to see if they had ink cartridges for her printer.

Officer Shrieve was waiting when she stepped outside.

"Is everything all right? Is Daphne all right?" she asked.

"She's fine." He held up a hand, as if he thought she would go running down the street to check on the little girl. Then he waved at someone down the street. "Her dad just wants to thank you." There was a twist to his mouth that made Saundra think this little errand didn't sit well with him.

Daphne's father looked like every small-town career politician she had ever had the misfortune to encounter in her many library duties. Despite being dressed for a day of manual labor, he looked starched and pressed, his auburn curls held in place with gel, his too-white smile polished and practiced. His hand felt cool and slightly damp-sticky. She imagined he had used hand sanitizer before she crossed the street to meet him, and he would probably use it again once she walked away. This was someone who considered supervision to be heavy manual labor, and only showed up on a workday to look good.

Head Trustee Roger Cadburn introduced himself exactly that way. Not as Daphne's father. Saundra labeled him politician first, and father somewhere several slots down the list. She hoped Daphne's mother was more like Officer Shrieve. Saundra let him shake her hand, thank her, and assure her that the rude idiot she had encountered was the exception when it came to the people of the township. Then he encouraged her to enjoy the street festival this coming weekend.

That was almost enough to make her consider not attending. What was it about the man that implied everything good was to his credit? Maybe she was just irritated because he said nothing about Curtis.

Then again, she had said nothing to him about Curtis, either. Not that she wanted to prolong the conversation. Saundra thought about going back to Book & Mug to ask Olivia how the big man was doing, but she got turned around and found herself at the parking lot when she thought she was heading back to the coffee shop. Maybe she was more shaken by the near-accident than she thought. She got in the car and headed home.

Back in her apartment by 10:15. How did all that happen in such a short space of time? Saundra made a pot of coffee that filled the air with the promised luxurious aromas and got to work. First, she did a search on her smart phone for the number for Book & Mug. She talked to someone named Ramon. He startled her a little when she gave her name and he knew who she was. He assured her Curtis was all right. They had made him take some aspirin and sit with a bag of ice on his back, gave him a big frozen drink, and he was happy.

Feeling better about him and herself, Saundra spent the rest of the morning organizing her personal library, making adjustments to the greenhouse, and setting up her kitchen and office to her liking. She had to laugh at herself, believing that, other than her books, she led a rather spartan existence. Why did she need more than four place settings, or a dozen rubber scrapers of different sizes? Granted, she had more shelf space and drawers than she needed by the time she finished putting everything away, but the time to put it all away made her feel like a hoarder. Just how much did a single girl need?

She started off with that thought when she sat down at lunch to write an email to Aunt Cleo. She passed on greetings from Patty and Roy, and talked about the street festival, the status of the plants and the greenhouse, and the little bit of maintenance she wanted to do right away. She described the people she had met so far, trying to follow the example of Patty and Roy and not talk about negative people or situations. Then she got up, the letter unfinished, and snapped pictures of her apartment to email to her aunt.

While she was online, she did a search of nearby stores that sold the supplies she needed to make the minor repairs and upgrades to her balcony greenhouse. She thought about going to Book & Mug and asking to talk to Troy. If he had a greenhouse on the roof of his building, then certainly he would know the best place to get supplies. Somehow, that just struck her as too much trouble. Saundra decided she would prefer to meet people socially instead of introducing herself to them by asking for help.

Chapter Four

Saturday, August 20

When Saundra woke up the next morning, she was still gnawing on the bit of insight that she had more than she needed. Why walk to the center of town and tempt herself with the goodies offered at the street festival? Especially when she didn't *need* anything.

Well, there was nothing wrong with enjoying the weather, was there? Or getting to know the people of the town, whom she had come to serve by helping their children love books?

"The problem is, you can always talk yourself into and out of anything." Saundra settled in her living room and looked out through the balcony curtains and the wrought iron railing to the park landscape below. She took a sip of her morning green tea. "That's your Mulcahy blood. Concentrate on being a Bailey."

As if her aunt was right there in the room, big blue-gray eyes snapping, she knew what Cleo would say. She would scold Saundra to stop planning her life to be the antithesis of people whose opinions didn't matter in the least. God was more pleased with her when she enjoyed life than when she played martyr.

"Okay, I'm going, I'm going," she told the quiet room.

An echo of Cleo's laughter rang in her ears as she got up and tried to drink the rest of her tea while she walked to the kitchen. Some of it went up her nose, which served her right. Saundra remembered to take a Welcome Wagon bag, and all the coupons she hoped to use. Marking herself as a newcomer would make it easier to meet people, at the very least.

When she reached Center Avenue, booths filled the street, from the western end, where it intersected Sackley Road, to the cement barricade where it dead-ended at the park. The barrier was painted with an American flag, the Ohio flag, and the Cadburn High School mascot, a hound dog. At least, Saundra assumed that was what she saw peeping out from behind the banners announcing the live entertainment scheduled to perform in the gazebo, and the hours for the festival.

Cadburn took its street festivals seriously.

Before she had visited more than the raffle booth and the popcorn ball booth, three people spotted the Welcome Wagon bag and asked if she was new in town. Saundra saw the Welcome Wagon booth and took a detour the moment she saw Ashley's platinum blonde hair. At the booth that sold bricks painted to look like stores and historic buildings, a woman with four children in tow caught up with her. All four looked enough like her to be clones. At least their mother didn't dress them all alike. The five Kenwards were delighted to have a new children's librarian in town and wanted to know when after school story time would resume. Did they actually have to wait for school to resume, or could they come in the afternoon anyway? Mrs. Tinderbeck and Saundra had already agreed on a long list of responsibilities, programs, launch dates, and ideas for new activities, via email and phone conversations. Her answers got cheers from the Kenward children. Always a good thing to make a great first impression.

From there, word got around the festival, reinforcing what Aunt Cleo had said about small-town gossip. Saundra hoped her aunt's warning about matchmakers wouldn't prove true as well. By this time, she had reached the intersection of Center and Apple. She decided to visit Book & Mug before she investigated any more booths. That coupon for a free large special of the day sounded awfully good about now.

A twittery kind of scratchy voice called out behind her.

"Sandy?"

No, that didn't sound anything like her venomous cousin Bridget. She and Edmund had taken to calling her Sandy when they were in elementary school. They claimed it was a pet name, as in Little Orphan Annie's dog, Sandy. Maybe she was being petty, but she refused to answer to a name that wasn't hers.

"Sandy? You're Sandy Bailey, aren't you?" A bony hand caught hold of her overshirt at the elbow.

A bony hand with long fingernails painted a dull yellow. Saundra moved in slow motion, following that skinny arm sporting at least fifteen bangle bracelets, to an oval head with a sharp chin and sharper nose, and a triumphant smirk that smeared hot pink lipstick on her teeth. Where had she seen that woman's face before? Her makeup was just heavy enough for Saundra to think *plaster job*, and then mentally slap herself for being catty. The woman dressed like she was in her twenties, but had to be in her fifties.

"It's Saundra." She tried to tug her sleeve free without catching on those talons. How did anybody do any work with fingernails that long?

"Sandy, Saundra, what does it matter?" That twittery voice turned into scratchy giggles.

"Her name is *Saundra*, and yes, Twila, it matters," a familiar, comforting, fresh-bread-out-of-the-oven kind of voice announced.

"Mrs. Tinderbeck?" Saundra guessed, as she turned to the grandmotherly, statuesque woman who had come up on their right while she was trying not to snarl at Twila.

Yes, this was Mrs. Tinderbeck, with her snowy white, stylish cap of hair, coffee-and-cream skin, and the same turquoise and emerald caftan she had worn in her profile picture on the library's website. Which, Saundra realized, was also where she had seen Twila's face before.

"Hello, dear. I'm so glad you were able to get down here today." Mrs. Tinderbeck held out both her hands and caught hold of Saundra's. "You're all moved in? Do you need help finding anything?"

"All moved in and doing my getting-to-know-you walk." She raised her elbow, where the Welcome Wagon bag hung, for explanation.

"Uh huh. If I remember right, Patty Hill said she was making the call, because she knows your aunt. I hope she invited you to our church."

"I wouldn't dare not go."

"Oh, please." Twila rolled her eyes. Her mouth flattened to half its thickness, like deflating balloons. Saundra wondered if she got collagen injections. "It's a violation of ACLU laws --"

"The ACLU doesn't make laws in this country, and I'm ashamed of any of my librarians who would make a mistake like that." The hint of laughter in Mrs. Tinderbeck's voice, like a thick layer of chocolate cream frosting, took the bite out of the rebuke. Twila didn't react. "Since you're here, dear, let me start the official introduction early, all right?" She held out her arm.

"That would be great." Saundra hooked her arm through Mrs. Tinderbeck's arm, anticipating a slow stroll through the festival, with lots of charming and amusing comments thrown at her. Even better if they left Twila behind. She hoped their desks wouldn't be near each other in the library, because if so, she needed to stock up on really strong pain reliever before going to work on Monday. Hearing that voice all day long would be uncomfortable, at best.

Saundra was wrong. Not about Twila, who did let them leave her behind, but the speed of their stroll. Mrs. Tinderbeck, for all she looked like a stereotyped pillowy grandma who spent most of her time in a rocking chair, soon revealed she was a power walker.

She wasn't above quick stops, darting into an enclosed booth, or stopping in an intersection between booths to make introductions. Saundra gave up trying to learn and remember the names of every child and parent she met. She was impressed that Mrs. Tinderbeck seemed to know every family with children in the township. She probably knew everybody in the township, period. Mrs. Tinderbeck had struck her from the first phone interview as a force to be reckoned with. A benevolent dictator.

By the time they reached the dead-end at the park and turned to go down the next row of the booths, Saundra had grown used to hearing, "This is Saundra, the newest member of the family. She has wonderful things planned for the children. Just wait and see. You'll be so pleased."

"Oh, lovely," Mrs. Tinderbeck said, as a gush of sweet, fruity, yeasty aromas escaped a booth ahead of them. "Sugarbush has a fresh batch ready to put out. I think we've earned a reward for all the PR work we've done."

"My treat," Saundra insisted, and shifted the Welcome Wagon bag from one shoulder to the other, so she could get to her purse.

A gasp escaped Mrs. Tinderbeck. A dark shadow slammed up against Saundra at the same moment a hot, calloused hand grabbed her arm and spun her around. She caught the stink of stale, fruity cigar smoke and looked into those same angry eyes from her apartment doorway. Then she was falling -- no, pushed -- and her purse strap slid down her arm.

No, you're not, she snarled inside her head. She twisted her arm around to catch the strap as Stinky Cigar Man turned to run.

Saundra's self-defense training kicked in. Hearing Nic West's voice in her head, she used her falling momentum to yank the would-be purse snatcher off balance and went her knees, instead of struggling to stay upright. He cursed and swung at her -- and let go of her purse. Saundra rolled as Mrs. Tinderbeck called for help and the people around them reacted. She felt those dirty shoes swipe past her backside. Fury had her pivoting to kick upward.

She didn't connect with the portion of his anatomy she wanted, but she startled the man, so he yelped and scrambled backward. Then people were running, gathering around him. He swung at them and snarled something, fury in his gaze focused on her for a moment more before he ran. Saundra glimpsed a lean shape in khaki, racing past her, going after the man.

Mrs. Tinderbeck proved those pillowy arms still had a lot of strength, when she pulled Saundra to her feet. The jabber of excited voices was almost deafening. The double-sized booth for Sugarbush Bakery and Confectionary had tables and chairs in the shade. Saundra wasn't quite sure how she got from the street to the booth, but she was grateful to sit down.

"Miss Saundra?" Ramon Columbine, seven years old, with two missing teeth, looked up at her, his big black eyes wide with worship. "That was the coolest thing I ever seen in my who -- o -- ole life!"

Saundra laughed and wished she could cuddle the little boy up into her lap. There were far too many rules nowadays, and hugging children the same day she had met them simply wasn't allowed. Still, she wanted someone to hold her. Now that the excitement and anger and shock were over, she felt rather shaky.

Common sense told her the man had to be after her key, since his key didn't work yesterday. The question was what he wanted in her apartment.

~~~~~

Kai knew that guy coming toward him. He couldn't remember where, but that ugly face was familiar, if not the black T-shirt.

Wait -- was Captain Sunderson chasing that guy?

"Just a sec." He nodded to Cilla and Melba and stepped out from the photo booth.

The running man snarled at him and dodged to the right. Kai lunged, reaching for him. The man swung a fist and Kai twisted aside to avoid a punch to his ribs. The other fist came up and slammed into his chin. Kai went down, grabbing hold of the black T-shirt. The man jerked sideways, falling on top of him.

In half a second, he was on his feet, aiming a kick into Kai's ribs as he leaped over him. Kai stayed down, seeing the police captain approaching. The Tweed cousins hurried to him once the chase continued into the park. Kai had a piece of torn, smelly black T-shirt in his fist. He laughed, just for a second. Then an ache shot through his chest from where the kick had landed.

Mike Shipman, who was running the photo booth, offered Kai a hand up and suggested he go to the first aid booth.

"Your shift is almost over," he added, when Kai opened his mouth to protest. "I'll take care of the ladies." He winked at the Tweed cousins.

Mike ran the theater program for the rec department and the Cadburn Schools. He had access to fifty years of costumes and props, and the dress-up photo booth was the most popular fundraiser every time it appeared at a street festival. Kai enjoyed helping out. He refused to leave because his pride wouldn't let him admit the fugitive had scored on him. He stayed to help the cousins choose their costumes and teased them as Mike snapped their pictures. The ladies, members of his Guzzlers group, were old enough to be his mother -- not that he could remember her. He wanted to take care of them, help them with their photos.

By the time the ladies had made their choices of poses and ordered prints from Mike, Captain Sunderson had returned from the chase, sans a prisoner. Festival attendees had been walking past the booth from the area where the chase had started, and Kai pieced together the story from the things they said. He discounted about half as wild speculation. Apparently, the guy in the black T-shirt had tried to steal something.

"Kind of hot for a race?" he said, seeing Sunderson step into the booth to greet the Tweeds.

They were distant relatives, on a different branch of the family from Officer Shrieve. A lot of people in Cadburn were related in one way or another if they traced their pedigrees back far enough. The nice thing about the township was that newcomers like Kai and his cousins weren't made to feel like outsiders.

"The guy had a helper." She wiped a long, lean hand across her forehead, then scrubbed sweat off her sharp-boned cheeks. "Jumped in a car on the other side of the wading pool foot bridge and got away before I could get the license or even the make. Too many black cars on the road nowadays."

"What happened?"

"He knocked down the new librarian and tried to steal her purse. Tough girl." She grinned and gestured with a tip of her head down the street. "Must know some self-defense moves. Used his movements against him and didn't lose her purse."

"Yeah, well, anybody who works with the kids in this town has to be tough." Kai grinned and tipped a salute, two fingers off his eyebrow, to Sunderson and Mike. Now he could gracefully retire.

Curiosity had him slowing when he saw the crowd gathered around the Sugarbush booth. He stopped short when the would-be purse snatcher's face popped into his mind, and something clicked. He sniffed at his hand and the piece of T-shirt he still clutched. That was a familiar stink. Specifically, a cheap, fruity cigar. Several people detoured around him. One little boy, focused on the cotton candy he was peeling off his face, ran into Kai from the left. He barely noticed, until Sunderson rested a hand on his shoulder.

"You okay? I saw he took you down. Sure you want to pass on the first aid?"

"I've seen that guy before," he said, and let her lead him into the shade of the booth. "But he's shaved since then -- he's the guy who messed with our door. The smell is the same." He held out the scrap of cloth to explain. Sunderson sniffed, her nostrils flared, and she winced. Kai had to laugh. How did the guy think he could break in anywhere with that stink warning people he was coming? "What's really crazy is Troy was checking the old security videos, in case he tried to case our place before, and we caught him trying to snag the old fire escape ladder, about a week ago."

Then he turned. Blue-gray eyes met his, framed in pale auburn hair and he couldn't remember what he was saying for a few seconds while he tried to put a name with the face. Just long enough for those elegant brows to lower a little in puzzlement.

Ditto that. He realized he had never seen her face before.

"Sorry," he said, and stuck out his hand to shake hers. Like popping the rewind button, he realized Sunderson had introduced him to her as the man who had tried to stop her attacker. Kai just remembered his manners and was about to introduce himself when the police captain did so for both of them.

Her name was Saundra Bailey. She thanked him. He thought he said something halfway intelligent, because she smiled and didn't seem in any hurry to yank her hand free of his grip. Which he had kept just a few seconds too long.

When feeling awkward, always offer hospitality, Miss Sylvan, the counselor at the orphanage, had always said. Kai recognized that narrowing of Sunderson's eyes. She was going to ask to sit down with him and Saundra and Mrs. Tinderbeck, to go over the attempted purse-snatching. He invited them all to the Book & Mug, where they could speak in relative privacy. Everyone was outside and enjoying the street festival on this gorgeous morning, so they weren't going to linger after stopping in to pick up their drinks.

He wondered what kind of coffee or tea Saundra would order. The extras or lack thereof, he had found, could sometimes reveal a lot about a person. He wouldn't be surprised if a tough little thing like her asked for her coffee black. Maybe a shot of cinnamon vanilla syrup.

~~~~~

Saundra studied Kai Shane as their little party of four wove through the increasing traffic of the street festival, heading for the Book & Mug. He was a head taller than her, so maybe six-foot-four, with a runner's build, a thick head of dark curls, big dark eyes, and a squared chin wrapped in a light dusting of beard. He wore a long-sleeve, dark green T-shirt proclaiming he was the property of the Book & Mug, written in Olde English script.

"Your usual, Mrs. T?" Kai said, picking up his pace to step ahead of them through the propped-open door, and lead the way to the service counter at the back. "I heard you thinking of it from halfway down the street."

"Balderdash." Mrs. Tinderbeck chuckled. "After the little ruckus we just went through, I need more than my usual. Surprise me. Be nice."

"You wound me." He winked at Saundra, pressing both hands over his heart and pretending to wilt. "I'm always nice." He walked to the side of the counter and lifted up a portion, like a drawbridge, to step behind it.

"Don't trust this charmer for a moment."

That got a snort from the lady police captain.

"Well, at least she admits I'm charming. Captain?"

"Iced chai. Small," Sunderson called back, heading for a booth in the corner, by the back wall.

"And you, pretty lady?" Kai braced both hands on the counter and grinned at her.

Saundra stepped up close enough to see over the counter, which was set up in three levels. The top level that customers could see, a second level maybe six inches lower, and then the third, a few inches lower, holding whipped cream cans and mugs, containers of sprinkles and bottles of flavored syrups. Several nozzles, probably for milk or cream or other liquids, stuck up through the counter.

"What's good?" Her face warmed. What kind of a response was that? Would he think she was being flirty? Or blame the after-effects of the attempted purse-snatching, when his big, dark eyes and that gorgeous smile short-circuited her brain?

"For a nice warm day like today? Iced. No, whipped iced, white chocolate syrup, latte, frozen whipped, cinnamon sugar sprinkle."

"That sounds incredible."

His eyes lit up. Saundra had the oddest feeling her reaction to his suggestion was important to him.

"Oh, but it's not a special." She pulled the coupon out of her pocket and waved it. Yeah, like that would explain everything. Maybe she had hit her head when she fell, and didn't realize it?

"This is official police business. On the house." He winked at her and turned to reach for four glass mugs.

She followed Mrs. Tinderbeck to the corner booth and took a seat where she could watch Kai put together their drinks. With elegant, economical movements, he spilled a creamy brown, thick concoction from the blender into three of the mugs, two plops of what turned out to be whipped frozen cream on top, a dash from a shaker -- cinnamon sugar, the big crystals she loved to have on mega-muffins. Then another container from under the counter, poured over ice in the fourth mug, topped with more whipped cream. He greeted several customers who stepped up to the counter, set the four mugs on a tray, ducked under the drawbridge, and picked up the tray as a lean, white-haired girl in a royal blue Book & Mug shirt stepped up to the counter to tend to the new customers.

Saundra took her first sip of the frozen coffee Kai put in front of her. She had to close her eyes and just sink into the subtle swirl of flavors. Then she swore she could actually feel him watching her. She opened her eyes -- yep, he was watching her, one side of his mouth quirked up like he was trying not to laugh.

"What do you think?" He took a long pull on the drink.

Saundra almost cried out. Something that good shouldn't be inhaled, it should be savored. Slowly.

"It's incredible. What's it called?" His shrug startled a laugh out of her. "You don't know?"

"Mad scientist strikes again," Sunderson murmured, before taking a long sip from her own drink. "He just made it up now."

"Wow." Saundra hoped her face didn't look as red hot as it felt. She was pretty sure anything complimentary she wanted to say would sound like she was gushing.

Sunderson saved her by turning the conversation to the man who had tried to steal her purse. Apparently, he had also been trying to break into the private floors of the Book & Mug building. Saundra shuddered a little as she listened to Kai describe the attempt to block the door open, and what was caught on security video. While the back hallway of the coffee shop was open, to allow people to access the public bathrooms, the door to the stairwell was kept locked. He explained, for her benefit obviously, that he and his cousins lived on the second and third floors and had their offices on the second floor. Anyone wanting to do business with Troy and Eden had to ring the doorbell and state their business through the intercom by the door to the side street.

Right then, two people with Kai's dark, curly hair, dark eyes, and sharp cheekbones, appeared from the back hallway. They were introduced as Eden and Troy as they joined the four in the booth, which was big enough for eight. Eden explained she had been on the phone with a client, who told her about the attempted purse-snatching. She alerted Troy and they both came down to see what was going on. Eden had a sketch pad and offered to take the description from Kai and Saundra, to help in the search.

"Don't bother," Kai said. "He's that stinker who messed with the door and tried to get up the fire escape."

"Unobservant doofus," Troy said with a snort and a wink for Saundra. "That fire escape is halfway dismantled. The section that goes from the second floor down to the street is completely gone, and ten seconds of looking would have shown him that. We left it up there for atmosphere, when we did our renovations."

"I think it's time we take it down completely," Eden said.

Troy pulled out his smartphone and tapped a few times, then swiped the screen a few more times. He turned it around and showed the image to Saundra. "That him?"

"I think so," she said. "But the man I saw was shaved."

"Did he stink?" Kai asked.

"A bad, fruity cigar," Eden added, when Saundra hesitated, stumped by the question.

"That's him." She looked at the captain. "So, he's not from around here?"

"What worries me is that he knew to shave," Sunderson said. "Change his appearance, as well as his tactics. I'd hate to think that there's a leak in my department." She looked like she was about to say something, then caught herself.

"Dudley," Kai murmured into his mug, then took a sip.

Eden pressed her lips flat, smothering a smile.

Saundra supposed there was an inside joke there. She felt, just for a moment, incredibly lonely and on the outside looking in.

"Maybe he's smarter than he looks," Troy said.

"Why pick on Saundra, with such a long way to run?" Mrs. Tinderbeck said. "Why not someone closer to his getaway car?"

"He wanted my keys. I think," Saundra hurried to add.

"Come again?" the captain said.

Saundra sighed and couldn't make herself meet Kai's gaze. "We hadn't gotten to that part yet. I was just about to tell you ... I saw him before. The day I moved in." She went on to describe the encounter at her door, the differences in the key she had noticed, and what Pastor Roy had said about the changes in the building.

"That's a starting point," Sunderson said. "I have the feeling it isn't a coincidence that the same guy is trying to get into your apartment and here. Both buildings were owned by the Cadburn family before the collapse."

"What? You think somebody hid something in Saundra's apartment and here in our building?" Troy shook his head, grinning. "They're out of luck. We took the place down to the studs when we did our renovations. Anything hidden, we found."

"Big-time," Kai said. "Found a sliding panel in the cellar, led into what was either a smuggler's bolt hole or maybe a hiding place dating back to before the Civil War. About twenty feet in, it collapsed, probably from digging for sewer lines and power lines." He shrugged.

"It doesn't hurt to ask questions," Eden said. "If you don't mind?" she added, with a nod to the captain.

"Did it ever do any good to say no to Jessica Fletcher?" Sunderson grinned and the others laughed. Saundra was pleased by the reference to the author-sleuth of the 80s TV show, *Murder, She Wrote*. "I'll do some follow-up with the managers for your buildings, past and present. See if anyone has the old keys. Might answer a lot of questions right then and there."

Saundra remembered what Roy and Patty had said about the cousins. Eden did private investigations. A wave of something sort of twisted and warm and a little queasy washed over her. She supposed that was what envy felt like. Kai and Eden had jobs she had daydreamed about from time to time. Running Finders had to be successful if the police captain didn't mind Eden investigating alongside her.

"You might get answers a lot faster, at least identifying the key, if you talk to Curtis," Troy said. "From what people have said, he was handling all the maintenance and the management, there at the end, before Cadburn had to sell everything."

"I'd appreciate if you asked him for me. The poor old guy is kind of afraid of anyone in authority."

"Is that what happened the other day?" Saundra asked. Then she wished she hadn't.

"Oh, that's right, you've met Curtis." Sunderson smiled at her. "Shrieve filled me in. Daphne wanted ice cream, it was too early in the morning, her father was too busy to be nice when he said no." Her mouth twisted, and Saundra could guess right there what the police captain thought of the head trustee. "Daphne went running in tears. Clint Rhodes came tearing up a side street. Nearly hit her, but Curtis was her guardian angel. Got bumped." She hooked her thumb at Saundra and grinned. "Clint was about to take a piece out of his hide, like it was Curtis' fault he nearly hit that sweet little girl? But our new librarian took a piece out of his hide instead."

"That was you?" Kai grinned at her. "Curtis just couldn't shut up about the pretty lady who was so nice to him."

"Is he okay?" Saundra's face warmed.

"Curtis looks like a big, shambling softy," Eden said, "but he's tough. You've got a friend for life. If he likes you, he'll take a bullet for you. He loves kids' books, so expect him at the library practically every day."

"Is he okay? I mean, he seemed kind of ..." She wasn't sure how to say what concerned her without coming across as either insensitive or mocking.

"He's a good guy, and smarter than people think he is." Eden nodded, and her expression didn't change, so maybe she understood what Saundra was trying to say, delicately. "He's one of those guys who is so quiet, people take him for granted. He's kind of ..." She shrugged and glanced between her cousins. "Not quite in step?"

"That's a good way to put it," Troy said, nodding. His smile cooled. "So the jerks pick on him. Some who used to be in power around here used police and city workers to do their dirty work and keep their hands clean."

"Before my time," Sunderson said. "Some of the fallout, maybe fifteen years ago, pretty much emptied the departments."

"Not soon enough from what I heard," Kai muttered. That got a sigh and a somber nod from the police captain. "Yeah, he sees the uniform, not the guys who are his friends when they aren't in that uniform. We'll talk to him, ask about the keys."

Sunderson, Eden, and Troy left soon after that. Kai took his and the captain's empty mugs to the counter, leaving Saundra and Mrs. Tinderbeck to finish their drinks.

"Well, that's a nice bit of excitement for your first day." Mrs. Tinderbeck chuckled. "I promise, things won't be quite so exciting for the rest of the year."

"Good. Dealing with all the different reading groups and coming up with activities is more than enough excitement for me." Saundra tipped up her mug to finish the last mouthful. "Oh, that was wonderful. I hope he wrote down the recipe, because I'd order that again."

"Flattery of the nicest sort," Kai said, startling her so she set the mug down a little louder than she meant to. He slid back into the booth. "So ... as the first people to taste test this one, what would you call it?"

"Don't you drag me into this." Mrs. Tinderbeck's mouth turned down, but her eyes sparkled. Saundra guessed this was a running joke between them.

"What does it remind you of?" he said, tipping his head slightly to the side and staring into Saundra's eyes.

"Well ..." She folded up her napkin and put it in the mug. "It reminds me of what klah *should* taste like. If it was cold and creamy. I know that doesn't make sense --"

"Makes perfect sense. Genius." Kai scooped up both of their mugs. Then he stopped short, his grin turned to puzzlement. "Why do you say *should*? You've tried to make it, haven't you?"

"We even had the *Dragonlovers* book and the official recipe. After maybe five attempts, we could never get it to turn out right, or even taste the same, each time we tried." Somehow, Saundra didn't feel so silly, confessing.

"Oh, now you've done it," Mrs. Tinderbeck said. "You're speaking his language. This one," she flicked her fingers at Kai, who just laughed at her, "is on a never-ending quest to come up with coffee and tea based on literary characters. I'm assuming this klah you were referring to is an actual drink from a book?"

"The Pern books. Science fiction," Saundra added.

"Mrs. T, make sure she gets to the next Guzzlers meeting?" Kai slid out of the booth. "Sorry, but duty calls." He gestured with a hand full of mugs toward the counter. "Nice to meet you, Saundra. Despite the circumstances." He winked at her and hurried away.

Saundra turned around and saw three people in Book & Mug T-shirts beckoning for Kai. So he wasn't making an excuse to get away from the crazy girl who tried to recreate food from books set on other planets.

"What are the Guzzlers?" she asked.

"His club of coffee enthusiasts who try to come up with new recipes." Mrs. Tinderbeck patted her shoulder. "You've made a lovely first impression, dear. No doubt about it."

Chapter Five

Sunday, August 21

Sunday morning, Saundra walked into the glassed-in foyer of Cadburn Bible Chapel, what had been the front porch before the big house was turned into a church, according to Pastor Roy. She headed for the information desk. The woman standing at the counter, studying one of several signup sheets taped to the surface, glanced at her. They exchanged smiles. Saundra returned to looking for the visitor card Patty had asked her to take care of, so she could be put on the newsletter and email and contact list. Then the woman's face registered in her mind. She looked up to see the woman glancing at her again.

"Saundra?" the woman said and laughed.

"Charli?"

What were the chances that a writer she had befriended over several yearly writing conferences, at her last library posting, would show up here in Cadburn?

"What are you doing here?" Charli Hall put down the pen she had been writing with and stepped to the other end of the counter where Saundra stood.

"I just moved here. I'm the new children's librarian."

"You are kidding. That's great! Wait until I tell the gang."

Saundra held onto her smile, but inside she felt like she was melting, relieved that Charli was glad to see her.

Charli Hall wrote under the pen name of Carlotta VanDevere. Her character, Anastasia Roman, was a private investigator. A tough chick who didn't depend on sex or violence or foul language to do her job or keep the attention of readers. Six of her last eight books had reached the *New York Times* bestseller list. Saundra had met Charli and her three writing friends five years ago. She had refrained from researching Charli to respect her new friend's privacy. However, comments during subsequent reunions at the conference had revealed Charli's "secret identity." She had laughed, rather than being angry when Saundra had approached her privately to verify her guess. Saundra and Aunt Cleo both adored Stacy Roman, and she had trusted her aunt with the precious secret.

The last thing she wanted was for Charli to think, even for a moment, she was stalking her. She never mentioned it, but the other members of their quartet of writers -- Rita Carmichael, Megan Romanoff, and Tamera Artierri

-- had confided in Saundra about some problem fans. As in rabid fanatics. People who had made life very uncomfortable for her.

"Are you with anybody?" Charli continued, gesturing at the double doors into the sanctuary. "Let me introduce you to Patty and Pastor Roy."

"Umm ... they're family friends. They're how I heard about the librarian job."

"What a small world. Got to warn you, Cadburn is my home library, and the girls and I take turns having our writing and research meetings at our libraries, so ..." She waggled her eyebrows. "We're going to show up when you're on duty and run you ragged helping us."

"Looking forward to it."

They took nearly twenty minutes getting from the sanctuary doors to their seat, because Charli had to introduce her to everyone. She sat with Saundra and Patty in the front row.

Cilla and Melba Tweed caught up with her just before the service started. Saundra had met them at the street fair the day before. They informed her she had been drafted into the Guzzlers. Would she like to have lunch with them and go to a last-minute meeting that afternoon?

When she hesitated, Patty urged her to go, promising she would have fun. It wasn't like she had anything planned for the afternoon, and the idea of having an instant group of friends, people to share a common interest, appealed to her. Besides, it was an excuse to go back to Book & Mug.

Thank You, Lord, for my new home and new friends and a new job and hopefully, I've finally found a place where the Mulcahys will never find me. Or at least Cadburn is such a small town, no high society, no wealth, they'll be too allergic to the wholesomeness to come here?

~~~~

Cilla and Melba Tweed lived on the corner in front of Saundra's apartment building. They accepted a ride home from church with her but insisted, when they went to Book & Mug for the meeting, they all had to walk. They gave her the basic information on the Guzzlers. Usually they met every third Thursday, but they were meeting today to welcome her. Otherwise, it would be three weeks until she could meet them.

They also had first pick of any new used books Devona brought into the shop, before Kai had them put on the shelf and added to the online catalog. Book & Mug impressed her more every time she encountered it. Early access to new-old books was reason enough to join the group even if Saundra didn't like fancy coffee drinks. Which she did. Plain coffee, she couldn't stand. It had to have syrup and lots of cream, preferably whipped cream and sprinkles.

The ladies informed her they shared a duplex, each taking one side, so they had plenty of room for their hobbies and libraries. They made her laugh on the short ride home from church by arguing about who would have custody of the next books in several series they both loved. After all, it was ridiculous to have two copies of the same book in what was essentially the same house. Their usual tactic was to buy one copy, and borrow another copy from the library, and then race each other to read the book.

Saundra was enchanted with the outside of their home. A curved flagstone path led through the wildflower garden of their front yard. She managed a few glimpses of the back yard while she helped them dish up the dinner that resembled an English high tea. They settled on the back porch, chattering about the Guzzlers and the candles the Tweeds were turning from a hobby to a business.

The three of them had such a lovely time over dinner, they were nearly late for the meeting. Saundra wished she had insisted on driving, when the clock on the corner of Apple and Center, kitty-corner from Book & Mug, showed the time was ten minutes after 2pm. When she pointed it out, slightly out of breath, Cilla just chuckled.

"That silly thing is always five minutes fast. We've been telling the old coot he needs to get a computerized clock instead of calling the phone company once a week to get it aligned or whatever you call it."

Saundra thought the big, brass-plated clock hanging from the intersection corner of the building, with three faces so everyone could read the time, was charming. However, Cilla had a point. The store was an electronics store, which made it odd to rely on an old clock that never told the correct time.

The Guzzlers were a grand total of twelve this afternoon and included Curtis. He grinned at Saundra, almost wriggling in his seat when she greeted him by name. He insisted she had to sit next to Kai at the head of the five tables pushed together, then said nothing for the next half hour. She didn't mind that, but Curtis watched her so intently, she felt a little uncomfortable. Especially when she remembered what Kai had said about Curtis being so loyal.

They sat in the back corner of the coffee shop where it extended behind the bookstore side. Everyone welcomed Saundra, and nobody put her through the third degree as the new kid in town. She was grateful, and had to laugh at herself for a little irritation, too. She had braced herself for the expected newcomer interrogation, and now it seemed that effort was wasted.

Most of the meeting passed in looking at the books Kai had just bought at a Friends of the Library sale in Toledo. Saundra got to know the members by listening to them discuss books and tease each other about their reading tastes. Kai spent most of the two hours either sitting and listening and laughing, or running back and forth with trays full of tiny sample cups for them to give input.

Saundra was almost embarrassed to see how seriously he had taken her comment about the frozen drink on Saturday. He took the basic recipe he had thrown together, and each variation had a different added flavor.

41

More cinnamon. More vanilla. Espresso syrup. Nutmeg. Almond syrup. Bittersweet chocolate shavings. Kahlua. By the end of the two hours, they had approved a formula and a name. It would come hot, iced, and frozen, and was dubbed Mo-Klah. Kai already had a magnet rough drafted to go on the menu board, with a dragon curled around the space where the name would go, and in small letters, "Dragonrider Approved."

Her relaxed feelings popped like a soap bubble when Kai returned from taking away the last taste test cups with printouts of photos taken from the security camera. Jacob Styles' face was slightly blurred from being enlarged, but the details were clear enough for target practice, as Cleo's protégé, Nic West, would say. Next to it was a sketch Eden had done Saturday, of Styles shaved and wig-less. Kai explained what the man had done and asked the group to be on the lookout for him.

"You're in the Courtyard Apartments, ain't ya?" Curtis said, after staring longer than anyone at the picture.

Something seemed to tighten in his jaw, and his gaze sharpened for the first time that afternoon. Saundra remembered what Eden had said about him being smarter than people thought. Then his head sort of snapped up, so their gazes met and locked. Her heart jolted for a moment until Curtis' gaze softened and he looked away. What was it about his eyes?

She tried to follow along with the conversation and push the question to the back of her mind where it could simmer until an answer came to her. Gnawing on stubborn puzzles wouldn't give her any answers, she had discovered early in life. She needed to relax and let her brain process things on the back burner, as Cleo always put it. She insisted Saundra would make an incredible researcher, once she had learned to relax, trust her instincts, and let her mind put all the pieces together without forcing or even conscious guidance.

Saundra was glad to have the conversation shift back to the subject of coffee, and tea, and changes in town as the school year approached. A new sandwich shop had taken over the space that had been occupied by the pet grooming and supply shop, Pampered Paws.

"Not sure I'd trust a place that serves food where animals used to be," Doug Wells quipped. "Hah! Deli-licious says everything is homemade. Maybe that's where they get their meat?" He waggled his eyebrows.

Cilla shook her head and sighed, while Melba muffled a giggle behind her hand. Others groaned. Curtis' face crinkled into slowly dawning horror, indicating he understood the reference.

"Don't give up your day job," Nelson said.

"Too late." More waggling of Doug's eyebrows. "That is my day job. Well, night job, technically."

More groans and teasing comments followed. Kai grinned and winked at Saundra, and nobody seemed compelled to explain anything to her.

Suddenly, she felt like she was home. Simply because these people included her in their inside jokes and could relax enough to be themselves around her.

Soon, though, the meeting ended. Everyone had something to do, things to take care of before Monday morning arrived. Saundra helped with the cleanup while Cilla and Melba hurried to the bathroom before their walk home.

"Something on your mind?" Kai asked, when she helped shove the tables apart and put them back in their original spots. "If bringing up yesterday bothered you, I'm sorry. I just thought ..." He gestured around the coffee shop. "The gang pretty much represents every section of town, and the different groups. They could ask around without stirring things up."

"Oh, no, I understand. That makes perfect sense. I just had that feeling of something ..." She waved her hand in a small circle. "You know, feeling like you're about to remember something or an important detail is just hovering there at the edge of your mind, but if you reach for it you'll lose it completely?"

"Yeah. I hate when that happens." Kai grinned and gave the last table a hip shove into place.

"I don't. I get the most incredible ideas, or it's like a puzzle half-assembling itself without me having to do anything. Just sit and wait for it to come together. Except --" A gasp escaped her as an image snapped into place in her mind. "That's it. His eyes."

"Cigar Man? He was wearing -- no, when you saw him, he wasn't wearing sunglasses. What about them?"

Saundra looked around, to make sure no one was close enough to overhear. A group of people had come in about the time the Guzzlers started to disperse, but they were on the other side of the shop, settling into booths and tables closer to the door.

"His eyes were kind of hazel, with a green ring around the outer edge. You really wouldn't notice the contrast except in bright enough light to make the pupil shrink."

"You want me to call the station and add that to the report?" He tipped his head toward the counter area, and Saundra followed him, helping him gather up a handful of napkins and spoons, and the wet cloth for wiping down the tables.

"Would you? I don't know how much good it'll do, except ..." Her momentary sense of elation, at having snagged that detail, faded. "The thing is, I didn't remember that until I was looking into Curtis' eyes. He seemed kind of upset, just for a second --"

"Yeah, he was head of maintenance for your building and a few others back before a lot of changes here in town. Kind of a family tradition from what I've heard. It makes sense he'd be kind of protective about the place. And the big guy really likes you."

43

"I like him, too, but ... It's weird, but I could swear Curtis has the same eyes as the man who came to my door."

"Yeah?" Kai stopped short. "Funny, but I was just thinking I've seen eyes like you described. Not Curtis's, though. These eyes are always angry. Like they're ready to shoot lightning."

"I can't imagine anyone angry with you. Certainly not enough to shoot lightning."

"Yeah, well, you come up against the movers-and-shakers, or at least they think they are --" He laughed and reached over the counter to drop his trash in the wastebasket. "Cadburn. That guy was in our faces from day one. Forget that, *before* day one. Like he could read our minds and knew when we were just thinking about buying this building."

Saundra thought back to her brief encounter with Daphne's father on Saturday. She shook her head. "He was wearing these blue-tinted sunglasses. His eyes seemed just brown. Not that I wanted to stand there, looking into his eyes and trying to guess the color. But yes ... " She shuddered.

"What?" Kai rested a hand on her shoulder, just for a moment.

"I thoroughly despise people who are angry, but they pretend to be all jolly and gracious. His little girl almost got hit by a car, but the message I got from him was basically he was doing *me* a favor, giving me the time of day. In front of witnesses, of course."

"Politicians."

"That's a dirty word, and I'll thank you never to use it in my hearing."

"You got it, pretty lady." He held out his hand and they shook, and suddenly everything was right in the world. She met his gaze. They grinned. Then Cilla and Melba met up with them, and it was time to start walking home, and the moment ended. Far too soon.

~~~~~

The Tweeds stood on the porch of their duplex and watched Saundra as she headed down the street to the apartment building. She looked back twice, and they were still on the porch until she reached the corner. They waved each time, and she waved back and laughed at how sharp their eyesight was to see her that far away and know she was looking at them. A few steps after she turned the corner, a tall box hedge blocked her view of the duplex.

Saundra sighed and picked up the pace a little, eager for the sight of the building. Funny, how dark the afternoon shadows seemed once she stepped into them. Thank goodness it was still broad daylight. In the future, if she was going to stay out past nightfall, she would leave a light on in her kitchen to welcome her home. The kitchen balcony faced the parking lot and the road. Maybe she would invest in a string of patio lights to hang on the greenhouse and brighten her balcony. Someone walking in the park might enjoy the lights. Her balcony was easy enough to pick out now in daylight, with the greenhouse filling it up.

She wondered about the previous occupant of the apartment, what had induced him or her to build that greenhouse, and why he or she had left it behind. Whatever the reason, she was grateful. Thinking of greenhouses made her wonder about Kai's cousin Troy, and what he was growing on the roof of the building. When she got to know him a little better, she would ask. Of course, she would have to ask Cleo's permission before she could talk about the special plants grown from rare seeds that she tended for her.

That prickling warning sensation ran up her back. She caught herself before she stopped short. Saundra knew better than to let someone following her know she sensed them. She had developed that instinct because the Mulcahys so thoroughly enjoyed sneaking up on her, scaring her, dropping nasty surprises on her, and especially making her shriek. Knowing she was being followed or watched helped her brace and muffle the expected reaction and took away a great deal of her tormenters' triumph. Nic had taught her that particular skill. She was grateful and honestly did like him, even if he did come across far too often as smug and I've-got-a-secret-and-I'm-not-going-to-tell-you.

What were the chances Bridget and Edmund had followed her to Cadburn?

Please, Lord, no?

Saundra prayed they hadn't yet realized she had left her previous library job and moved. It was only a matter of time until they needed her to do some delicate research work for them, or they would make another fruitless attempt at getting Cleo's antique Venetian glass heart locket. When Saundra's mother died two years ago, the Mulcahys had gotten a court order to search the house. They insisted Corrinne had heirlooms that Samuel Mulcahy had taken without the family's permission. For as far back as Saundra could remember, her cousins were constantly trying to get her to admit the heart existed and to let them see it. She had been five by the time she learned that she might never get back anything they got their hands on. She had been four when Aunt Cleo impressed on her how important it was that no one ever know the heart locket existed. The Mulcahys had found nothing when they got their court order and searched the house because the heart had always been in Cleo's possession.

Despite the intelligence that had built a fortune and made Mulcahy-Dresden Pharma a name to respect, the Mulcahys never seemed to learn. They would try again, just because they couldn't let someone else win.

The irony was that when Aunt Cleo headed to Europe for several months of research travel, she had left the Venetian heart locket in Saundra's care.

So, did that creepy feeling digging thorny boots into her spine mean she was about to be ambushed?

"Supid, stupid, stupid," Saundra whispered. The front door of her building was only another fifty yards away, but it could have been five hundred. Or a mile.

Why was she thinking about her nasty relatives when she had a new and local nemesis to worry about? Saundra felt for the breeze, to determine the direction it came from. Her heart skipped a few beats when she decided it came from ahead of her. That didn't do her much good if Cigar Man was behind her because she wouldn't smell him.

Ten more yards. Now was the perfect time if he was going to attack. Saundra reached in her purse and pulled out her cell phone. She could at least be ready to dial 911 if anything happened.

The heck with trying to out-psych her enemy. She picked up the pace for the last five yards. When her feet touched the curb of the front sidewalk, she felt like a faerie tale heroine who had passed through a magical boundary. Four more steps and she was in the foyer -- and couldn't find her keys. She could almost laugh even as she fumbled through her purse. From now on, she would make sure she had her key in her hand before she reached the door.

Living in anticipation of attack wasn't fun, but it certainly got her blood pumping.

She turned as she pulled the door open and glanced across the parking lot in front of the building and the borders of the park on either side. To all intents and purposes, it was a perfect, quiet, late Sunday afternoon in August. Warm with soft breezes -- which had just shifted direction. Saundra paused to sniff the air. She couldn't be sure she *didn't* smell cigar stink. She had the awful feeling that sweet, burned smell might just be nervous sweat.

By the time she reached her apartment, her sweat didn't stink, her heart had slowed to normal, and she could laugh at herself. Chances were good she had just imagined it. After all the things that had happened in her first few days in Cadburn, was it any wonder she was a little jumpy? Plus, feeling a little alone now, and the anticipated stress of the first day at work, it all added up to heightened alertness. Cleo always said it was better to be alert than to be nervous.

Would Cleo agree with how she had rationalized away the scare she had given herself? Maybe it was time for an email. The last one to her aunt had been short, essentially just saying, "I'm here, love the apartment, exhausted, can't wait to explore tomorrow." Now she would paint the pictures in words that Cleo expected.

In moments, she had her computer open and chatted through the keyboard about events as they happened. The delicious coffee she had bought and how Cleo would love going to Book & Mug. The friendly people at Green's Grocer and Sugarbush. The aroma of fresh bakery. Meeting Mrs. Tinderbeck and how she took Saundra under her wing and introduced her to everyone.

Holding to her resolve to only say positive things, she didn't mention

Twila or Trustee Cadburn. That meant editing the encounter with Daphne and Officer Shrieve and that oblivious, nasty Clint. She spent a whole paragraph on Curtis and Daphne, just didn't mention that Curtis was hit by the car, only that he pulled Daphne out of the way in time.

She didn't want to tell Cleo about the attempted purse-snatching but knew better. Cleo had motherly instincts ten times stronger and fiercer than Corrinne's had ever been. She quite made up for the affectionate obliviousness of Saundra's parents and had been known to call from the other side of the country or even from overseas when Saundra had faced some kind of trauma or tough decision. She had simply sensed when her niece needed her.

Cleo would know. The longer Saundra took to relate what had happened and what she was doing about the problem, the worse the sense of disappointment when they finally did talk.

Even though it was skipping ahead in the timeline, Saundra then related the scare she had on walking home after the Guzzlers meeting.

> *Do you think I should contact Kai and warn him? If this guy really is trying again with me, maybe he'll try again to get into the Mug Building. What do you think he could want? Eden said he was looking for documents or journals or whatever. Sure, I can see that in that old building from the founding of Cadburn. The thing is, it's been totally renovated inside, so they would have found something during that time. What could this man want in my apartment? Thank goodness the keys and locks were entirely changed when they renovated this place.*

She was tempted to relate what she had heard about how the Cadburn family had lost so many buildings. Saundra moved on to meeting Kai and his cousins, and being taken under the wing of the Tweeds, and the pleasant surprise of meeting up with Charli Hall at church that morning. She looked forward to meeting up with Charli's writing friends and seeing them at the library.

> *You know what would be fun? I won't do it without your permission. In fact, maybe we should wait until you come visit so you can tell her the whole story behind it. Charli has all those glass hearts on her Carlotta VanDevere website. She collects them, and fans send some to her, and she even donates the really special ones for fundraisers. I'd love to show her our Venetian heart someday. Of course, that's assuming she ever invites me over. But she was so glad to see me, and she wasn't upset when I figured out her pen name. Do you think talking about her glass heart collection would feel like I've been stalking her?*

Silly, I know, to worry about something like that. I'll wait until she decides to tell me where she lives. But still, do you think it would be okay?

She chatted for a few sentences about the duplex the Tweeds shared and all their beautiful landscaping, then detoured into the greenhouse on the roof of the Mug Building that she had heard about. She ended with a report on how well all the plants and rootings and seedlings had taken the move. She reported that she planned to hit the local garden centers next weekend to shop for supplies to take care of the greenhouse. She signed off by wishing her aunt safe travels and wonderful discoveries in all her research, told her she loved her, and asked for prayers for her first week of work.

Despite ending the day on an upbeat note and feeling even more sure she had just imagined being followed, Saundra checked the locks and chain on her door twice before she washed her face, changed into her pajamas, and spent an extra half hour praying over her coming week.

Chapter Six

Monday, August 22

Saundra detoured to Book & Mug on her way to the library for her first day of work. Well, why not? The coffee drinks were incredible, and she wasn't ashamed to want to look at the used bookstore again. A true bibliophile could never have too many books. The problem wasn't the number of books but not planning ahead and getting extra bookshelves, after all.

Kai wasn't at the counter when she stepped up, but Olivia was on duty. She had sat two pews in front of her at church yesterday. Her roommate, Phoebe, had squealed when Pastor Roy introduced Saundra to the congregation and announced she was the new children's librarian. The two of them had made sure Saundra met Devona and her brother, Rufus.

"Hi, Olivia." Saundra stepped up to the counter and decided right then to make a habit of always choosing the first item on the specials board, no matter what. *Live adventurously.*

"Hey, Saundra. Thought I tagged you as a morning person." Olivia reached for a glass mug, then gestured at the cardboard to-go cups on the counter behind her to. "On your way to work?"

They laughed together, and Olivia confirmed the cinnamon cappuccino was a good choice. Saundra chuckled when she was a block away and realized she hadn't checked out the books. Well, there was plenty of time for that later. She did want to get to work early today.

Twila was spraying the front desk and the switchboard with disinfectant spray when Saundra came in the side door using the key Mrs. Tinderbeck gave her yesterday after the service. She muttered as she scrubbed with a neon yellow sponge. Saundra hurried past her while the woman's back was turned and headed for Mrs. Tinderbeck's office.

Twenty minutes later, Mrs. Tinderbeck completed the last official tasks of the hiring process. That meant signing Saundra into the computerized time clock, logging her into the library computer system and settling her at her desk in the children's corner of the library. Saundra deposited her lunch bag in the refrigerator in the kitchen/break room, refilled her cup from the pot on the counter, and headed back to Mrs. Tinderbeck's office for what she termed the Monday morning circle-the-wagons meeting. Twila got to the door first, stomping up from the other direction, crossed her arms, and nodded twice with a loud snort.

49

"It's five minutes after 9. Where is this wunderkind you were so excited about? Late, and on her first day of work. Didn't I say you should have given me the job?"

"No, you did not tell me, and no, you said nothing about wanting the position." Mrs. Tinderbeck's voice was pleasant, but with a coolness that made Saundra stop, five steps away, and vow to never have that disappointed tone directed at her. "In point of fact, Saundra was almost half an hour early this morning."

"No, she --" Twila's head turned quickly enough to generate a loud crackle from her neck. Her nostrils pinched together, and her eyes widened as her gaze met Saundra's. She snorted, turned, and stomped back to the front desk.

Mrs. Tinderbeck shook her head and sighed loudly when Saundra stepped into her office. She said nothing about Twila, and that was both irritating and comforting. Saundra itched to know what compelling reason kept Twila working and stopped the library from firing her. Maybe she was only this way toward people she didn't know? At the same time, Saundra didn't want to know. She sensed Mrs. Tinderbeck wasn't the kind of person to talk about others behind their backs. Even when they deserved it. While Saundra's mother had been oblivious about far too many things, she did have moments of deep wisdom. Long ago, after hearing Saundra and her playmates chatter about a school nemesis, she had pointed out that people who said nasty things to Saundra about other people most likely said equally nasty things about her to those same people.

After that, Saundra's first day of work sped by with fewer new-kid-on-the-team awkward moments and mistakes than she had anticipated. She was ready and eager to get to work when the daycare story group trooped through the doors at 10am. The school year started on Wednesday, and once everyone had settled in, Saundra would be handling story times and book discussions throughout the day for each grade in the elementary and middle school. The high school had access to the library during the day, but the students had to have passes to come over during study hall. All three school buildings sat on the far side of the municipal parking lot that separated the Cadburn Schools property from the library. Someone, years ago, had decided it was more efficient to have the children trot the hundred yards to the library, rather than maintain libraries in all three buildings.

Everything about Cadburn pleased Saundra. The layout of the town was logical. She supposed when she got more acclimated to her new surroundings, she would find inconvenient things that irritated her. Right now, she felt as if someone had sat down decades ago and designed everything for maximum efficiency. She looked forward to being able to walk everywhere, until the weather turned nasty. Then she would drive from her apartment and park in the municipal lot, with access to all the shops and businesses of downtown Cadburn.

~~~~

Tuesday, August 23

Tuesday morning, Saundra met up with Mindy Sommerfield, the apartment building supervisor, on her way out the door. Mindy wanted her to know that new security cameras were on order and twice the number would be installed in the building. Upgrading the security system for entering the building would take some time, but again, she wanted Saundra to know the management company was working on the issue.

Saundra thanked her, grateful even though the news just made it harder to forget Cigar Man.

When she walked up to Green's Grocery to get some fresh produce after work, the sensation of being watched was expected. The problem was that she couldn't tell the difference between an actual warning of impending trouble or paranoia mixed with an over-active imagination.

The clouds scudding across the sky, making 6pm feel like 9 at night, didn't help her mood, either. Maybe she should stop being so health-conscious, virtuous, and energy-efficient and drive to and from work for the next week or so? At least until they located Cigar Man, aka Jacob Styles, and could determine what he wanted, and he was just creepy and not a threat.

She had just walked past the school buildings on her way home down Longview Road when a dark green sedan slowed a little as it passed her. Since it turned left at the next corner, only a hundred feet or so ahead of her, she didn't think anything of it.

The car reappeared almost immediately, turned right, came back down the street, and slowed again as it passed her.

She counted under her breath, waiting for the car to return. There were several shops ahead on the next section of street, in among the houses, as the business district of Cadburn gave way to residential. She crossed the street at the intersection and saw the lights were out in the first one, Cadburn Hardware. Seriously? How could they justify closing a hardware store before 7pm?

The next business was a landscaping supply store. The lights were on, but there were no cars in the parking lot.

When the green sedan hadn't returned, Saundra relaxed and told herself she was being stupid. She stopped counting after 100.

"Paranoid, anyone?" she muttered but picked up her pace. Just a little. Those clouds moving in had gotten darker and were nearly overhead now.

A car slowed, and she looked without thinking. When would she learn not to let the creeps know she knew they were there?

Her gaze locked with Cigar Man. She caught her breath.

At least, she thought it was him. He was wearing a baseball cap, and he hit the accelerator as soon as their gazes met. Saundra shivered and thought about turning around. Take shelter in the landscaping business, or take her chances that the next business, the art supply store, was still open? She had to go past six houses to get there.

She kept walking, despite knowing that brought her closer to the green car, which meant less time for it to come back and chase her down. Maybe run her down and steal her purse while she was stunned?

"You have got to stop watching those *Investigation Discovery* episodes," she scolded herself, and managed a slightly shaky laugh. Aunt Cleo had gotten her addicted to the channel that covered one mystery, disappearance, and horrific murder after another. They teased each other that all those shows accomplished was to encourage people never to trust anyone and make home security systems installers and self-defense trainers rich.

Why did it suddenly seem like no one was traveling this street?

Saundra caught movement in the doorway of the art supply store. Just three more driveways ahead of her. Someone walked out and toward a car sitting in the parking lot. There were two more cars in the lot. Okay, that was a good sign. She just hoped she wouldn't need --

Movement beyond the store caught her attention. A car pulled out from behind those other two cars, onto the street, and headed toward her. A dark car. Too far away to tell the color, but instinct insisted that was the green sedan.

"Discretion is the better part of valor," she told herself and turned around. Was anyone home in any of these houses? She didn't see any cars in the driveways. Saundra strained her ears for the sound of the green sedan coming up behind her.

"One of these days," a familiar voice said, coming from the shadowy front porch of the house ahead of her, "you're going to listen to me and invest in a taser. A can of pepper spray, at least." It was low, rich with laughter, and her memory supplied the smirk that went with that lazy, teasing tone. "Keep walking. I want to see what this guy will try."

"I don't," she retorted, fighting down a bubble of laughter that was partly relieved and partly a scream of frustration.

Nic West, Aunt Cleo's protégé and sometime investigative partner, peered out between the thick, luxurious grape vines covering the trellis that cast the deep front porch of the Victorian house into shadows. He winked and tipped his head in the direction of the car she heard coming up behind her. Then he ducked back into hiding.

Chances were good part of that sensation of being watched today came from Nic spying on her. That was just how he operated. He showed up and watched her for a few hours, checking out her situation, before he made contact. Half the time, she wanted to accuse him of being terrified of running into the Mulcahys. Now what was his excuse? Testing her self-preservation instincts? Probably. Nic delighted in teaching her little tricks guaranteed to save her neck if she ever got into a really tight situation. Saundra hoped she would never need them, but she was grateful for the lessons. Not that she would ever tell him that.

Gravel crunched under tires. Cigar Man was pulling off the road, onto the berm. Saundra calculated how far he was behind her. She kept walking, straining her ears, focusing to block out the thudding of her heart.

Well, at least she was wrong. Cigar Man wasn't going to --

Instinct screamed. Saundra leaped forward, off the sidewalk, across the ditch, angling up the front lawn of the next house. Behind her, the car's engine roared into life and tires crunched and shot gravel behind them.

Bang -- the car thudded. The engine screamed. Saundra turned, swinging her arm back, ready to sacrifice her groceries by flinging the bag into the windshield. She nearly pulled herself off her feet with the momentum of the bag.

Cigar Man shrieked curses and scrambled out of the car, now tipped sideways, with the front tires trapped in the ditch. Nic leaped out of hiding, trailing a few grape leaves behind him. Cigar Man fled across the street and up the driveway of the creepy-looking pink house with a yard full of gnomes.

Nic vaulted over the hood of the green sedan and raced across the street. Cigar Man turned, and a gunshot startled a shriek out of Saundra. Nic hit the berm and rolled into the ditch on that side of the road. Cigar Man vanished between the houses. Suddenly there were cars coming from both directions. Where had they been when she needed witnesses to protect her just two minutes ago?

Saundra dropped her groceries and darted across the street as soon as the last car passed. Nic had pulled himself out of the ditch and bent over, brushing dirt and grass off his knees and left thigh. She fought the urge to grab and turn him and check him over for injuries. He led a charmed life, as far as she could tell. Bullets wouldn't dare hit him.

"Are you okay?" she asked anyway.

He muttered something in that odd language that seemed to be a mix of French and Spanish with some Latin thrown in and took a few steps like he would follow Cigar Man. Then he sighed and summoned up that trademark crooked grin she sometimes wanted to slap off his handsome, square-cut, olive-skinned face. This wasn't one of those times.

"Well, I was going to take you out to dinner. That English pub back in town looked interesting." He brushed at his clothes again. "Not fit to be seen in public with a lady." A chuckle. "One tough lady. I could almost hear you, calculating your chances. You caught on to him fast."

"Not fast enough. How long was he following me?" She let him lead her back to where she dropped her groceries and her purse.

"He was lying in wait. I checked on you a few times through the day -

-"

"Nice to know I wasn't imagining things."

That got a laugh from him. He brushed her cheek with his knuckles, then gallantly leaped forward a few steps, to pick up her bag and purse for her.

"You were safe, nobody threatening. He was waiting behind the school buildings when you came back. He's not a professional, otherwise he would have noticed me trailing you."

"I don't suppose you left your car anywhere nearby?" The day seemed about twenty hours too long, all of a sudden, now that the excitement was over.

Or maybe it wasn't. A van pulled into the driveway of the house that now had the green sedan sitting in its ditch. Francine Kenward leaped out of the driver's seat and came running.

"Are you all right? What happened?"

Nic gave Saundra a little hushing sign and stepped forward. "We're not sure. I was asking for directions -- new in town -- and this man just swerved into the ditch and took off running. Might want to call the police."

"Daddy's gonna be hacked off," the oldest Kenward boy said with a delighted grin. He headed toward the ditch with his younger siblings in tow. One stern look and a shake of their mother's head, and they stopped. Visibly disappointed.

"Allen lives for his yard," Francine offered. "Somebody get my purse?"

While she was calling the police station, Nic took Saundra aside. She wasn't surprised when he told her to stay there and talk to the police. He had left his car at her apartment building. He would wait for her there. The less the police saw of him right now, the easier it would be for him to keep watch over her.

"Plan on driving yourself everywhere until this guy is caught," he added as he headed across the street and between the houses, following the path Cigar Man had taken.

"Duh," Saundra muttered.

She knew she had recovered most of her equilibrium when her usual irritation with Nic kicked in. It wasn't just the need to inconvenience him a little in retaliation that prompted her to break from the story he had told. She stayed with Francine until a patrol car pulled into the driveway behind the van. The officer on duty turned out to be Allen Kenward. He didn't seem as upset about the gouges in the velvety grass as Saundra expected. He was irritated when Francine told him one of the witnesses had left, but relaxed when Saundra covered for Nic by saying he had gone to try to follow the man who fled the car.

Allen took pictures, wrote down all the pertinent information, then reached in to turn off the engine, pocketed the keys, and locked up the car. He offered to drive her home. She accepted, but as soon as she was in the car, she asked him to take her to the police station, instead.

"I need to talk to Captain Sunderson," she admitted once they were heading up Parkview toward Center.

"Uh huh. Something to do with the guy causing trouble for you and the people at the Mug?"

"I didn't want to frighten Francine."

"Appreciate it." A snort escaped him. "Although, she's a lot tougher than she looks. We've got five kids, after all."

Allen dropped her off on the front steps of the police station because he had to get back to patrolling. When she offered to take the paperwork into the station for him, to help speed up filing his report before he went home, he thanked her, but had to decline.

"About half the time, that wouldn't be any problem even if it does kind of break procedure. Today is not one of those days." He rolled his eyes and wouldn't say anything more.

The front reception area of the police station was quiet. Saundra didn't have any experience with police stations but knew better than to expect what she saw on TV to reflect what real ones should look like. It was too clean and neat, with dark green tile and pale green walls, and metal folding chair. And empty of people. Shouldn't someone be on the front desk at all times?

She waited by the window that reminded her of a bank teller's station, with a grill for speaking and a deep indentation in the counter, to pass things through under the glass. Just what kind of crime did Cadburn deal with that they needed what could be bulletproof glass between the desk officer and whoever came into the station? Or was this just standard, required by law, no matter how nice and quiet or crazy-busy-dangerous a town might be?

"Yeah? What do you want?" The man who strolled across the reception area, from behind her, looked her over with a sneer lifting the left corner of his mouth. He had a little bit of a swagger that just accented the pot belly straining his khaki uniform.

"I need to speak with Captain Sunderson. Please," she added and hoped the slight pause wasn't noticeable.

He paused for a moment, looking her over again, then stepped up to a door she thought was a closet. It turned out to be the entrance into the area behind the glass. He sat down behind the counter, bending forward enough for her to see the bald spot, and what looked like about a quarter inch of gray roots under his dull black thatch of hair.

"What's this about?"

"The purse-snatching on Saturday, mostly."

"Captain's got better things to do. When we've got more information, we'll contact you."

"I have more information for her. Officer Kenward said --"

55

"Kenward's on the road. He's got no say in what happens here in the station."

"Neither do you, Carruthers," Captain Sunderson said, her voice coming from the right of the front desk area. A moment later, she stepped into view, coming from behind the officer. "As a matter of fact, I'm expecting Miss Bailey." With a tip of her head, she gestured for Saundra to go to the door Carruthers had used.

Saundra decided Carruthers was the reason Allen hadn't taken her up on the offer to deliver his report.

Later, she couldn't quite explain why she didn't tell Sunderson everything about the run-in with Cigar Man. Yes, she knew the name he had given Eden was Jacob Styles, but was that his real name? Cigar Man seemed more appropriate. Captain Sunderson even smiled a little when she used it. Saundra left out the details relating to Nic -- specifically, that she knew him, and he had been checking on her. She could honestly say that the man who had leaped out to defend her when Cigar Man tried to run her down, and trapped his car in the ditch, hadn't given her his name. She phrased it as speculation that he might have some training, since he didn't seem frightened by the one shot her attacker had taken at him, and gave chase.

Captain Sunderson let her know the officer who had gone out with the tow truck was on his way back with the green sedan, and they had already traced it to a rental agency. She wouldn't be surprised to learn Jacob Styles used another name for the rental.

Nic was waiting two parking spaces down from the police station when Saundra came out. She knew it was him the moment she saw the low-slung black sports car, before he opened the door and stood up to wave her down. Nic always rented a black, late-model sports car when he came to check on her or meet with Aunt Cleo when she was home from her travels. It was one of his signatures. Saundra muffled a chuckle when she wondered what his reaction would be if she mentioned that to him.

"Were you worried?" she said, once she was seated in the car and he was checking the mirrors before pulling out into the dwindling, dinner-hour traffic.

"I came back in time to see you get in the patrol car. Smart move, talking with the authorities."

"So glad you approve."

That earned a chuckle from him. "Nice little town. I keep meaning to stop in and introduce myself to the reverend and his sister, but ..." He shrugged. "What did you do to my cover story?"

She related most of it on the short drive to her apartment building. There were people in the lobby, and an elderly couple rode up in the elevator with them, so the remainder had to wait until they got upstairs and had ordered pizza to be delivered. Nic approved of what she did and didn't tell about his part in the encounter. He was amused to learn that the responding officer was the homeowner. Saundra didn't ask why. He went over the details of both encounters with Cigar Man, then got everything she knew about Kai, Eden and Troy, and the bits of history of Cadburn she had picked up.

"You know, a vacation home might be nice. I like what I see of this town," he commented, after there was nothing left of the pizza but the box and the paper liner and their dirty dishes. "Mind if I stick around for a few days?"

"Would it matter if I did?"

He laughed. Despite herself, she had to laugh with him. Nic West, despite how he irritated her, really was a good man, dependable, and his presence truly did make her feel safe. Not that she would tell him.

Chapter Seven

Wednesday, August 24

Wednesday morning, Saundra went to retrieve a voicemail she had left on her work phone on Tuesday, because it was easier than writing down the information. The message was gone. She went through the voicemail system three times, just to be sure, and each time the computerized voice insisted there were no messages, new or old.

Odd.

She came back from lunch to see Officer Carruthers leaning on the front desk, talking with Twila. He stopped and glared at her as she walked past the desk. Saundra had all she could do to nod and smile. She couldn't force herself to say it was nice to see him again.

Then she almost stumbled when she saw his hand resting on top of Twila's on the counter, mostly shielded from sight by their bodies. The implications were enough to make her slightly queasy. The thought of anyone being emotionally involved with Twila was slightly mindboggling. Then again, Carruthers did seem to be her sort, just after that one unpleasant encounter with him.

Half an hour later, Twila was on the phone with her back to the front desk, two patrons who were trying to sign out books, and the flashing switchboard. Saundra considered going up there to help out, but chances were good she would just cement Twila's dislike for her. She could take some of those calls, though. If she could remember the instructions Mrs. Tinderbeck gave her on Monday.

"Cadburn Public Library," she said, after successfully finding the right buttons to push on the first try.

"Saundra Bailey, please," a semi-familiar woman's voice asked.

"Speaking."

"Saundra, it's Charli Hall." She laughed. "I was wondering if something was wrong with the system or I got the wrong number or something."

"No, the switchboard's just very busy right now. Sorry if you had to wait. What can I do for you?"

"Well, tonight is the first night of the church choir practice. In fact, we're having a picnic to start off the new year. Choir doesn't sing during the summer, so our year officially starts when the kids go back to school. Anyway, I was hoping you'd join us."

Saundra glanced at the lights on her extension. None were flashing any longer, meaning Twila had answered them, or someone else had jumped in to help. She relaxed and chatted a little with Charli. Joining the choir at church sounded like it might be fun. The library was closed on Wednesday nights, so she didn't have to worry about the scheduling conflict there, at least. They agreed to meet at the park, and Charli would take care of the food contribution to cover both of them since this was Saundra's first time with the choir.

If they still had the energy afterwards, Saundra suggested they get dessert at Book & Mug. She had to laugh when Charli confessed she hadn't had a chance to stop in for months. Usually, the coffee shop was busy when the writing meetings ended at the library. Besides, she was trying to be virtuous and avoid bookstores, because she had over 100 print books waiting to be read, not counting all the e-books on her tablet that she hadn't read yet.

Then Charli said something just before hanging up that took a little of the shine off the morning.

"I was starting to wonder if I had done something to upset you," she said. "I left a message yesterday and this morning, and you didn't call back, so ... well, you know us writers. So insecure. That's why we write instead of handling a day job or working with the public."

"That's funny. Funny-strange, not funny-ha-ha," Saundra hurried to add. "I've had some messages vanish from my phone that I know I kept. Maybe there's something wrong with the system." She thought about the hope to become better friends with Charli. "Remind me, and I'll give you my cell number when we meet up tonight. Then you won't have to go through the switchboard."

"Sounds great. I swear that gargoyle on the switchboard will recognize my voice one of these days, and then I'll never get anywhere." Charli laughed and they said goodbyes and hung up.

Saundra glanced over at Twila's desk as she put the phone in the cradle. Why did she have the sneaking suspicion the other librarian might be involved in her missing messages? First impressions weren't always right, however ...

~~~~~

Troy had left before dawn to drive up to Lansing for a meeting with a botanist. Eden and Kai were having a late lunch in the back corner booth when Captain Sunderson walked into Book & Mug.

"Can we go up to your office?" she asked, her voice pitched low, clearly not wanting to be overheard.

"It's not Troy, is it?" Kai asked, when they were in the old brass elevator and riding up.

"Not that I've heard. This has to do with that Styles character." She paused as the elevator clanged to a stop on the second floor and the metal gate folded up to let them out. "He struck again."

Quickly and simply, Sunderson related how Styles -- if that was his real name -- had gone after Saundra and crashed into a ditch the night before.

The car rental agreement was under another identity, using a stolen credit card. The Cadburn Township police had to send the prints to another jurisdiction to get them traced. Hopefully what they took off the steering wheel and door handle of the car would provide a breakthrough. Eden would have a chance at finding what the fingerprints could show them once the police had gone through the regular channels.

Kai didn't like it that the only witness to the attack had taken off. Ostensibly to chase down Styles. Once Sunderson was gone, he and Eden planned what to do with the information when it came from the police. The first step was talking to Saundra to get a description of the witness to the attack. Eden could do a sketch -- and share it with the police, of course. They both knew better than to do anything that would irritate the authorities. They had spent too much time banging up against walls that others had thrown in their way in their personal quest for answers and information. Being rude or nasty or refusing to cooperate with the authorities never made the relationship any easier to navigate. Cooperation now would contribute to an easier time obtaining answers and maybe having favors granted in the future.

He called Saundra in mid-afternoon to ask her to come to dinner. She thanked him and apologized, but she was joining the choir at church, and tonight was a picnic before choir rehearsal.

"So ... we wanted to ask you about this run-in with Stinky yesterday."

"Oh. I'm sorry. I should have come by, but ..." Saundra let out a sigh that was hard to interpret. He wished he could see her face. "I had a visitor last night, and then it's been a little crazy, with the start of school. And honestly? I'm kind of used to not having people involved in my problems who weren't *causing* the problems. I just didn't think about going to you. And I'm sorry."

"Well, can you make it up to me by stopping by after rehearsal?" He closed his eyes and was glad Saundra wasn't in the same room with him. Did he look as pathetic as he sounded to himself?

"Actually, I'm planning on it, but my friend Charli is coming with me."

"And he is?"

"*She* is a resident of Cadburn who goes to our church."

"Okay. Bring her along. If it's okay to talk about yesterday?"

"That might not be wise. She's a writer. That's how I met her. She and her writing group came to a conference my former library used to hold. We met and became friends, and it was a total surprise, a nice one, when we ran into each other at church."

"That's great. Why wouldn't it be smart to talk about Stinky in front of her?" Kai mentally kicked himself for keeping this going. Why did he keep digging?

"That's the kind of stuff she writes. Mysteries. Suspense. You want this whole mess to end up as a *New York Times* bestseller in a couple years?"

"Hey, why not? We're both bibliophiles."

"True." She laughed with him.

He did feel better when they finally had to say goodbye. Kai thought he heard the front desk librarian's snarky voice somewhere in the background before Saundra said she had to get off the phone. He hoped he wasn't responsible for getting her in trouble. There were a few times he left the library without the books he wanted, just because that nosey old bat was the only one on desk duty. She had it in for him and Eden and Troy because her boyfriend, Carruthers, insisted they were trouble. And Carruthers, aka Dudley Do-Wrong, was in Roger Cadburn's pocket.

Somebody should really warn Saundra about Cadburn's nasty politics, the snakes in the grass or shadows or whatever. He wasn't sure if he should be the one, because he enjoyed watching Saundra learn about Cadburn. He didn't want to ruin this new home and experience for her. He also didn't want her to be ambushed. Although he was pretty sure Saundra was smart and observant and could identify most oncoming troublemakers and sticky situations in plenty of time to avoid them.

He just wished the library would bring in those automated systems, where he could scan the book and scan his library card, and not have any contact whatsoever with crazy Twila at the checkout desk.

~~~~~

"There she is," Eden said that evening, reaching over the counter to touch Kai's arm.

She had been sitting at the far side of the order counter where she had a good view of the door of Book & Mug. They needed to separate Saundra from her friend long enough to get a basic description of the man who had witnessed Styles trying to hit her. They had no plan, just waited to use whatever opportunity provided.

Growing up, Kai, Eden and Troy had become good at improv, identifying opportunities and openings. That had been necessary for self-defense, and to stay together. They had been thrown into the child welfare system so young, Kai couldn't remember any other life. He was the youngest and had clung to Eden and Troy, the only faces he recognized. Eden was the oldest, and insisted they were cousins, and she had fought to keep them together. They had learned through necessity to work around well-meaning and ill-intentioned social workers, and other authorities who tried to separate them. Their biggest obstacles were the false identities and histories Sybil Orwell had slapped on them when she threw the three children into the system and hit the metaphorical handle to flush them away.

Kai looked up in time see Saundra point at the counter, and then change the gesture to wave at him. He could almost read her lips as she pointed at him, then Eden, and gave their names to the woman with her. Charli was a few inches taller than Saundra, with a short mop of dark chocolate curls, dark eyes, sharp cheekbones and pointed chin. She was all sleek lines and an easy, rolling sort of stride. She wore a *Guardians of the Galaxy* T-shirt and faded jeans. Kai liked her already.

Light glinted on something resting approximately on her collarbone. She turned and the sparkle vanished.

"Nothing as wonderful as punctuality," he greeted them as Saundra and Charli stepped up to the counter.

"Just what every woman wants to hear," Eden said with a groan and a roll of her eyes. That got chuckles from both women.

"No, what I mean is that it's nice that ... oh, heck." Kai hoped the light was soft enough this late in the day that his face didn't look red. It felt warm enough. "Okay, I calculated how long it would take to get from your church if you were walking or if you drove. You're pretty much on time." He held out his watch, as if that explained things. "Give or take five minutes."

"Walking time or driving time?" Charli rested her forearms on the edge of the counter and leaned into it. That dropped the collar of her T-shirt just enough to see a glint of something red and glossy. She had on a short necklace, or maybe a choker of some kind.

"Walking."

"Sorry." Saundra shrugged. "We stood around gabbing for a while after choir, and I drove. After yesterday ... well, some friends advised me not to walk to work for the time being. Which kind of reeks. I love that I live so close to everything in this town."

"What happened yesterday?" Charli asked.

"Saundra witnessed an accident." Eden slid off her stool and moved closer. "The driver was kind of nasty to her, and you know how some people are. The more at fault they are, they more they think they have to punish the people who saw them being morons."

"Oh, don't I know it." She nodded, her grin going crooked. "I have a friend who's an investigator. People sure don't like having their secrets uncovered, and especially when uncovering them protects other people. I hear you're an investigator, too."

"I try." She shrugged. "Speaking of which ... Saundra, would you mind describing the other witness, the one who ran off after the driver? If I can do a sketch, that might help track him down."

"Oh, this sounds juicy," Charli said, nudging Saundra's arm. "Do I need to pump you for details?"

"Pump?" Kai said. "Oh, that's right. Saundra said she met you at a writing conference. What do you write?"

"I don't know anymore, honestly." Some of the sparkle left Charli's eyes. She reached up to touch her collar, and pulled out that red, glossy object, maybe two inches wide, to rub between the first two fingers and her thumb. "Getting a lot of grief from a would-be agent and a pretty nasty publisher and ..." She shook her head. "Nothing like feeling like a beginner no matter how long you've been chasing the dream."

"It's not you, it's them," Saundra said, reaching to rest a hand on Charli's shoulder. "I've read everything you've written and --" Her forehead crinkled, just for a moment. "Well, you're incredible. That's all I can say."

"You're biased."

"Have I read anything you've written?" Kai asked, then a moment later wished he hadn't. If a bibliophile like him didn't recognize her name, then probably she wasn't published yet. She might be sensitive about it.

"Have you read anything by Charli Hall, would-be sleuth and apprentice investigator?" Charli asked, with a toss of her head for punctuation. She tucked that red bauble on her necklace back inside her collar.

"Hmm, sorry. No."

"Nothing to apologize for. Now, what about this sketch? Are you a sketch artist? With the police?" she said, focusing on Eden.

"Before you get all official-like," Kai said, "what can I get you ladies?"

"Saundra's been raving about your version of klah. Iced, please."

"Make it two," Saundra said.

Kai thought about teasing her that she wanted twice as much as Charli, but Eden's thoughtful little frown caught his attention. She led Saundra and Charli to the back corner booth to sit and talk. When he brought their drinks to the table less than ten minutes later, all three turned to look at him.

"What? Did I spill something on myself? Do I have spinach between my teeth?"

"According to Saundra, our mysterious witness looks like you and Troy. Maybe a long-lost cousin," Eden said.

"Don't even joke about that." Kai forced himself to grin, to make a joke out of it.

"I'm just saying, the eyes, the hair, the nose, but ..." Saundra turned a little in the booth to look straight at him. "The face is squarer, the skin a few shades darker, more olive. Maybe the tip of the nose is more pointed. The shoulders a little wider. And I'd guess he's in his mid-thirties."

"That's a lot of detail to pick up in a face-to-face that lasted, what, ten minutes at the most?" Eden said slowly.

Saundra blushed. She shrugged and picked up the tall glass Kai had put in front of her, so quickly she almost swept it off the table and into her lap before she got her hands around it.

"Oh, I've seen it happen. And Carson, my PI friend, he's told me about it. In a really tense situation, you focus on something, anything, to kind of block out the really horrid details," Charli offered. "If there's someone else there with you, especially someone who's a stranger, you focus on them.

Kind of a drowning man situation."

"Makes sense," Kai said.

He had to go back to the counter because he was working, after all. Wednesdays could be busy later in the evening. All the churches had choir rehearsals, or Bible studies, or family activities. Clubs met somewhere, such as the book club that met in the pavilion in the park every other week. Once September hit, they would switch either to the café at Third Street Bakery, or Book & Mug to meet indoors until spring and pleasant weather returned.

A larger handful of people than usual came in after the square dancing club finished for the evening. He was barely halfway through their orders when Eden came up to the counter, leaned over it to put her glass in the dirty dishes pan, and waited. He looked over at her. She tipped her head toward the corner booth then gestured up toward her office. He nodded, guessing she meant she was finished getting the sketch from Saundra.

The square dancers were succeeded by a bunch of guys talking baseball. They looked sweaty and dusty, and loudly compared people whose names he didn't know to the current Major League team rosters. Kai guessed they were baseball players themselves and had just had a game or practice. From their high spirits, he guessed they had won. After they placed their orders and moved to the other end of the counter to wait for them, Charli stepped up with her glass.

"I have to get going. Let me settle up for both of us," she said.

"Nope. On the house. As long as you promise to come back."

"Oh, definitely." She grinned and took a few steps backward. "I've avoided the goodies you have here just to try to be virtuous. Too much sitting in my line of work. But after tonight? I've searched the world over, looking for someone who could make a decent klah. The Dragon Lady would be proud."

"Blame Saundra. She's the one who gave me the idea." He slapped the lid on the blender carafe and set it on the stand.

"I'm bringing my writing friends, next time it's my turn to host."

"Ah, see? There's a method to my madness."

She waved and turned to leave, and he was busy with the blender, and shaving chocolate, and pouring espresso syrup, and piling double whipped cream on glasses for a few minutes. Then Eden was at the end of the counter, looking a little frantic.

She was wearing her Venetian glass heart locket.

Out in plain sight. Where anybody could see it.

Kai swallowed down the need to shout for her to at least tuck it away out of sight, inside her collar. Eden had learned to pick locks, thanks to interfering social workers and other authorities who had decided that three abandoned children who couldn't even speak English had no right to possess expensive antiques. All three had been wearing heart lockets, nearly identical on the front, and only differentiated by the stripe of color on the back. Eden had retrieved their lockets at least five times during that first year of confusion and fighting to stay together. Finally Kai and Troy entrusted her with all three lockets, and she kept them hidden. Certainly no one thought it odd for a girl to have glass hearts, but boys wearing heart lockets always caught attention. Attention led to questions, which led to too much interest. Which led to someone taking the lockets away.

So why was Eden wearing the locket now? Why out where anybody walking into Book & Mug could see it?

He finished the last drink, a Mississippi mud frappe, with layers of caramel and fudge lying in the bottom of the glass, and more sinking through the chocolate whipped cream on top. Kai sent it sliding down the counter into the hand of the too-skinny-for-his-own-good guy who had ordered it. He definitely needed the calories. Then without waiting to see if it reached its destination, he left the dirty containers on the counter and hurried down to Eden.

"Where are they?"

For a second, he nearly asked who she meant. He could see the door into the back hallway. Saundra stepped through as he opened his mouth to answer.

"Well, Saundra's just coming back from the bathroom. Charli left maybe five minutes ago. What's up with --" He nodded, glancing down at the locket.

"Charli has one. I was close enough to get glimpses, and then I couldn't keep trying to look down her shirt, so I just asked. She showed it to me." Eden caught up the locket, hanging on a chain long enough to put it securely down inside the collar of her shirt, safe from slipping out or being glimpsed. Like that blob of sparkly red Kai had glimpsed inside Charli's collar several times. She cupped it in her hand, as she had done hundreds of times over the years, as if waiting for the locket to open and spill its secrets.

"So you thought if she saw yours, like a secret password ...?" He wasn't quite sure where he was going with that thought.

"Charli isn't much older than us, but who knows? She might not be an orphan like us, and maybe her parents told her about the hearts, what they mean, what the seeds are for."

"We're not orphans. We just got separated from our folks, and they can't find us yet."

"Kai, I love what an optimist you are, but ..." She sighed. "I've been searching since high school. Either they don't want to be found, or ... they can't look for us." Eden rested her hand on his for a moment.

"Hey," Saundra said, joining them. She opened her wallet as she stepped up to the counter. "Let me settle up for me and Charli."

"She already tried." Kai glared at Eden, trying to tell her with just his gaze to put the heart away.

"That rat. I told her tonight was my treat." Saundra laughed and put her wallet back in her purse. "No wonder she wanted to take off before --" Her gaze caught on the heart cupped in Eden's fingers. "Wow ... that's just like ... Charli's."

"I was hoping we could compare them," Eden said.

"Well, Charli is the expert. She has a humongous collection of glass hearts. She said it started with one her grandmother had. She loved it so much, she just wanted more." Saundra shrugged and looked around the shop. Kai had the oddest feeling she didn't want to look at them just then.

"I probably shouldn't have told you that. It's kind of ..." Another shrug. "Personal? You know, I hate to eat -- slurp?" A breathy chuckle. "Okay, I hate to guzzle and run, but it's been a really long day and we're doing a lot of back-to-school stuff tomorrow, and ... See you in the morning? Gotta have my morning jolt to get the brain going," she said, backing toward the door.

"Absolutely." Kai held onto his smile until she turned around to face forward. He watched her as she went out the door and walked three spaces down to get to her car. After that remark about being advised to drive rather than walk, he was relieved that she was able to park in front, where he could see her get into her car.

"I think we scared her." Eden had finally tucked the heart into her shirt, out of sight. That let him relax. "We got kind of intense for a few seconds."

"Ya think? E, I thought we agreed, never bring them out into the light of day."

"Maybe we should. Maybe if I wore my heart, let people see it, maybe talk about it, even ask questions, that might bring people to us who know the secrets."

"Yeah ..." He exhaled, forcing a good chunk of tension out of his muscles. "I mean, what can they do to us now? It's not like they're going to try to take the hearts to make us pay for the cost of raising us, ten years after we were set free."

"You make it sound like we were in prison. We had great house parents."

"Once we got them trained. Once we got them to understand we wouldn't let anybody separate us."

"Once Troy earned enough money to give us a cushion, and we learned enough to make the system work for us." She turned to look out the front of the shop. Saundra's car had vanished into the night. "We have to be careful, though. Someone wanted us lost in the system. We don't need to get them angry if they're out there checking up on us."

"Oh, lovely thought. Guess who's not getting any sleep tonight?"

Eden snorted, and grinned, and slapped his arm.

~~~~~

Saundra had been composing the email in her head from the moment she jumped into her car to head home. She could almost wish the drive was longer, or she had ignored Nic's advice and walked to choir practice and the Book & Mug, so she had the walk home to give her more time to think.

What did Kai and Eden think of her, hurrying out like that? Hopefully, they chalked up her behavior to the after-effects of Cigar Man coming after her.

She pulled into her designated parking spot at the apartment building and got out of the car without thinking. Four steps, and she remembered Nic's lecture on being careful in parking lots, especially late at night. Well, too late now to park in a different spot every time, to avoid being so visible, and to look in all directions before walking in the open. She kept alert as she crossed the parking lot and made sure she stayed away from dark places where someone could leap out of hiding at her. Would Nic at least be satisfied she did that much?

Safely inside the building, and alone in the elevator that clanged and rattled a little as it rose to her floor, she turned her thoughts back to the email. Such a simple message. Should she just leave it at the facts and not waste time with questions and ideas? No extraneous details?

The worst part in all this, she supposed, was that she had no idea of the importance, the significance, of the Venetian glass hearts. Only that Aunt Cleo was scouring the world for them, and Saundra must never let slip the slightest hint they were anything more than just glass hearts. Not their age. Not their value. And certainly not the secret for opening them. The craftsman who made the hearts decades ago had created the hinges hidden inside, so a cursory examination wouldn't reveal the hearts were lockets. To protect the secret.

Whatever that secret was. Saundra didn't know. She didn't ask -- Aunt Cleo never told her, specifically to protect her.

Despite gnawing on the task for the last fifteen minutes, by the time Saundra sat down in front of her computer, her mind blanked. She stared at the cursor pulsing in the message field of her email program and still couldn't decide how to start.

Sighing, she got up, giving in to temptation. It wasn't like her aunt had told her never to do what she was about to do, but she still felt like she was betraying a trust.

Patty and Roy's friend who had once lived in this apartment had made some modifications that Saundra doubted the landlord knew about. Saundra wondered for a moment if Curtis, who apparently acted as handyman for a lot of people, had helped make those changes. Did he know about the compartment in the window seat, or the other one behind the medicine cabinet in her bathroom, tucked among the pipes?

Saundra pulled the curtains down to hide what she was doing, then she lifted the cushion off the window seat. Even if her living room windows looked out over the park, and the trees were still thick and luxurious, just because she couldn't see anyone down there on the ground -- or even in a tree -- watching her, that didn't mean she was hidden from their view.

She tipped up the lid, reached into the window seat, and moved aside a few boxes of personal papers sitting on top. She caught hold of the handle of the strongbox, then slipped the fingers of the other hand under the opposite end. It was a tight fit. She had to be careful lifting the box out so it wouldn't scrape and catch against the sides. She took the strongbox to the kitchen and dug out the key from the bottom flap of the baking soda box she kept in the freezer. Cleo had taught her many tricks of hiding and disguise and erasing clues that anything of value was present. Not that she had needed to learn many of them by the time Cleo included her in the family secrets. Saundra had learned quite a bit on her own before she was ten. Doing so had been necessary, to defend her favorite books and treats and other treasures from the prying, spying, and thieving tendencies of Bridget and Edmund. Starting way back in kindergarten.

Saundra wiped the retrieved key on the dishtowel before sliding it into the lock of the strongbox. For a moment the key refused to turn, and she had the awful feeling she had mixed up the keys. Cleo gave a handful to her when she passed over the guardianship of several safe deposit boxes in different cities, along with files and papers in that odd language that was partly French, partly Spanish, and maps that looked like they belonged in museums.

A little more pressure and the key turned in the lock with a thick kind of stiffness that could be blamed on dust and disuse. Inside the strongbox were several bundles of photographs, inside airtight boxes with desiccant packets, and wrapped in plastic. Several long jewelry boxes, just the right size for necklaces, with metal straps holding them closed. They rattled slightly and made sliding sounds when she gave each one a testing shake. A cube of plastic in multiple layers, like a stack of CD cases, was filled with dozens of leaves and bits of stems, roots, and seeds, ranging in size from dust to the shape of wild rice. All of them preserved in the plastic. The descendants of all those samples thrived now in her balcony greenhouse and greenhouses tended by trusted friends and allies. Saundra had only met a few of them. She supposed some of Cleo's travels involved visiting those greenhouses and allies on a regular basis. Sometimes Cleo returned from her travels with new plants for Saundra to tend, but more often, she took samples of Saundra's plants to those allies to add to their collections.

At the bottom was a brown velvet-covered jewelry box. Saundra held her breath as she brought out the box and tipped it open. A sigh escaped her, and she smiled as the overhead lights caught on the bits of sparkle embedded in the clear glass that surrounded the red core of the Venetian glass heart. It was just as enchanting as her first glimpse when she was in kindergarten.

Her mother had been ill, and Aunt Cleo had come to stay with them and look after her. Saundra should have known then that it was more than just being feverish and coughing for nearly two months. It was the first of four bouts with cancer that finally took her mother away. Aunt Cleo had brought the heart for Corinne to hold. It seemed to help her. Saundra had waited until her mother fell asleep before daring to pick up the heart from her thin, feverish fingers, and examine it for herself.

Aunt Cleo had told her then that she must never tell anyone about it because it was very old and very rare and expensive. Saundra had never asked, but she had the oddest certainty that her father didn't know about it.

Within days of Aunt Cleo's arrival, her Mulcahy relatives made an unexpected and inexplicable visit. The Mulcahys despised Aunt Cleo, according to Cleo, Corrinne, and Samuel, but they put on a big show now of wanting to welcome the world traveler "home." Saundra didn't know what they discussed with her parents, but Bridget and Edmund asked if her aunt had anything interesting in her luggage. Would she be a best pal and prove she was a "real" Mulcahy and distract her aunt while they looked through it? Before she could muster the courage to say no, they ran off. Aunt Cleo caught them trying to open her suitcases. Several times. After that, her aunt never brought the heart into the house again.

The heart in her hands now was just as beautiful as the first time she saw it, despite the cloud of sad memories and mystery enclosing it.

"Idiot," she whispered. "Coward. Just get it over with."

Saundra sighed and put the heart back in its box. She carefully put everything back in the strongbox in the order she found it and put the box back in the window seat.

Aunt Cleo --

I finally got a good, up close look at Charli's heart. It's the real thing. The stripe on the back is royal blue, and the pinhole is on the right side of the tiny curve in the tip of the heart, which points to the right, when I look at it from the back.

Even more important: my new friend, Eden, has a heart that looks like ours. She kind of froze for a second, when she saw Charli's.

Here's what's weird. She went upstairs to put her sketchpad away -- she wanted me to describe the "other witness" from yesterday. I tried to be vague. She sketched a guy who is pretty generic, but does look a little like Nic. I need to warn him if he hangs around much longer. But Eden came back down after Charli left, and she was wearing the heart.

You told me not to approach Charli about her heart, so I don't have to ask about Eden. I know you'll be checking her out, though I

70

*don't know how much you'll be able to find out about her
background. From what Kai has said, the three of them were
orphaned when they were little kids. For all I know, Eden bought
the heart.*

I won't say anything or do anything until you tell me otherwise.

~~~~~

Kai supposed he had cursed himself. The power of suggestion and all
that rot. When he joked with Eden that he wouldn't be able to sleep now, he
hadn't meant it.

Just after 1am, he gave up trying to sleep. He had tossed and turned
until his sheets threatened to come off his bed, then lay still by willpower,
until his muscles ached from the effort. Now he thought about all those
magic potions Troy was always fooling with. Better living through organics
and nutrition. What were the chances Troy had labeled something he had
created in his laboratory kitchen, and he could look through the triple-wide
refrigerator and find something to help him sleep? Why did his cousin have
to pick tonight to be away?

He tugged up his sleeping shorts as he padded across his living room
and opened the door to the little foyer area between their apartments. It
smelled stuffy. Why was the stairwell door closed? For ventilation, they left
the doors open on the second and third floors and had installed a screen
door on the little hut that covered the stairwell on the roof. Kai opened the
door. He didn't get the immediate gush of air laden with paper and plastic
and the smell of warm circuits that usually filled the stairwell on hot
summer evenings.

Something sweet-burned and acid-metallic, like dirty sweat, drifted on
the warm air.

In all the monster movies, someone was always dumb enough to go
into the darkness, following whatever weird sound or light or smell caught
their attention. Kai knew better, or at least he thought he did. He backed
away from the dark stairwell that was suddenly worse than those dream-
memories that had awakened him screaming when he was six and seven
years old. The memories of hands picking him up and dragging him away
amid bright bursts of light and loud sounds that made his ears ring so he
couldn't hear anything for days. He backed up to the window that opened
out onto the fire escape and opened the window. Slowly. To avoid the
screaming of the polymer frame that always seemed to stick worse than
wood.

Warm air flowed past him, into the building, heading toward the
stairwell. It carried the now-familiar scent of fruity, cheap cigar and sweaty
male. He knew he wasn't imagining. Stinky, or Cigar Man, as Saundra
called the failed purse snatcher, was close enough for his body odor to carry

on the warm air to Kai.

He doubted the wind would carry the scent all the way up from the sidewalk. So, what did that leave him?

Voices filtered down through the too-quiet, warm night.

Okay, so someone was on the roof.

How did they get on the roof without going up the stairwell? *Inside* the building.

How did they get in the building?

The heck with monsters lurking in the shadows. He was twenty-nine. He wasn't scared of movie monsters or faerie tale monsters. More important, Eden was alone on the floor below him. Stinky had already shot at Saundra. Eden was skilled in self-defense, hand-to-hand fighting. But how much good was that against a gun?

All three of them hated guns. There were guns in their shared nightmares. Right now, Kai wondered if it was time to change their policy and get conceal-carry permits. Avoiding tense situations didn't seem to ward off danger anymore. He darted into Troy's apartment for the biggest cooking knives he could find. He could throw knives. He settled for two bread knives with wickedly serrated blades and dashed down the stairs.

He tried not to think of how stupid he was facing intruders with at least one gun, wearing nothing but sleeping shorts, armed only with two bread knives. Eden could be in trouble. She had taken care of him when he was little. He had to take care of her.

Kai mentally kicked himself. He should have taken ten seconds to call the police and report an intruder. Too late now to go back upstairs and find his phone. He had to find out what was going on, where Stinky was lurking, find a way to stop him. Yeah, and make sure there really was an intruder before he called the police. With his luck, Carruthers was on duty tonight. He'd really love that if Kai turned in a false alarm.

The stairwell door on the second-floor landing was closed. Stinky had obviously closed it. Kai half-expected it to be locked from the other side when he hit it running, but the knob turned easily. He skidded a little in his bare feet on the dusty tile of the supply room as he barreled through, into the office. Eden's apartment door was closed. When he opened it, he found her sprawled on her couch. The dribble of melted ice cream in the bottom of a carton and a book that had fallen on the floor explained what she had been doing when she fell asleep.

He almost forgot to put the knives down as he reached to shake her awake. Eden's reflexes were two steps ahead of him, as always, and she woke before he touched her.

"Somebody's on the roof. One of them is Stinky, and he's arguing with someone," he whispered. Just in case her window was open, and someone was listening instead of joining in the low-key argument. Then he turned and dashed out to the office to check the security system. Something had to be wrong for Stinky to get into their building without setting off the alarms. How?

Eden proved her common sense by not asking any stupid questions, such as "Are you sure?" She was on his heels and settled at her own workstation, so in moments, they both were checking different parts of the building security system.

"All the cameras are off. How did they turn them off without coming up here?" she murmured.

Kai clicked to another screen. "They're not off." He turned the monitor so she could see, although the print on the screen was too small to read from where she sat. "Power's been cut."

"Someone could cut the cables or just pull the power feed ... but they'd have to do that from inside. How did they get inside?" She shook her head. "I'm calling the cops. Where are you going?" She flinched when her voice rose.

Kai almost laughed. He hadn't even realized he was moving until he was halfway to the supply room door heading for the stairwell.

"Won't do us any good to have the cops come if they leave before they get here."

"Kai --"

"I'm just gonna test that security bar Troy said we might need someday."

"Yeah in the event of an aerial attack," she muttered, as he headed into the storeroom.

Troy had insisted during the remodeling that they needed to secure the roof door. Two heavy iron brackets on either side of the door, screwed deep into the wood, held two-by-four planks that kept it from opening inward.

Kai didn't think of the bread knives until he was halfway between the third floor and the roof. This was proof he would never survive past the first ten minutes in a horror movie. He made it up to the stairwell door. The intruders had made a big mistake closing that door. How they did without making enough noise to rouse him, when he wasn't sleeping, he didn't know. Odd -- the hinges sort of glistened in the red emergency lighting at the top of the stairs. He touched them.

"Okay," he whispered, "who would know they need oil?" He shuddered, then shuddered again. He was wasting time, standing there and thinking when he had to *act*. Fast.

Troy was right about the security bar. Fortunately, he wasn't the kind to say "I told you so." Not too much, anyway. For good measure, once he had the planks in place, Kai pressed the button on the lock for the door. Not that it would do much good, but --

The door rattled and the doorknob clicked. Someone tried to turn it. Voices came from the other side of the door, muffled enough to blur the words, but not the emotion. Anger. Surprise.

Kai skidded down the stairs, trying to be quiet, shoulders hunched in anticipation of a bullet smashing through the door. Did people really shoot locks out of doors? How many bullets would it take to break those two-by planks and get the door open?

"Stupid," he growled at himself, and skidded to a halt on the landing.

The rattle of the old-fashioned, iron-pipe fire escape came clearly through the warm night air.

The trespassers were climbing down the fire escape.

What would they do when they got to Eden's floor and found out the ladder to drop to the street level was gone? Stupid answer to a stupid question: go through Eden's apartment to the stairs.

Kai dashed to the window to lock it. In his imagination, he was already racing down the stairs to warn Eden, get her off the floor, and fly down the stairs to the coffee shop. He grabbed the bottom of the sash window to slam it closed. It stuck. The cigar smell he had come to loathe slammed him in the nose. A black-clad figure slid down onto the landing outside his window.

Stinky Cigar Man Styles turned and looked Kai in the eyes. Terrified anger lit up his face. He reached into his bulging pocket. Kai knew it was a gun. He stumbled back two steps.

Styles raised the gun and aimed.

An inarticulate, baritone shout rang through the darkness and bounced off all the buildings up and down Apple. A huge, dark shape dropped down on Styles. He screamed like a girl, and the two forms banged against the railing. Kai glimpsed two sets of legs flailing, then they vanished. The fire escape framework clattered and banged. He stumbled to the window and looked out, and down, through the grid of the third-floor landing. Two dark shapes struggled, tumbling down the steps to the second floor, where they landed hard. A terrifying screech of old iron bolts pulling out of bricks filled the air. The glass of Eden's bedroom window shattered. A man shouted, cursing, and tried to pull free of the tangle of two bodies on the landing. That same muffled, clogged, baritone voice cried out.

Moonlight glinted on the gun pointed at the man lying in shadows on the landing.

"No!" Kai shouted. He had no idea why, until later. Everything had happened so fast, he had no time to think, just react. When the whole mess ended, he realized it was because the man with Styles had saved his life, stopping him from shooting.

The gun swung up, pointing at Kai. He ducked back out of sight and braced to hear the fire escape rattle as Stinky climbed up to shoot him.

He still hadn't shut that window.

Styles shouted and the fire escape rattled and banged more. The shout turned to a scream. The gun went off.

In the distance, sirens finally streamed through the air. The police station was only a block away, but it sounded like miles.

A horrid, wet, dull thud ended the scream.

Kai looked out. No one was on the fire escape below him.

A dark shape slowly moved on the sidewalk two stories below him. It separated from another shape and staggered away into the darkness beyond the streetlights. The second shape didn't move.

His imagination painted pictures of what a body had to look like, falling from the second-floor fire escape to the pavement, smashed under another body that looked at least twice his size. Kai tried to push the bloody images from his mind as he stumbled down the stairs to Eden.

She met him in the storage room, with sweatpants pulled on over her pajamas, holding a T-shirt he had left in the office in one hand, and her cell phone in the other. Troy answered her call when they were halfway down the stairs. She told him in minimal details what had happened. He didn't say anything except that he was on his way. Kai wrapped his arm around Eden as they went out the side door to meet the police.

Jacob Styles, Stinky Cigar Man, lay sprawled on his back, eyes wide with shock, still clutching his gun, with one leg hanging off the curb. Blood slowly spread across the sidewalk from the back of his head.

~~~~~

Carruthers didn't conduct the preliminary investigation on site, but he had the night shift this week, just as Kai feared. He lingered on the sidelines, making his opinion very clear with snorts and mutters. Shrieve conducted the questioning downstairs in the coffee shop, while Kocevar went around on the roof and up and down the fire escape, taking pictures, and dusting for fingerprints, and gathering any evidence he might find.

"Do you want to weigh in on something?" Shrieve finally said, when Carruthers snorted and made a hacking noise, like he would spit. Even he wasn't stupid enough to spit indoors.

Kai wondered if he should have offered to make coffee for the investigating officers. Would that be considered a bribe? Maybe the leftover pastries? Then again, he doubted anything would sweeten Carruthers' disposition.

"Cut and dried," Carruthers said, swinging his awkward shape around to perch on the edge of the table opposite the booth where Shrieve sat facing Eden and Kai. "The guy's been making a pest of himself. This one --" he hooked his thumb at Kai, "-- let him in and took him up on the roof to talk, then when the guy threatened him, pushed him off the side."

"There would be a lot more damage from a fall of three full stories," Eden said, her voice soft and so emotionless, it was a rebuke in and of itself.

Carruthers, of course, didn't catch it.

"You actually expect us to believe someone got in here and cut your security system? Turned it off? Convenient, don't you think?"

"Any theories how someone got in and managed to do that?" Shrieve said.

"Someone who knows the system, someone who got a key." Eden shrugged. "We've been here six years now. Plenty of chances for someone to figure things out, maybe get someone we trust to help them."

"Maybe you ain't so popular as you think," Carruthers muttered. He settled in more comfortably on the end of the table and crossed his arms. The table creaked under him.

Kai almost wished the heavy, reinforced table would break under him. With his luck, that wouldn't even stun Carruthers, or shut his nasty mouth for more than ten minutes. Then he would have another gripe to add to all the false accusations he constantly made against Book & Mug. Granted, Carruthers didn't think of most of them. Everything he said quite clearly parroted the claims and accusations and complaints Cadburn and his new wife made against Book & Mug and the cousins, every chance they got.

Kai wondered what I-told-you-so stories Cadburn would get out of this morning's break-in and death.

Chapter Eight

Thursday, August 25

Saundra arrived fifteen minutes before the library doors were supposed to open. Carruthers was inside, leaning on the front desk and talking in low tones with Twila. She thought about asking why Twila let the man in, when she was such a stickler for holding strictly to the posted library hours for everyone else. Just yesterday, at 6pm closing time, she had snatched books out of the hands of two people waiting to check out their books. The library was officially closed. It didn't matter that both those people had been waiting while Twila gossiped with Ashley Cadburn.

Saundra sighed, turned her gaze off those two troublemakers, and headed for the breakroom to put her lunch in the refrigerator. She had learned long ago to choose her battles wisely. Mrs. Tinderbeck was seated at the lunch table watching the coffee pot as it brewed the first pot of the day.

"Oh, there you are, dear." She smiled, but the usual chipper morning person brightness didn't touch her eyes.

"Mrs. T? Are you all right?"

"Fine, fine. Do me a favor and meet me in my office? Some things shouldn't be discussed out in the open."

Saundra agreed, put her lunch away, and headed to her desk to turn on her computer. She kept watch, and when Mrs. Tinderbeck migrated from the breakroom to her office with her mug of coffee, she followed.

"Close the door, please," Mrs. Tinderbeck said without turning around. She settled at her desk as Saundra complied and waited until she had taken the chair facing her. "Now, this is one of those situations where good news is mixed with bad, and things will likely get worse before they get better. Just remember that I'm here for you, and I've already called Patty and Pastor Roy."

"It's not --" Saundra caught herself and pushed down the panic rising up in her. No, it couldn't be Aunt Cleo. Patty would call her, rather than leaving it to Mrs. Tinderbeck to tell her. "Something awful has happened, hasn't it?"

"Quite an appropriate word. That awful man who tried to steal your purse. He was breaking into the Book & Mug and fell to his death from the fire escape."

"Are they all right? Kai, and Eden, and Troy? They didn't get hurt, did they?"

No wonder those two nasties were gossiping and having a good time at the front desk. Saundra had been raised on puzzles and putting disparate pieces together to get a whole picture. She had already picked up the skeins of some of the rivalries and feuds in Cadburn.

Eden had called this morning, to ask Mrs. Tinderbeck to break the news to Saundra. Since she had been threatened by Styles, she should be ready when the police came to get her side of the story for their investigation. Captain Sunderson also called Mrs. Tinderbeck, as a courtesy because she had been there on Saturday and because calling Saundra in for questioning would disrupt the library which was under her jurisdiction.

Plus, sitting in the breakroom had allowed Mrs. Tinderbeck to hear a good portion of what Carruthers and Twila were chuckling over. She thought Saundra should be braced for all sorts of wild stories and speculations.

"Thank you. I've had more than my share of dealing with people who choose speculations over facts. The kind of people who get nasty when what they want to believe is proven wrong. Like their rights have been violated." Saundra tried to smile. "When should I go to the station?"

"Oh, Danny Shrieve is the lead investigator, and he's coming here. Lovely man. We all agree that you've had to endure enough already. Besides, it might be wise to keep a low profile for a few days. Stay away from Center, if you know what I mean."

"It's a good think I packed my lunch today, isn't it?"

~~~~~

Officer Shrieve did indeed live up to Mrs. Tinderbeck's description of him. He was kind when he asked his questions and apologized when he had to show her pictures of the dead man, to verify that yes, this was the man she had seen Saturday and Tuesday. More important to Saundra, he answered her questions and either verified or denied the gossip that had reached the library before he arrived. The overheard whispers and outright questions just proved how quickly rumors flew and twisted far away from facts. Saundra had a better idea of the political loyalties now. People either scoffed at or sympathized with Trustee Cadburn's take on the incident. After all, he had predicted the cousins would cause trouble someday.

Rumors said the security system at Book & Mug had been turned off. Shrieve said the power cables to the cameras had been cut. Gossip made Kai the lead suspect, on the verge of being arrested. The popular method of murder was a baseball bat. Shrieve assured her the police considered Kai and Eden innocent, and all evidence proved Styles had fallen to his death. Two security cameras on two buildings showed him falling, and Kai visible at the window while two dark figures struggled and fell from the fire escape. He had never touched the dead man.

The authorities were concentrating on finding the second person who had been on the roof and had fallen, fighting with Styles. Saundra's spirits were in better shape when Shrieve thanked her for her time and left the little conference room on the far side of the library. However, when she passed the front desk a short time later, her spirits fell again. Ashley Cadburn was gossiping with Twila, in almost the same position and posture as Carruthers had been three hours ago. Their voices, sugary and raspy, made a sort of hissing and crackling background hum.

"Serves them right," Ashley said, as Saundra passed by the desk at the closest point. "After all, they stole that lovely old building from our family. It took long enough, but trouble caught up with them, just like my hubby said it would."

Saundra held her breath and picked up her pace. She absolutely would not turn around and give those two catty idiots the satisfaction of knowing she had heard them. Chances were good Ashley had raised her voice to be heard on purpose.

This was the last straw. The heck with keeping a low profile. Saundra went to her desk and retrieved her purse and clocked out of the system. For good measure, she shut down her computer completely. Just in case some busybody tried to get in and erase some of her files, like those phone messages had been erased. There had to be a way of proving someone erased them before she could listen to them. Maybe Eden could do that?

Would it help if she went to Book & Mug on her lunch break and talked with Kai and Eden? Or would showing her face there just make things worse? Stir up more gossip?

By the time she reached Center Avenue, Saundra didn't care. She paused on the corner. Turn right and go to Book & Mug and order one of their decadent sandwich plates? Maybe go straight for dessert? Go for ice cream, at Goody Two Scoops on the other side of the river? If she had been thinking, she would have taken her lunch from the refrigerator and gone to the park to eat. Well, she hadn't been thinking, had she? More feeling than anything.

"Buy you lunch, pretty lady?"

For two seconds, she thought Kai had come up behind her. Saundra turned. Her smile didn't die, it just froze, as she looked up into Nic's eyes.

What was wrong with her to mistake his voice for Kai's?

"That's not funny," she said, feeling her heart jolt back to normal rhythm. Why did it feel so wrong for Nic to call her that? After all, it wasn't like Kai had a corner on the right to call her that -- though she did like it when he did.

"Guess you heard." He hooked his arm through hers, and she didn't resist when he led her across the street and they turned left. "Did you hear there was someone else with your shadow? You're not out of the woods yet, *quera*."

"Did you see anything?"

"I wasn't watching your new boyfriend, I was focusing on keeping you safe."

"He's not my boyfriend. I haven't even been in town a week." Saundra's face warmed.

"Yeah, well, the guy strikes me as pretty smart. Good taste, too. Can't see why he wouldn't be interested." Nic winked when she glanced up at him.

"What did they want, breaking into the building in the middle of the night?"

"That's something for the police to figure out. Or maybe Eden will figure it out. After all, the dead man was her client. Did you know Eden means 'bear'? Wonder if she is one, when it comes to taking care of her family."

Saundra couldn't respond because Nic led her into Celestial Dragon, and they were no longer alone. Well, the food suited her perfectly. She was in the mood for hot and sour soup and Szechuan dumplings. They took their food to go and walked down to the park. Several people turned to watch them walking past, and Saundra couldn't seem to stretch her mind enough to remember if she had met any of those people, and they knew who she was. How much of the gossip included her in the mess, because Stinky Cigar Man Styles had attacked her at the street festival?

Then she caught someone at the right angle and realized they were staring at Nic, not at her. Why? Granted, he was good-looking. She had always been partial to dark curls and big, dark eyes, and that wicked twist to his mouth, despite being so irritating at the same time. She never would have fallen for Nic West, maybe because he had always been there, part of the work and mysteries Aunt Cleo couldn't share with her. Yet at the same time …

"What?" Nic said, pausing in unpacking their lunch on the one picnic table that wasn't in the shelter of the pavilion.

"I messed up. I thought I was misdirecting Eden when she asked me to describe you. As the other witness to Cigar Man running into the ditch."

"How?" The usual glitter in his eyes turned cold, even though nothing else about him had changed. He kept unpacking and dividing up their food, and still smiled.

"I basically said you looked like Kai and Troy, just with a few changes. Darker skin tone, squarer face. That sort of thing."

"And how is that messing up?"

"Because you *do* look like them. You even sounded like Kai, back there when you first caught up with me." She wondered if that was why people stared at Nic. They thought they saw Kai, and were startled when she and Nic got closer, and they realized he wasn't the man they thought they saw.

"Huh. Interesting." He pried the lid off his wonton soup and picked up the white plastic spoon. "I might just have to stick around here a little longer, once I'm sure you're safe." He took a mouthful of the soup, then that wicked sparkle returned. "Just not sure I want to stick around and see you fall for my doppelganger, when you wouldn't fall for me."

"Don't be an idiot."

"*Moi*? I am crushed." He snickered and paused, his humor fading into something almost wistful. "The only thing that would make this situation perfect is if one of them had a glass heart."

Saundra fumbled the lid of the dumplings container. Nic put two fingers under her chin and tipped her head up, so she had to look him in the eyes.

"Tell me."

For two seconds, she considered stalling him. She hadn't prayed over her meal, after all. Nic wasn't the kind of man who would put up with such tactics. Besides, using God as an excuse just felt so sacrilegious. And lame.

There was no good in refusing to tell him. Once Cleo read her email, she would tell Nic anyway. The Venetian glass heart lockets, and whatever they contained and protected, were at the heart of Cleo's quest.

"Eden has a glass heart. I have no idea if it's another locket, because I just saw it for a few seconds. But she brought it out after we both got a good look at my friend Charli's glass heart, which is a locket. There has to be a connection, or she at least recognized what Charli had."

"Huh." A tiny smile flicked the corners of his mouth, and his gaze went distant. "Makes sense."

Then Nic blinked and dug into his soup, and that was all the reaction he gave her. Saundra was seriously tempted to douse him with hot and sour soup. She focused on her lunch, because she refused to give him the satisfaction of knowing he had frustrated her.

Again, she wondered just why she not only liked Nic West, in a grudging sort of way, but more important, she trusted him.

~~~~~

Friday, August 26

"Hi." Saundra sounded a little breathless, her voice coming from behind Kai.

He flinched, almost dropping the stack of mugs he was putting on the shelf on the wall behind the counter. He had been going back and forth between hoping to see her and common sense saying she wouldn't come by until things calmed down.

"Hi, yourself." He turned and rested his arms on the counter and slouched forward to grin at her. Three minutes after he had opened the door for the day, she was the first customer.

"How are you doing? Stinky didn't hurt you, did he?"

"Nah. Not even close." He forced a grin, despite having flashed back to that moment facing the gun. "How about you?"

"Glad I can walk to work again. Have they tracked down who he really is yet?"

Kai shrugged.

The door thudded open, pushed hard enough to make the hinges shriek. Roger Cadburn stomped into the coffee shop.

"Where is she?"

"If you're looking for Eden, office hours are 9am to 4pm --"

"I've been banging on her office door for the last ten minutes. What kind of business is she running?"

"Impossible." Kai didn't care about being more mature than Cadburn. He was fed up with all the ugly, ridiculous rumors that mostly originated from Carruthers, Cadburn's minion. "Eden's office is at the top of the stairs, and the stairwell is locked."

"You know what I mean."

"No, I've found it's safer to never guess what you mean." From the corner of his eye, he saw Saundra backing away from the counter. "You can't get to the office door to knock without someone letting you up the stairs. And don't even ask. It's 7am."

"You're not getting away with this."

"With what?"

"Spreading all those lies about me, my family, the paperwork that sneak thief was looking for. You three have been trying to cause trouble for me and my family, tearing down our reputation, since you swooped in and stole this building."

"This building? The one you lost by declaring bankruptcy? How could we steal it when we paid good, solid money we earned honestly? The bank owned it. Prove they stole it. The county and federal government say we own this building fair and square."

"You know what I --" Cadburn ground his teeth hard enough to be audible. "Getting involved where you've got no business being. Strutting around town, telling everyone you're digging up my family's heirlooms, telling everyone you're looking for documents and ledgers that will take everything away from us. Trying to rewrite the history of this township."

"No, we haven't. We haven't," Kai repeated, louder, and braced himself to lean halfway across the counter.

To his surprise, Cadburn backed up a step.

"Find witnesses that we said all of that. Not the mental midgets repeating what they've made up in their spiteful little imaginations. Actual *witnesses* that those words came out of our mouths. You can't, can you?" he hurried on, when Cadburn's mouth opened and closed a few times, but no sound came out. "News flash, Roger baby. You don't own this township. Keep it up, keep giving us reason to file harassment complaints against you, and you'll own even less than you do now. See those cameras?" He flicked his fingers, gesturing around the room. "Got it all on video."

Cadburn opened his mouth, probably to spew more threats and accusations. Kai could see the thought sparking and fizzing behind those angry brown eyes.

Brown, ringed with green.

Cadburn's mouth snapped shut, and something that might just have been fear, or at least some discretion and common sense, dimmed the angry fire.

"You wouldn't dare," he finally ground out.

"Don't give us reason to."

The tableaux held for several more heart-thudding seconds. Then Cadburn inhaled deeply, his nostrils flaring like a crazy horse, and turned to march out.

"Tell her to call me."

"Leave a message on her phone," Kai shot back. As the door swung slowly closed behind Cadburn, he spread his arms and collapsed forward across the counter.

"My hero," Eden cooed in a falsetto like nails on a chalkboard. Saundra's muffled chuckles seemed to clear the air.

Kai opened his left eye and looked to the left side of the counter where Eden and Saundra came out of the shadows. He debated just staying there, collapsed with his face pressed against the cool marble. No, he was already getting a crick in his neck. He sighed and pushed himself upright.

"Did you catch all that?" he asked.

"Most of it. I figured it was easier coming down here for what was fresh than fussing with making something for myself." Eden snorted. "When is that *nimnul* going to figure out that Carruthers is more a liability than an asset?"

"What's a -- oh, I know that reference." Saundra leaned against the counter next to Eden. "From *Mork and Mindy*, right?"

"Marry the girl. She's a pop culture genius." She grinned when Kai just gaped at the two of them. "Interesting tidbit: I told the captain what Styles was hiring me to investigate. *Nobody else.* I know you wouldn't spill those details. As far as I know, nobody else should know that, and our speculation that Styles was going after Cadburn documents. Nobody else could know, unless they looked at the report. And it's not open for public consumption."

"He made the connection though, didn't he?" Saundra said, her voice soft. "Styles said family information, lost documents, and Cadburn made the connection to his family. Maybe he thinks Styles was trying to claim he's a Cadburn? Maybe he met up with Styles before, and wouldn't give him what he wanted?"

"Hire the girl," Kai said. His heart made another funny little leap, replaying Eden's comment before. "She's got the gift for making deductive leaps." That painted a blush on Saundra's cheeks. He grinned at her. "We know who passed on that information to his evil mastermind. Think we got enough evidence to get Carruthers fired?"

"If only those cameras really did exist," Eden said.

"Those aren't cameras?" Saundra said.

"Pin spots. For when we have parties, or when we do an improv night, or music night. We can program in different colors." Kai shared a grin with her. "Yeah, it'd be great if we could get that kind of proof. Might be smart to install some cameras inside here, even if they're dummies. They'd keep his royal lowness and his really rabid, loyal followers from coming through the doors."

"So that was what Stink -- what Styles wanted you to do? Rewrite township history?"

"We never got that far. That's purely speculation on Carruthers' part, and Cadburn's," Eden said.

"Yeah, but this guy said specifically *family* documents, and combined with trying to get into two buildings formerly belonging to the Cadburns ..." Kai shrugged. Then he thought of something and froze while he waited for the idea to crystalize.

"What?" She reached out to rest her hand on his.

"Did you ever notice his eyes? Roger's." He watched Eden think and wasn't surprised when she shrugged. "Yeah, it's kind of like looking into the eyes of a basilisk. You don't want to do it. Well, I got caught and guess what? His eyes sure look like Styles' eyes. Brown with green rings. Family trait, maybe?"

"I think I feel sorry for Styles," Eden murmured.

"Kind of supports his accusations. If you had taken the job from Styles, maybe you'd be looking for documentation proving Styles' side of the family was cheated of their inheritance. Meaning, if he's also a Cadburn ..." Kai shrugged and spread his arms, gesturing to take in the entire township.

"Okay, I'm going to take my coffee upstairs and write up a report for Sunderson, and figure out if I want to take this job after all, even though the client is dead."

"To hack off Cadburn?" Kai said.

"To figure out who was working with him and killed him," Saundra said. "You said you heard voices arguing? Would it be safe to assume that the other person helped Styles get into your building and onto the roof, and maybe he's actually working for the trustee?"

"Oh, you're good," Eden said with a slow, weary smile. "I think we need to adopt you, if this idiot doesn't marry you."

Chapter Nine

Saturday, August 27

"Saundra? Oh, it is you." A whirlwind of white-blonde curls scooted around Saundra's desk in the children's section to give her a hug. "Although why I would think Charli was teasing us, I don't know. Blame the fried-brain syndrome. It always hits during the third and fourth drafts of a book."

"Don't tell me your writing group decided to meet here this month?" Saundra got up and looked around for the other three writers. It was a delaying action while she tried to place a name on the young woman grinning at her. She knew all their names -- she just couldn't put the other three names with the faces correctly. She only had Charli's name fixed with her face because she had done a little cyber-stalking to match Charli's real face with what hid under the thick black curly wig and makeup and dangle-bangle earrings for her public face as Carlotta VanDevere.

As if she knew what Saundra was doing, the petite blonde grinned and pulled a digital camera out of her satchel-sized purse.

"Tamera. Sorry. You caught me off guard."

"Well, I'm early. I thought I'd come see if you wanted to have lunch with us before the meeting." Tamera Artierri often joked that she took up photography because she so often told people how to pronounce her name by saying it was "Camera, but with a T in front." Her friends alternated calling her Tamera and Camera, and she willingly responded to both.

"Oh, I'd love to," Saundra said, "but I'm having a lunch meeting with my boss and some of the teachers. School is in session, and it's part of my job as children's librarian."

"How about after? What time do you get off? Or do you have plans? Please tell me you have a guy on a leash by now?"

Saundra firmly pushed Kai's face out of her thoughts -- but of course, trying *not* to think of something or someone was impossible. She agreed to meet with the foursome after their writing meeting and walked with Tamera to the door. They hugged again and she sighed, wondering how she could feel so worn out already at just 11:30am. Tamera did that, so peppy and so visibly enjoying life.

"Please don't tell me you know those troublemakers." Twila sounded especially nasal this morning.

Maybe she was just upset that she had to work this Saturday. Every librarian took turns working Saturdays, so everyone had an equal chance to enjoy their weekends. Those who were habitually late lost the privilege of requesting specific days free for activities. Twila was late coming to work or coming back from lunch so often, she was stuck at the bottom of the scheduling ladder.

Saundra couldn't understand why Twila paid so much attention to everyone else's comings and goings when she couldn't seem to control her own.

"What troublemakers?" Saundra asked, honestly confused for a few seconds. Then she remembered Charli's comment about their questionable welcome when her quartet of writing friends met at her local library. It figured that Twila would be the one who rolled out the un-welcome mat for them.

"Those twits who think they're writers." She crooked her pointer and index fingers on both hands, indicating quote marks around *think*. "Gypsies, that's what they are. What right do they have, going from library to library, taking up tables that belong to our patrons? Taking out books that our patrons should have access to first? They're just so smug and arrogant, sitting there, talking about writing, about the books they're working on. Yeah, right, like they really do have agents who are advising them and waiting for them to turn in books?" Her snort-and-sniff combination almost yanked a giggle out of Saundra.

She found herself listening, stunned and fascinated, like someone at a roadside accident scene. Twila grumbled about conversations she had overheard, the books Charli and her friends had asked for, "the gall of them" when they saw people looking at various authors and offered recommendations. That seemed the most offensive to Twila, because it was her job to make recommendations, not "those nasty outsiders."

Didn't Twila realize she had ignored the advice she now threw at Saundra, to "ignore them, they're just nuisances, they have no grasp of reality, romance is just soft porn for lonely, desperate women"? If she could remember the conversations the four writers had had at previous meetings, then Twila had focused on them instead of ignoring them.

Saundra knew better, after a week's exposure to Twila, than to point out her inconsistency.

"Somebody should just tell those gypsies to stay at their own libraries. Our taxpayers don't pay for them to come in here and take up our space and time and use our books." Twila's eyes widened, and her head tilted back, and the angry hunch of her shoulders relaxed.

Saundra wished she had headed back to her desk about five minutes and forty grumbles ago.

"You know them. It's your job to tell them to just go away. Stop intruding. They don't belong here."

Yep, she should have walked away and hoped Twila would give her the silent treatment, to "punish" her for not listening.

"Just what criteria do you use to determine who belongs and who doesn't?" Mrs. Tinderbeck said.

How long had she been standing there, a few steps out from the break room door? At just the right angle that Saundra hadn't seen her superior, and Twila probably hadn't, either.

"Well... residency, of course," Twila said after a few seconds when her jaw moved but no sound came out. Her complexion faded to a yellowish cast under her usual heavy coat of makeup.

"Then you have no business being here, either," Mrs. Tinderbeck said, her expression one of soft, sorrowful regret. "You don't live in the Township. That dear Charli Hall *does*. She has the condo two spaces down from mine."

"Well -- that doesn't give her the right to invite the other three."

"She doesn't have to invite them. The alliance of libraries throughout Cuyahoga County invited them. All our libraries work together, sharing books and resources. We invite their patrons to attend events here, and our patrons are invited to events at other libraries. In fact, our little library enjoys twice as many benefits as we share with the other libraries. What if the librarians at the other branches decided *you* aren't welcome, when you go to all those meet-the-author events you enjoy so much?"

"But -- but -- you just don't understand." Twila turned to Saundra, who wished again she had had the sense to beat a retreat when she had the chance.

The plea for support was clear in Twila's eyes. Saundra wished she could feel some sympathy for her, but the nasty things Twila and Officer Carruthers had been saying about Kai and the dead man and Trustee Cadburn made that hard. The honest truth was that Saundra wasn't as nice a person as she wanted to be.

"How about I take care of Charli and her writing friends when they come after lunch?" Saundra offered. "Then you won't have to be bothered by them. In fact, the little conference room isn't reserved for the rest of the day. They could meet in there, instead of out among the stacks, and not bother anybody. How about that?"

"Lovely idea." Mrs. Tinderbeck glanced beyond Saundra. "Ah, there's our lunch order. And there are Judith and Cheryl and Morton, right on time."

Saundra had placed the order with Deli-licious, so she hurried to take care of the delivery. With some relief. She led the two delivery girls to the small conference room and showed them where they could place the trays of sandwiches and brownies, bucket of potato salad, and cold jugs of lemonade and iced tea. The three teachers followed her to the conference room.

"Twila is partial to ham and Swiss with horseradish," Mrs. Tinderbeck said, after she had made introductions and invited everyone to fill their plates. "Be a dear and fill a plate for her? Like Pastor Roy said last Sunday, we really do need to feel sorry for the irritants in our lives. The oyster ends up with a pearl, but the grain of sand ends up smothered and invisible."

Saundra knew Twila was also partial to the cheesecake brownies. There weren't as many on the dessert tray as she would have liked, but she gave Twila two anyway. Just to make up for feeling so gleeful over the gentle dressing-down she got from Mrs. Tinderbeck. Saundra hoped someday, when she finally grew up, she would be as kind and patient as her new boss. She had truly learned the art of letting the selfish, self-righteous stupidity of others just roll off her with no lasting effect.

The school year preparation meeting lasted longer than anticipated. Saundra knew that was partially her fault. She had so many ideas for programs for the students, to get them excited about reading. This wasn't the standard meeting the others were used to. When she apologized for breaking the mold, the others laughed. They pointed out that they were taking her ideas and running with them too, so they were just as guilty.

Saundra reflected over the meeting as she took care of the cleanup. Part of her excitement and ease in offering ideas came from the sense of welcome here. She felt as if her input was wanted, not just tolerated. She was a partner and not an intruder.

When Saundra finished cleaning up the small meeting room, the writing group was nowhere to be seen. She was sure Tamera told her they would be at the library around 1:30, but it was now nearly 2pm.

Twila hadn't been more snotty than usual, had she? Had she driven them away? Maybe the day was nice enough they decided to use the picnic tables outside the library?

While Saundra pondered her options, a plump brunette stepped out from behind the bookshelves that masked a table tucked into the far-right corner of the library, farthest from the front door. She would recognize Megan Romanoff anywhere, with her long, blue-black hair hanging to her hips and the gray-blue gauzy shirt she dubbed her writing outfit. Saundra glanced around, to make sure there were no parents and children needing her help on this beautiful day that demanded outdoor activities. Then she headed for the back corner.

Megan gave her a smile when Saundra caught up with her looking through the European history section. She looked away, then looked back. Her eyes got wide. She slapped a hand over her mouth just before a yelp escaped.

"What are you doing here? Oh, the girls are going to go nuts when they see you. Is there a conference here?" She hooked her arm through Saundra's and guided her toward the table where the other three were talking in library-appropriate half-whispers.

"Umm, no. Didn't Charli tell you? Or Tamera?"

"Tell her what?" the fourth member of the group asked. Then her face lit up, and Rita Carmichael turned to Tamera and Charli, who just grinned. "That's our surprise?"

"Saundra was supposed to be a surprise for me, too but I am the master of interrogation," Tamera announced.

"This is my library now," Saundra said.

"That's great! Like, you live here now?" Rita pulled out a chair at the end of the table, gesturing for Saundra to join them. "Oh, wait, you're working, aren't you?"

"She's having afters with us," Tamera said. "Two Scoops or Sugarbush?"

"If you don't mind, I'd like ice cream." Saundra gestured for them to get up. "Mrs. T says you can use the small conference room today, if you'd like."

"Fantastic." Megan scooped up her book bag and took possession of Saundra's arm again. "So, are you too new to the area to have any kind of inside scoop on this murder Wednesday night?"

"Guys," Charli began. The rest of them hurried to pick up notebooks, tablets, and bags.

"It sounds so mysterious. A break-in gone wrong," Rita said. "All they'll say in the paper is that this detail and that detail are unconfirmed, they're still trying to identify the victim, and that he was harassing people in town. What was he doing? Why doesn't anybody know who he is?"

"Just hold off," Charli continued.

"It'd be a good start for a mystery, or a complication in any of the other genres we write," Tamera added. "Not that any of us have time to start a new book. We're all in the middle of projects. Coming along quite nicely, if I do say so myself," she added, buffing her fingernails on the front of her shirt.

"Huh, just what I thought," a familiar, congested voice said.

Saundra noted that Officer Carruthers was speaking above normal street volume, but nobody shushed him. Twila took a step back from the front desk where he leaned, and crossed her arms, eyes glittering with satisfaction. Now Saundra regretted being generous with her sympathy and those brownies at lunch.

Charli rolled her eyes and gestured with a twitch of her shoulder for her friends to keep walking. Megan didn't take the hint. She fluttered her eyelashes and put a saucy sway to her hips as she stepped closer to Carruthers, whose scowl deepened.

"Is there a problem, Officer?" Her voice took on a syrupy drawl.

"Heard about you. Think you're writers. Don't go getting involved in things that ain't none of your nevermind." Carruthers stood up a little straighter. "Nothing worse than a bunch of wannabes thinking because they write detective stories, that makes them experts."

"Why would we think that? Speaking as an expert yourself, of course,"

Tamera added.

"Don't you go getting involved and interfere with the investigation, that's all I'm saying."

Saundra kept walking and tried to herd the foursome away from the front desk. She had already learned that when Carruthers stated, "that's all I'm saying," he was getting ready to pontificate.

"We weren't thinking about it," Megan said, with another sashay of her hips and a deepening of the Southern syrup. "Bless your heart."

As Megan had explained years ago, when she went into Southern Belle mode, "bless your heart" meant the exact opposite, with many variations depending on the circumstances.

"Yep," Tamera added as they retreated into the conference room. "Not until you opened your big mouth."

"Guys, she has to work here," Charli said, *sotto voce.*

"Oh, sorry. Really." Megan's voice went back to normal. She leaned back as if she could see out the door. All five of them were now safely in the room. "That was kind of stupid."

"Yeah, well, she does have a tendency to bring that out in people, and he's her … whatever. The guy is kind of sore when it comes to the murder. He's been spreading rumors and got a dressing-down already from the captain," Saundra explained, keeping her voice as soft as possible while still being heard.

"Guys, the dead man was harassing Saundra." Charli put her bag down on the conference table with a thud of punctuation.

"And I really do need to get back to work. Save your questions for over ice cream?" Saundra asked. "If you need any research help, you need to find anything, come to me. Mrs. T's orders." She slipped out of the room before they could respond.

The only route back to her desk was past Carruthers and Twila. Saundra ignored their muttering as best she could.

Several times through the afternoon, the foursome took turns coming to ask for help. They were obedient and never said anything about Cigar Man, but Saundra thought she could see the questions in their eyes. And the concern. No matter how obsessive any of the four could get about their writing, about research, about refining a scene, and defending their chosen genres against literary snobs, she knew their hearts were good and they truly cared. Another unanticipated benefit of moving to Cadburn: a chance to see the foursome regularly, instead of just once a year, at the conference.

Her workday ended at 5pm on Saturdays. The four were waiting, sitting on the park benches out front, when she walked out with Mrs. Tinderbeck. She wasn't surprised when her boss and the foursome greeted each other with smiles.

The five of them took only a few moments to decide to walk from the library to the ice cream shop. To work off some of the calories they would be eating.

"That sounded like a pretty serious discussion you were having when we came out," Saundra said, mostly to delay them asking about Styles and all the problems he had been causing.

They headed up Apple, to cross Center and the bridge, with Goody Two Scoops on the other side.

"More griping than discussing," Charli admitted with a shrug.

"Publisher problems," Rita said.

"Jerk publisher problems," Tamera added.

"What would you think if I killed off Stacy in my next book?" Charli said, not looking at any of them.

"Why?" Saundra muffled the yelp that wanted to burst out of her. She adored Charli's PI character, Anastasia Roman.

"The problems and perils of working with a smaller publisher," Megan said. "The house was bought out by a larger publisher. Still not one of the big five. They want to take Charli's books in a new direction, reach a wider audience. They say."

"They want Stacy to turn into a prosti-toad," Tamera said with a giggle.

"Prosti -- oh, I get it. Jumping from bed to bed." Saundra couldn't even muster a smile. Not that it was a joking matter, but she had to admit Tamera's play on words was at least semi-clever.

"Fortunately, my current agent is holding them to the contract we signed. I am so glad that I specified which books I was writing, titles and synopses, so they can't make me switch gears mid-stream," Charli said. "Not without a lot of negotiating and making concessions and paying me big bonuses."

"But," Rita said.

"But," Tamera echoed.

"But my agent made it pretty clear he'd like a bite of those bonuses they're offering me to scrap my contract and write new books. Including giving the publisher some control in planning the next five books."

"Five?" Saundra didn't care that her voice cracked. "A five-book contract? That really isn't common, is it?"

The conversation paused as they crossed Center. The bridge across the river was ahead of them.

"Nope. That's the power behind a bigger publishing house with a really good marketing department. But they want to take away some of my power. They want to tell me what to write, and change Stacy. Thank goodness they don't own Stacy. I could take her and go to a new publisher when this contract is up, and there's nothing they could do about it."

"Except threaten to buy the next publisher she goes to," Megan offered. "The industry is a bunch of cannibals, all running around devouring each other."

"So what does your agent think about that?" Saundra asked.

"He's getting ready to retire, his agency got bought out by a bigger, more aggressive agency, and the guy waiting to take over repping me says making Stacy a 'more realistic' woman will make her more popular." She emphasized the two words with air quotes.

"Realistic as in making her a skank? How realistic is it to expose a woman to all the STDs out there and *not* expect her to catch one?" Rita asked. She flinched when her voice bounced off the cement sides of the bridge wall. "Sorry."

"The almighty dollar." Charli sighed. "I'm really thinking of starting over. A new character. New publisher. New genre. Or maybe get out of writing altogether and get my PI license and work for Carson full-time. That'd be fun, don't you think?"

"I guess it depends. Eden seems to enjoy her investigative work. Despite the creeps she has to deal with," Saundra offered.

Of course, the other three wanted to know who Eden was. That meant explaining about the three cousins and the building they shared, with the coffee shop and greenhouse and investigative office. Saundra thought about relating the uncomfortable encounter she had witnessed between Kai and Cadburn, but as much as she had come to dislike the man, that didn't feel right. Not because she didn't want to embarrass a public figure. He had a responsibility to act with maturity and discretion. If he didn't want people saying nasty things about him, then he shouldn't give them legitimate ammunition. No, most of her concern was for Kai. Saundra had a vision of one or all four of her friends using the scene in a book someday. They would make it funny, or a pivotal scene that pointed out the next victim of a murderer, or even the villain. However, Saundra could see Roger Cadburn or his friends reading the scene, recognizing him, and immediately blaming Kai. That would make the harassment even worse. Cadburn might even remember Saundra had been there and guess she was the source.

Saundra had little faith in her friends' belief that when nasty people were parodied in print, they never recognized themselves, no matter how accurately it was done.

The conversation turned back to the death of Cigar Man, by the time they had ordered their ice cream and settled at the umbrella tables outside of the shop. The four were more concerned about Saundra's safety than the gossipy details of the last week. When she wasn't willing to give more details, they didn't press. Too hard, anyway. They were writers, after all, and Saundra knew from the seminars she had helped run that the very thing she was going through would make a decent sub-plot in any number of genres.

Chapter Ten

Monday, August 29

Monday, the Welcome Wagon committee met at the library. Every member of the committee showed up, which meant the only conference room not already booked up with regular meetings wouldn't hold them all. They ended up pushing together all the tables throughout the library in the open area between the front desk and the reference librarian station. Saundra overheard a lot of grumbling as she helped move furniture.

She reasoned that she wasn't really eavesdropping because the women airing their complaints and seeking information couldn't seem to remember they were in a library. They spoke at normal volume, and she suspected some of them raised their voices a little to make sure the other side heard them. There were two sides, she caught on quickly. The regular attendees, who considered themselves in charge of the Welcome Wagon, and the ones who didn't attend regularly because they couldn't. The committee meetings kept getting changed from evenings to afternoons and even mornings. The non-regular attendees, she deduced, had jobs, or children to ferry to and from practices and lessons. According to the grumbles, everyone ignored their protests and requests for a regular meeting schedule when everyone was free.

Her theory started to gel when one woman from the "regulars" made a snide remark to a woman from the "irregulars" about "finally" showing up, and "how nice you found the time to do your civic duty." The other woman shot back that the bylaws required meetings to take place on the evenings and weekends, but the current chair kept changing the meeting times for her own convenience and to lock people out. Someone else remarked that it seemed odd the chair herself couldn't manage to arrive on time, especially since she made it so hard for other people to attend. Pot shots were exchanged about how some people never found out about the changed meeting time until after the meeting had taken place, with the other side denying it happened.

Then Ashley Cadburn walked in, looking self-important with a hot pink folder marked *Welcome Wagon* and clutching a gavel. She walked up to the table that had been left empty facing all the chairs and dropped her materials on top of it.

Saundra ducked back behind a half-wall of bookshelves and scurried to her desk. She didn't want to be seen close enough to be accused of eavesdropping, after all.

No surprise, Twila abandoned her post at the front desk to settle in a seat at the edge of the meeting. Saundra anticipated having to answer phones because Twila would be too busy to do her job.

Patty Hill sat in the center of the handful of women who weren't participating in the accusations and snide remarks. Almost half an hour after the meeting was scheduled to start, Ashley called everyone to order.

Two members of the Welcome Wagon group were realtors, and they reported on houses that had been sold and the move-in date for the new residences, along with a little personal information -- if they were married, if the couples worked, if they had children, and their ages. Information that would help with putting together the Welcome Wagon bag.

Several women competed for the chance to be the Welcome Wagon visitors for one of the houses. Saundra was surprised, until she overheard several women who sat closest to her desk, at the back of the group. They remarked on a feud that had been going on between those women and the former owner of the house, and how long it had been since any of them had been invited inside.

Was that the only reason people were on the Welcome Wagon committee? To get a look inside of newcomers' homes, spy on their decorating style, their possessions, and see what the previous residents had done to the house? Saundra remembered her double Welcome Wagon visits and shuddered. Had Ashley and Colette hoped to spy on her? Was welcoming her to Cadburn far down the list? She was grateful Patty had been there first, to protect her.

Saundra overheard a few complaints about how the number of houses for sale was declining. Someone remarked the committee should be reduced since there wasn't so much need for welcoming parties. That led to some back-and-forth comments among the people in the back few rows. Saundra almost didn't hear when the conversation turned to the man killed outside Book & Mug.

A gasp seemed to ripple through the group. People hissed for others to be quiet. Someone called from the back of the group, asking Ashley to repeat what she had just said.

Ashley stood up, and jammed her fists into her hips, and looked like she couldn't decide if she was irritated or traumatized.

"I said yes, we did know the man. Not personally, of course. I just knew of him. Roger had the awful duty of having to actually talk to him. He was just simply horrid. I swear, he was crazy. He was making claims against us, just like that big idiot, Curtis."

That caught Saundra's attention, just when she thought she could ignore Ashley's posturing. What kind of claim would Curtis make against Trustee Cadburn?

Other people asked, but Ashley emphasized her apparent suffering, being put-upon by rude, nosey people who had no right to ask about her personal business. Lots of sighs and eye-rolls. Those she didn't cow into silence through guilt looked thoroughly disgusted. Saundra suspected they didn't believe her act for one moment. The topic was dropped. The meeting ended after a team was assigned to the second house that had been sold.

It was nearly quitting time for Saundra, by the time they got the library furniture shoved back into the proper positions. She wished she could erase the whole meeting from her memory because she hadn't heard anything useful. Just enough to pique her curiosity. What could she make of the statement that Styles and Curtis had made some sort of claim against the Cadburn family?

Saundra rolled the idea around in her head as she worked, until she decided what interested her more was finding out what the Cadburns thought was going on.

Yet how could she go up to either Roger or Ashley and ask? He had to know by now that she was a friend of Kai. If he hadn't seen her name on the report that Carruthers had illegally shared with him, he had to have seen her at Book & Mug the other day when he made those accusations about Eden.

Saundra saw Twila standing in the doorway talking with a few Welcome Wagon stragglers. People she had mentally tagged as "regulars," who could adjust their schedules to accommodate Ashley. It made sense that Twila would be in their clique. The people who agreed with the Cadburn version of reality.

Saundra debated the best way to get Twila to tell her what was going on. Could it be as easy as asking what she knew? Would Twila's addiction to gossip be enough to get her to spill? Or would she be nasty enough to refuse to tell, and then inform Cadburn that Saundra was asking questions about an unpleasant situation?

On the plus side, Twila might be so offended or even frightened by Saundra's questions, she might leave her alone from now on. Cadburn might order her never to talk to Saundra again. A win-win situation no matter how it turned out.

Well, no way to find out except by trying.

"Wow, Ashley Cadburn certainly sounded like the world is on her shoulders," Saundra commented when she and Twila were the only people visible in the main room. Mrs. Tinderbeck had her door closed, and Phyllis, the part-time reference librarian, had gone to the breakroom. "Anything I can do to help? I mean, the guy was harassing me, and now it turns out he was harassing her, too? That's awful."

"Whatever he wanted from you, he probably needed it to hurt Ashley." Twila sniffed and looked away. Maybe she hadn't bought the expression that Saundra hoped looked sympathetic?

Then she looked back, and that spark that was part excitement and part malice lit her eyes. Saundra felt only slightly guilty at this sign of successfully manipulating the older woman.

"Did I hear correctly? This guy was trying to get Curtis to make claims against Trustee Cadburn?"

"No, you didn't." Another disdainful sniff. "The nerve of some people. Why is it so hard to remember they're in a library, and they should be using respectful library voices?"

"You're absolutely right."

Twila didn't look shocked to have Saundra agreeing with her. She was already too caught up in the tidal wave of complaints.

"This man wasn't even using his proper name. Not that I know what his real name is, but Roger said time and again," Twila lowered her voice to a rasp, and leaned closer to Saundra over the desk, "he was wearing masks and telling false stories and pulling evidence out of thin air. He was claiming that he had a right to share in the Cadburn legacy. Can you imagine the nerve?"

"No. That's awful. Do you think he was responsible for all the trouble that hurt the family a few years back?"

"I wouldn't be surprised." Another sniff. "He claimed he had a right to one of the buildings. He claimed that his grandfather was supposed to be given one of the daughter buildings when Roger's grandfather died. He claimed he had Cadburn blood, and that gave him the right. The nerve of him."

"That takes a lot of nerve. How awful for them, and everybody standing up for them." Saundra thought Jacob Styles, or whatever his real name was, had a lot of guts to want to be included in the Cadburn family. Or maybe he was insane? She had heard that earlier generations were quite admirable. However, starting with Roger's father, the family ethics and reputation had taken a nosedive. She wouldn't have been surprised to learn Styles did have a legitimate claim, but it had been stolen from him.

So did that make one of Roger Cadburn's supporters a prime suspect in the murder? If so, was it to prevent Styles from providing real evidence that would give him a right to what little Cadburn property remained?

"What's totally sad is that everybody believes those lies about that big idiot, Curtis," Twila went on after visibly soaking up Saundra's sympathy. "The story has been going around since his grandmother's time, that they came from the wrong side of the family. The wrong side of the blanket, they called it in the old days. Roger's grandfather was just stupidly tenderhearted enough to believe those ridiculous stories. He gave the Bridgewaters homes at half rent. Supposedly he was stupid enough to promise Old Man Bridgewater the deed to one of the daughter buildings. Can you believe that?"

"No, I can't."

Saundra couldn't believe Curtis was related by blood to the Cadburns.

It just went to prove that genetics did not have anything to do with people's dispositions or their fates.

"Old Man Cadburn was just so stupidly soft-hearted. Soft in the head, I say. He wanted to take care of them. He gave them jobs doing maintenance for all his properties. And what did those ingrates do? They turned everyone against Roger and his father with all their lies. The nerve of them!"

Saundra bit her lip against replying that if anyone turned the people of Cadburn against Roger Cadburn and his father, those people were Roger and his father. She could easily imagine Curtis had been a diligent, reliable, and trustworthy maintenance man, liked by everyone. She thought about how Curtis had thrown himself between Daphne and that driver who ignored the barricade at the end of the street. It was easy to imagine him willingly getting hurt to help other people.

And for every person who thought he was a great guy, Saundra didn't doubt, there were just as many who agreed with the Cadburns, that Curtis was a dummy. Slow. Unworthy of even admitting he was a distant relative, let alone an inheritance.

Twila went on, grumbling about how Curtis and his father had a reputation for doing utterly stupid things. She didn't give any examples, though. She claimed the Bridgewaters were sneaky, scheming folk. Look at how they led everyone to believe they were imbeciles, only good for working with their hands, and yet they tricked so many people into thinking they were abused and had been cheated, so the township felt sorry for those lazy ingrates.

Lazy? Saundra almost snorted at that. It sounded like Curtis and his father had been the only Cadburn offshoots who actually did something worthwhile with their lives. They hadn't been the ones who made bad investments, and got themselves cheated, and hired embezzlers to handle their money and property.

Everything she had heard made her willing to believe Jacob Styles might have had at least a semi-legitimate claim. Maybe he hadn't been lying when he came to Eden to hire her to do some investigating for him. Maybe he had crept around and investigated until he couldn't get any further and had to turn to more legal, visible avenues to reclaim his inheritance. Or at least what he considered his inheritance.

After all, Jacob and Roger had the same brownish eyes with the same green ring around the pupil. She thought Curtis' eyes had that same green ring, but now she couldn't really be sure. Curtis didn't look people in the eyes. He was always looking down, or away, shoulders hunched, or his lids drooping like he would fall asleep. Was it possible to use those eyes as the foundation to prove his claim to be a Cadburn?

What good would that do Curtis? There was practically no Cadburn heritage left, except a soiled family name.

Finally, Twila wound down. She actually smiled at Saundra when the phone rang and she turned away to answer it. A wintery sort of smile, but it wasn't that self-satisfied, triumphant, you-messed-up-now kind of smile she usually wore. Saundra walked away with a lot to think about. And the slightly nauseous feeling that the only way to get and stay on Twila's good side was to listen to her gossip and make her think she had been believed. Not a pleasant prospect for the rest of her career at the Cadburn library. Especially when she had the awful feeling that tactic would mean lying. Constantly.

She gnawed on what she had learned as she closed up her desk and went through the security check for the evening. What was truth, and what was wild speculation based on fragments of truth? And what was simply nasty gossip that people made up because the truth was boring or they didn't want to believe it?

All that thinking made her tired. There was something about standing and listening to Twila gossip that made her feel somehow gritty and greasy. Maybe even a little scorched. There was a lot of frustration in Twila's soul. The sad part was the realization that Twila could be a solid, loyal friend, totally devoted to the people she chose to support. If only she didn't take such delight in complaining and accusing.

By the time Saundra walked out the door, she was close to wishing she hadn't walked to work today. It would be nice to climb in her car and head straight down Longview, and be at her apartment door in ten minutes, if traffic was on her side. Of course, maybe by the time she got home, she would have worked through all the bits and pieces swirling around in her head, and she would have some kind of decision.

"You dummy," she whispered, and paused at the edge of the sidewalk in front of the library.

Deciding what was fact and what was nasty speculation wasn't her job. Sorting through all the stories and claims and counterclaims was the sort of thing Eden did. Maybe for her own peace of mind, and some professional obligations, she needed to get to the bottom of things and find out what the real story was?

With that decided, Saundra headed across the library parking lot, aiming for Apple, to go up to Center and Book & Mug. She pulled out her phone to text and let Eden know she was coming.

~~~~~

Kai got a text from Eden asking him to send Saundra upstairs when she arrived. She was in the middle of a Skype chat and couldn't come down herself. That caught his interest.

Saundra's somber, slightly troubled expression when she walked into the coffee shop snagged his interest even more. He jerked his head toward the door to the back hallway, she nodded, and he hurried to finish ringing up an order of five vanilla creams and five subs that would have made Dagwood's eyes bug out. The testing partnership with Deli-licious seemed to be working out fine. They provided their two-foot-long subs, for the baristas to sell in four-inch-wide increments, and a placard on the counter and the window announced their special of the day.

That task done, he hurried under the drawbridge in the counter and pulled out his key for the back stairwell.

"What's up?" he asked when he caught up with Saundra.

"I heard some things today. About Cigar -- about Jacob Styles." She shook her head, and her mouth relaxed its hard lines just a little. "I should really use his name instead of that nickname. It's kind of disrespectful now that he's dead."

"If that's his real name." He tried to think of something encouraging to say as he unlocked the stairwell door. He couldn't. "What did you hear?"

"A lot of gossip." She sighed and obeyed his gesture to step through. "I should probably leave Eden to sort it out. I'm just passing along what I've heard. If it helps at all."

"That makes sense." He stepped back, letting the pneumatic hinge slowly shut the door. Saundra headed for the stairs.

"Kai?" She shrugged a little when he reached forward and blocked the door from closing. "Jacob Styles has the same eyes as Roger Cadburn, and Twila said ..." She shook her head. "I should tell Eden. Sorry."

"Oh, thanks." He wrinkled up his nose at her. "That's just going to go around and around in my head for the rest of the day. It's your fault if I don't get any sleep tonight."

That got a muffled chuckle from her. He let the door close, feeling he had accomplished something worthwhile for the day.

The Monday evening traffic finally died down to the point he could leave the shop in the hands of Olivia and Jorge, so he headed for the stairs. Just to see if Saundra was still there. And yes, find out what she had come to discuss with Eden. He passed Rufus coming out of the elevator and thought for a moment of asking the young hardware genius and electrician what Saundra and Eden were talking about. He hesitated long enough for Rufus to wheel into the front area of the coffee shop and give a yelp for his sister before wheeling his sleek, low-slung racing wheelchair for the front door. Devona popped up from behind a bookshelf, looked around, and waved to Kai. He waved back and headed for the stairs. He would find out in a few moments, wouldn't he? Saundra had said it was a lot of gossip, but if she thought there was no truth in it, she wouldn't have come to Eden, would she? He had a right to know because like it or not, he was involved in Jacob Styles' falling death. Except for the dark man-shape that had fallen with and landed on Styles, Kai was really the only witness.

"Right on time," Troy said, as Kai stepped into the office.

"For what?" He looked around. A deep sniff told him the cartons on the conference table between Eden, Troy, and Saundra held Chinese food, spicy, and still fresh enough for the aromas to linger in the air. "Did you leave me anything?"

"Poor baby. We neglect you horribly," Eden murmured, cradling her jumbo-sized mug with the scarlet and sapphire dragon curled around it, the tail forming the handle. It steamed and she took a slow sip, her eyes sparkling.

"Good news? Weird news?" He grinned when Saundra gave his desk chair a nudge, so it rolled out from the table and revealed the three closed cartons sitting on it. "Guys, we're keeping her."

He scooped up the single-serving cartons. Kung pao chicken, rice, and Szechuan dumplings. As usual. The three of them had gone through too many years when others decided what they would eat and wear, what they would study and where they would go. If he wanted to eat the same food every time they ordered from the Celestial Dragon, his cousins wouldn't argue with him. Habit made ordering easy. He just called the restaurant, Vinnie saw his number on the caller ID, and told him when the order would be ready. No need to waste time asking what he wanted.

By the time he had retrieved a fork from the little cabinet that held the coffee maker, tea kettle, and basic supplies for eating at work, Eden started in on a condensed version of what she, Saundra, and Troy had been discussing. He glanced at Troy when Eden repeated the allegations that the Bridgewaters claimed to be an offshoot of the Cadburn clan. His cousin cocked an eyebrow at him. When Eden finished, the four just looked at each other for a few moments in silence.

"So ... you guys think this makes sense?" Kai ventured. He knew they had probably been discussing all this as Saundra reported the spew of gossip from Twila.

"The pieces are sort of sliding into place." Eden picked up her dragon mug to cradle it again. "Of course, the first thing they teach you in sneaky school is to never trust the easy explanation. The one you want."

"The one that gives his royal lowness a black eye?" Troy said. "Kind of sucks for Curtis, that there's nothing to claim, if he ends up having a claim."

"So, if Styles had a claim, if he was getting close, maybe even stupid enough to make threats against Cadburn, maybe one of the minions was there on the roof and threw -- no." Kai dropped his fork back in the carton. He still had two dumplings left, but his appetite had fled. "I can't see any of those errand boys stopping Styles from shooting me."

"The Cadburns care about public image more than anything else," Eden said. "Think of the mess, the scandal, if you were killed or injured by someone who was out to get them. It might dig up a lot of dirt, raise a lot of questions. At the very least, people would blame them for you getting hurt. You'd be a town hero, and they can't have that."

They agreed that Captain Sunderson needed to be told about this new development. Chances were good she had already heard the speculation, especially the indignation from Cadburn supporters, and the glee from those they had insulted or cheated over the years.

Eden admitted she didn't expect the police to keep her or any of them updated, even though they were involved in the investigations. However, she had a duty to keep the authorities updated, if only to keep her relationship good with those same authorities for future needs.

Saundra promised she would keep her eyes and ears open for more talk in the library. It seemed to be a good place for people to meet and gossip and share news about events in the township.

"Just don't ask me to pump Twila for a while. My ears are still ringing from the last session," she joked.

"Hey, thought of something," Troy said while they were all still smiling. "You have easier access to things like land records and deed transfers, right? Stuff that's really old in the archives. All sorts of documents, legal things, right?"

"It depends." Saundra nodded, frowning a little in thought. "A lot of things have been handed over to historical societies and organizations with the resources and the training for preservation and restoration. Why?"

"Might be interesting to see who held what property since the township was founded. How many times it changed hands, or when it became Cadburn property. And maybe even any disputes further back. Like people who weren't Cadburn in name, but inherited anyway. And if they did, how it came back into Cadburn hands and ..." Troy shrugged. "Okay, that sounded a lot smarter in my head. Sorry."

"No, I get what you're thinking. Birth records would help. Just tracing back the Bridgewaters, see if they have common ancestors with the Cadburns."

"Yeah," Kai said, with a funny little thump in his chest, "we definitely got to keep her. She's really useful." That thump returned when Saundra blushed.

~~~~~

Going on midnight, Kai came back downstairs to the office to get into the massive photo files he and Troy had been compiling since they settled in Cadburn. Saundra's observation about Curtis' eyes kept popping into his thoughts. Somewhere in there, he had to have a picture where Curtis was looking directly into the camera lens, with his eyes wide open, so he could determine their color.

Eden was still sitting at her desk. That wasn't so unusual. She wasn't surfing the Web or reading or making notes, but sitting with her feet up on her desk. Her hands were clasped on her chest, and she had her head tipped back and studied the ceiling. Directly over her desk was a map of Middle Earth. Kai had painted the map of Pern over his desk. Troy had star charts from several different Star Trek role playing games.

"You okay?" Kai tugged his desk chair around so he settled down facing her. He doubted she was traveling with Bilbo in her imagination.

"It's kind of ironic, you know?" She closed her eyes, but otherwise didn't move. "Styles searching for family connections. Us searching to see if Curtis has those connections. How come I'm a whole universe better at finding stuff for other people, but I can't find what we've been looking for since middle school?"

He knew better than to say what they both knew. They hadn't been accidentally dropped along the way, forgotten or ignored or even stolen. Sybil Orwell and any associates she had, maybe someone she worked for, had deliberately put them in hiding and destroyed their identities. Enough strange things had happened to leads Eden had found, they had reason to believe even now someone was out there, keeping walls up, erasing every trail she uncovered. On the other side of that blank wall, so cleverly hidden in the shadows, was either a massive treasure that would change their lives -- whether information or wealth, it didn't matter -- or an enemy, a danger huge and vicious and all-encompassing. Enough odd things had happened during the course of their search since childhood, they couldn't be sure if the people or person destroying the trail was enemy or defender.

"It's time," Eden whispered. She tipped her head toward him and opened her eyes. "Saundra knows books. She knows people who can restore and protect them and find their secrets. We can trust her not to betray us. Not like that scuzzbag botanist."

Kai snorted. "Troy is still kicking himself over that. Lesson learned."

The heart lockets had mysterious seeds hidden inside, which they believed would provide a clue to their identities. The first expert they had turned to for information had sold the seeds to a major pharmaceuticals company. The company's agents occasionally showed up, trying to find the source of the seeds, but the cousins had years of practice in protecting their secrets and playing dumb, when necessary.

"If we can help Curtis, maybe stop some of the gossip, and yes," she smiled now, and tipped her chair to an upright position, "give his royal lowness a black eye in the process, then it's time to bring the books out, and ask for Saundra's help."

Chapter Eleven

Wednesday, August 31

Saundra nearly cancelled out on choir practice that evening. The school year library programs had officially commenced and were more exhausting than she had anticipated. Letting the younger children go hands-on at the library took a lot more energy than simply having them sit on the floor mats and listen to her read, or make puppets act out the stories she read to them. She was glad she went to choir, though, when Charli slipped in ten minutes after rehearsal started and sat next to her in the back row.

Her writer friend had dark smears under her eyes and looked distracted. Just showing up late was a bad sign of something going on in her life. Charli was one of those people who was ultra-organized just because she needed to get so much done. She held to a tight schedule so she could have as much time as possible for purely writing.

Saundra couldn't ask her question until choir was over and they were relatively alone, headed across the church parking lot. Their time was limited, though. While they both lived close enough to walk to church, Charli's townhouse was a right turn from church, and Saundra's apartment was a left turn.

"Are you all right?" Saundra asked. "Do you need to talk?" As soon as she said that, she knew that was a silly question. Charli had Rita, Megan, and Tamera if she needed a shoulder to cry on.

"Honestly?" A strained little chuckle escaped her. "I could use a triple chocolate sundae and someone who will really listen and not analyze things to see how it fits into a plot."

"Ice cream, especially chocolate ice cream, is my drug of choice."

They headed toward Goody Two Scoops.

"I don't know if it's my imagination. Maybe I really do need to stop writing all this suspense and danger and spying or ..." Charli sighed. "Carson is supposed to be at my place right now, installing some of the latest security gizmos on the market. He gets to test drive a lot of experimental stuff, so I guess I get to be a guinea pig for him. But that makes no sense, does it?"

"You think someone is spying on you? Maybe trying to break into your place?" Saundra guessed.

"Are you psychic? You can read minds? I could use someone with that skill right now, although, when you think about it, what a horrid thing to wish on anyone. Do we really want to know what goes on in other people's heads?" She shook her head and looped her free arm through Saundra's. "Back to your question. Yes. I've found footsteps in the flowerbed and seen movement from the corner of my eye, and I swear someone is sitting in a car down the street watching my place. I hope it's just my imagination because I do not want to have to move again. I know I've been in Cadburn for nearly two years now, but I just got my townhouse set up the way I like it. Moving is such a pain because I have so many books. And then there's my glass heart collection." She chuckled. "It's gotten to the point of being embarrassing."

"How could it be embarrassing?" Saundra hoped Charli didn't feel when she flinched at mention of the glass hearts.

"I just bought another display case for them. Not a bigger case -- another one. I tell myself it's my only real indulgence, but ... "

"How many do you have?"

"Hundreds. And it all started with Granny and her glass heart locket, and all the crazy stories she used to tell me, about a treasure hunt and a royal family and ... " Charli tugged her arm free so she could rub at her face and then raked back her dark curls. "I think I learned storytelling from her, if you really think about it. She always claimed it was a good luck charm, but ... Well, I don't think that luck is following me. In fact, maybe I should get rid of my collection."

"Why?"

Charli linked their arms together again. "I adore you for not telling anyone about my alter-ego, and for not going gah-gah screaming fan over me."

"Oh, no. Wacko-psycho fan problems again? How do you stand it? I was creeped out just from the two encounters with Stinky -- with Styles."

"My dear girl, there is a lot more Anastasia Roman in me than you might guess," she said, in a rich drawl with a hint of European accent that couldn't be traced to any one country. That was the signature voice of Carlotta VanDevere, which Saundra had heard in several radio and podcast interviews. A wicked twinkle touched her eyes for a moment, then Charli slumped, and the light vanished. "You're right. A fan out there can't tell Stacy and Carlotta apart, can't keep it straight in his head which one he's in love with, and he's determined to meet me face-to-face. In private. I just got my third glass heart from him, sent through my publisher. What if ... oh, there's so much that can be done with micro-miniaturized electronics nowadays. What if he traced the package and he knows where I live now?"

"You think that's who's spying on you?" Saundra shuddered. And she thought she had had problems with Jacob Styles?

"Who knows? Between the creepy fans who say I'm their soulmate, the psychos who threaten to sue me for invasion of privacy because Stacy's adventures are their life stories, and my lazy bum in-laws ... I should get out of this business."

They reached the ice cream shop by then. Saundra thought some of the tension had eased off Charli just from being able to talk. By the time they had their ice cream and settled down on one of the benches outside to enjoy the late summer dusk and warmth, Saundra had an idea of what to say to help Charli. If talking released the tension, maybe asking her about things she probably didn't discuss often could act like a safety valve.

"Lazy bum in-laws?" she asked, after they had both eaten a few spoonsful in blissful, sticky silence. "I didn't know you were married."

"I was. For about a year, in college. I actually thought I had dated and married an orphan. The perfect man, when you come to think of it. No strings or obligations, and none of the rivalry between families to worry about. At least, that was what I thought. Al was just too lazy to tell me. Or maybe he was trying to forget that the hopes and dreams and future support of the entire clan of Martinellis rested on him. Which meant they would rest on me when I graduated from college and started earning a decent living as an accountant."

"You? An accountant?" Saundra tried to muffle laughter, afraid this was a sore point with her friend.

"Yeah, I know. I was a whiz at business math. Ruined the curve for everybody in the class. I thought that meant I should go into the business program. Al was a junior on the six-year plan and trying to make it the seven-year plan. Who takes seven years to get a stupid bachelor of arts? Besides someone who won't choose a major and wants to live the rest of his life on summer jobs?"

Three more spoonsful of dark chocolate ice cream with peanut butter sauce.

"It was one of those stupid college romances. Al was a real charmer. Granny had her reservations, but he made me happy, so she gave us her blessing. Who knew that laughing and playing games all the time wasn't the same as being happy?"

"When did you dump him?"

"I didn't. The big idiot got a craving for burritos at 3am and ran down to the convenience store on the corner. Walked in on a robbery. His relatives blamed *me* because I didn't keep our breadbox-sized college apartment stocked with junk food to keep him safely at home. The guy ate every hour on the hour. How could I keep up?"

"Ouch. I'm sorry."

"Yeah, me too." Charli sniffed and summoned up a pained smile and knuckled one corner of her eye. "I had a narrow escape, if you think about it. Lifetime slavery. At the funeral home, while I was still getting used to the fact that I had any in-laws at all, I overheard some of Al's aunts talking about how to get me out of school and earning a living, and who would move in with me. They figured since I *let* Al get killed, I could just step in and support all of them for the rest of my life. Learning how to keep them from tracking me down and using crooked lawyers to confiscate my paycheck introduced me to Carson Fletcher, my main research resource." Another sigh. "Tracking down the jerk who robbed the store and shot Al was the basis for my first Stacy book."

She gave Saundra a sideways glance, visibly waiting for the question that burned on her lips. After all her years of reading and talking with writers and researchers, Saundra knew better.

"You found him, and you got the evidence to convict him, but I'm guessing you didn't have that really tricky, dangerous confrontation where you forced him to confess."

"That stuff only works in the movies. The guy actually tried to take a shot at me, when I was tailing him, and that started everything unwinding on him. I had all the proof, and he insisted through the whole trial, which was nothing like you see on TV, that he never went into that convenience store. He didn't know where it was. And all those receipts and torn up lottery tickets with the address were all planted by the cops to railroad him." She sighed. "I got justice, just not the justice I really wanted. And not a word of thanks from the in-laws. It was still my fault Al died, so I had to pay. Yeah, I learned a lot from that investigation."

"And you took the pen name to keep Al's family from demanding a share of your income?" Saundra scraped at the bottom of her sundae cup. She had eaten most of it without even tasting, she had been so caught up in Charli's story. "Wow."

"Yeah. Wow. I can't figure what's worse. Wacko fan kills me because I won't run off to paradise with him. Or he blabs my secrets to the world, and Al's family tracks me down and sues me to support them for the rest of my life. I should just pull up stakes and hit the road. But I finally have my townhouse the way I want it, and I'm getting too old to become a nomad!" She tried to laugh.

"I could take your books and those hearts and put them in storage, if you wanted ..." Saundra didn't finish the thought. She would love to get her hands on the Venetian glass heart locket so Aunt Cleo could examine it and determine if it was genuine.

"Maybe Carlotta VanDevere should auction them off for charity. Wouldn't that be a hoot? Or I could just work off some frustration, especially when writers' block hits, and take a hammer to the whole dang collection."

"No!" The thought made her dizzy.

Charli laughed.

"Most of it is junk. Pretty junk. Expensive junk. The only piece that's really worth anything is Granny's locket. I guess I'll have my proof if it really is a good luck charm."

"What do you mean?"

"Granny is going on a world tour in the spring, and she's taking the heart with her. If it protects her, and my life goes completely to pot when it's out of my hands, then we'll know."

"Just take it in steps," Saundra offered. "Finish the books you have under contract, then look for a new agent and a new publisher if they keep pushing you to write trash. After you get that new security system set up."

"Yeah, steps." She let out a long sigh and seemed to deflate a little. "Ye gads. You know how good it feels to let it all out? I mean, the girls know a lot of this, but just telling someone who doesn't know, so it doesn't feel like I'm just going in circles, boring someone to tears with the same old problems … Have I thanked you for not being a super-psycho stalker fan?"

"Who says I'm not? Maybe I just have a lot better self-control?"

Charli laughed, and Saundra wished she had never divulged her secret identity to Aunt Cleo. Not even for the sake of the hunt for the Venetian glass hearts.

~~~~~

Thursday, September 1

During the afternoon lull, Kai phoned Saundra at the library.

"Hey, would you mind if I came to ask for some advice? About books," he added before she could respond.

"Of course. Anything having to do with books, I'm interested. I'm here until 7. It's my late night."

"Oh, well -- I meant come by your place after work. Keep it private. With the talk around town lately, the last thing I need is Prince Roger accusing me of stealing family heirlooms."

"Why would he --" She caught her breath. "The … items that former client was looking for. You've had them all along?"

"I love a brilliant woman." He laughed despite the dropping sensation from his throat to his gut. After years of silence, this was harder than he had anticipated. "I need a restorer, for one thing. This stuff is ancient. We can't read it. Maybe it's time we get some experts involved. So that's why we're starting with you."

If he hadn't been in the stairwell for some privacy, he wouldn't have said that much.

"Okay, that gives me an idea of where to start. I should get home about --"

"How about I pick you up at work? I'll even bring dinner. What do you have a taste for?"

"Oh, I don't know. Surprise me?"

He spent so much time trying to decide where to order, and then what to order, he nearly forgot to order. The clock seemed to leap forward to 6:30. He barely had time to finish packing up the books in their padded boxes inside the sturdy cotton square-bottom shopping bags before he had to run down to the corner of Ivy and Shackle, to Frenchy's. It made perfect sense to him that an English-style pub would be named Frenchy's and served fish-and-chips on Thursday, not Friday. He hoped Saundra would laugh.

The aromas spilling through his car made his stomach rumble on the short drive down Longview to pull into the parking lot for the library. Perfect timing. There were no cars in the parking lot, meaning everyone else had left. Including whoever might be prone to gossip. Saundra was locking the door as he put his car into park. She turned around, tucked the heavy set of keys into her purse, and waved. Fifteen seconds later, she was in his front seat, and buckling her seatbelt, wearing what he hoped was a look of hungry ecstasy as she inhaled deeply.

"Don't tell me. Fish? And chips?"

"Is that okay?"

"More than. You have no idea how hungry I am, and how incredible that smells." She pressed her hand over her stomach and laughed. "Please tell me you didn't hear that."

He didn't, but he could guess because his stomach was clenching and making demands known. "Warp speed, engaging engines now."

On the short drive up Longview to her apartment building, he gave her the bare bones of how he and Eden and Troy had found the books hidden in multiple different spots in the walls throughout the building when they were renovating the Aurora Building. Despite the care that had been taken in wrapping the books, damp and insects had done damage. Much of the writing was hidden under mildew or other stains, or the pages were riddled with pinprick holes.

"We made the mistake of donating the first couple books we found to the historical society," he said as they pulled into her parking lot.

"How can that be a mistake?" Saundra asked. "Oh, wait --"

"There is no historical society for Cadburn Township," he said, in almost perfect chorus with her. They laughed together. "Nothing official, with any real authority. Except maybe the nuisance factor. They call themselves the historical society, but they're basically a bunch of older folks who sit around talking about the good old days and get in the way of the slightest change anyone tries to make in the township. Such as electricity and running water. Or at least, that's the way it feels," he said over her laughter. "Half the group was grateful and considered it validation when we handed them the books. The other half accused us of trying to bribe them. They spent a lot of time in the courts trying to stop the sale of a lot of the buildings the royal family lost."

"Royal family," she muttered.

"How about you think up your questions while we get all this inside? You carry the food, I'll carry the books."

Saundra agreed. Once inside, they had the elevator to themselves, so he continued.

"Anyway, the dust had settled long before we bought the building and got all the permits and regulations straightened out. The area was zoned for residential and commercial, so no one could stop us from setting up shop and living in the building. There was a lot of arm-twisting we didn't know about during the whole process. We were blamed for a bunch of old rivalries coming back to life, and some big shouting matches in the trustee meetings. So, when we found these historical treasures, devious motives were assigned to our donating the books. We didn't find the handwritten journals until a week or so later, and by then we knew better. We'd already had our first nasty run-in with the clown prince."

"You really despise Roger Cadburn, don't you?"

"Oh ... no, I wouldn't say that. Despise is such a friendly, warm word." Kai picked up the bags of books he had set on the floor and stepped off the elevator. "He's just such a pain when you contradict what he wants to believe are facts."

"Belief doesn't alter facts. The teacher who failed to teach him that should have had her license revoked."

"Welcome to my world." He meant to say more, just to get her eyes to sparkle again, and hear her laughter, but he had just realized which apartment was hers. Humor was too much effort as he fought the sensation of drowning in a sudden surge of questions and speculations.

"We tried to offer him the books when we made out enough of the words on the first few pages to guess they had something to do with the Cadburns," he continued, after what he hoped wasn't a very long pause. "The guy already had it in for us, and when we talked about family history, something he might find interesting, he cut us off every time. Once he accused me of doing a ham-handed job of working up to blackmail. I had enough of him after the first try, so ... to the historical society the books went. For a little while, we thought about offering him the next cache of books we found, just to smooth things over," he said as Saundra unlocked her door and led him inside. "We kind of felt sorry for him, I mean, how would you feel if a bunch of strangers showed up and discovered things your family might have lost, and handed them over to other people without giving you a chance to speak up?"

"But something happened to stop you?" She led him into the kitchen and put the food down on the little table tucked into the corner.

"You've got a greenhouse." Kai kicked himself for saying that. He remembered too late that Saundra had asked Troy for advice on where to get greenhouse repairs done. He knew this particular apartment had one on the balcony off the kitchen. Had Saundra chosen this apartment specifically for that? Or had she just decided gardening would be a fun new hobby? "Sorry, where was I?"

"Something stopped you from feeling sorry for the prince who was turned into a pauper."

"Ah ha! Clever." He wagged a finger at her. Saundra just smiled and pulled plates out of the cupboard. "Do you like ginger beer? Frenchy's gets it from some import place in Cincinnati. It's the best thing to drink with their fish and chips."

"Sounds incredible."

"Yeah, before we found out about the bankruptcy sales and some embezzling manager, we saw him in action. Picking on Curtis. Then he got in our faces about flaunting our wealth, and that pretty much sealed his fate. We figured silence was better than trying to be more mature than him. The so-called historical society here didn't have any idea what to do with old books in such bad condition. They handed them over to the library. We held onto everything we found after that and didn't tell anyone."

"How did you keep the construction crew from telling people?"

"Well, we aren't *that* rich. We did a lot of the demolition work ourselves, taking everything down to the studs, to save money."

"I bet you worked off a lot of frustration, too."

"Give the lady a cigar. Made it easy to keep people from knowing what we found."

While they ate, he described what he and his cousins had done to protect and preserve the old books when they had no idea how to restore them, or even if it could be done. Saundra asked questions about their condition, revealing some of her experience and knowledge. Kai came to the conclusion that they had been very lucky in dealing with the old, mildewed, crumbling books. They could have made things a lot worse.

When the unveiling moment finally came, Saundra handled the books with a delicate touch that had him feeling like a ham-handed clod. She commended him, Eden, and Troy for their commonsense approach to protecting the books and preventing any further decay.

"I have a few friends who are very good with books far older, in far worse condition," she said, after looking through each of the eight books. "These would be considered quite valuable just for their age and the handmade aspect. They're either journals or civic records, maybe minutes of township meetings, or even legal records. The historical aspect could render them priceless. Too bad they're so hard to read."

She carefully wrapped up each book and put them back into the same containers they had arrived in, sealed tightly to keep out moisture and light, and protect from jostling, or falls.

"You said some of the books you found are in the library?"

"Turned out to be the most legible of the bunch. Some are printed, a very old-fashioned looking print. I don't know if that makes them newer than these books. The funny thing is, someone who fancied himself an expert in old documents looked through one of the books and claimed it held a history of the township before it was a township and talked about the Cadburns. Then the book turned to dust and scraps of paper, because he didn't know what he was doing."

"Ouch." She hunched her shoulders as if it had been an actual physical blow.

Kai knew exactly how she felt. He had been sick when he heard, through the grapevine, what had happened to the book. It was like he had sent his own child to play in the middle of the highway. Cadburn blaming him for the damage and loss hadn't helped their already sour relationship.

He stayed until Saundra got off the phone with her friend who did restoration work, and the arrangements were made for him to take the books. He wanted to stay, but there was the Book & Mug to close up, and a new load of books from an estate sale he still had to look through. After Devona made the first assessment of what to repair or scrap or price and put out on the shelves. Besides, Saundra looked tired. He liked the idea of sitting together on that couch, watching a movie, and her falling asleep, leaning against him. Realizing how much he liked the idea jolted him. She had only been in town two weeks. They barely knew each other, and most of their time together had been dealing with this whole Styles mess.

On the drive home, he tried to remember that totally lame conversation between Keanu Reeves and Sandra Bullock in *Speed*, about relationships based on stressful situations, or whatever they had called it. All right, so he had had a gun pointed at him, and Saundra nearly had her purse stolen, but could the events the last two weeks truly be considered dangerous? Granted, dealing with the politics and cliques in Cadburn Township could be dangerous for their sanity, but it wouldn't kill him. At least, he hoped so.

He did like the idea, though, of spending time with her after this whole mess had been cleaned up once and for all.

Not until two days later did he remember the slightly uneasy feeling he had when he realized that Saundra lived in the same apartment where they had expected to find the woman they believed knew their true identities. They still weren't sure Sybil Orwell was the right person, because she had left town shortly before they arrived. It was a thin chance, with very low odds that they were right. After all this time, their leads had worn thin enough to be desperate to follow every lead, to invest effort and time for even the slimmest breakthrough in their hunt.

It hadn't been a wasted effort, though, because they had fallen in love with Cadburn. And now it was home.

Maybe Saundra coming into their lives and that apartment was a sign, or at least a step in the right direction. Who knew? Maybe when their relationship had solidified, he would tell her about the lifelong quest for identity, and she would let him search her apartment for anything Sybil might have left behind.

After all, Sybil Orwell had left abruptly. No warning, because there really wasn't anyone she was close to, other than her pastor. The chapel hadn't yielded any clues, and they hadn't been able to dig up an excuse to investigate her apartment before it was rented out again. It had been furnished, and all she had were her clothes and some plants in that greenhouse built on her balcony.

Chapter Twelve

Friday, September 2

Saundra got to work an hour early on Friday so she could look for the books Kai had told her about. Common sense said if the wrong people found out she was reading those books of township history, she could face harassment, if not worse forms of trouble.

She didn't expect to find the books on the shelves in the history section, so she checked the guidebook Mrs. Tinderbeck had given her on her first day of work. It was full of tips from the previous children's librarian, and useful instructions. Such as how to turn on the auxiliary power generator, in case of power outages. How to open the storm shelter, in case of tornados or severe weather. How to find the survival supplies and medical kits, in case of true disasters. Even a list of troublemakers and aliases they had used in the past, so Saundra wouldn't be duped into giving them access to materials and information they could use to harm others.

She found an interesting note on four people who had been caught five years ago trying to rip pages out of "rare reference books of local interest." They had a notation as being "highly active in politics," and the books were now located in TPC.

Those initials meant *Tinderbeck Private Collection*. They were under lock and key in the closet in Mrs. Tinderbeck's office.

Saundra had the keys and permission to access anything in TPC that she felt necessary to investigate. She could understand why such a measure of security and secrecy had been instigated. Easier to make certain touchy items and information simply vanish, rather than keep fighting with troublesome parties who would try to take them to use against others.

The closet containing TPC was deep, like a dressing room, with shelves lining the three walls. They weren't jammed full and were as neatly organized and labeled as Saundra expected from Mrs. Tinderbeck. The ones she wanted were in archival boxes. Saundra found it amusing to see them labeled as "historical interest, four volumes, removed from renovations of Aurora Building," with notations of each book by color, size, and sensitivity. Mrs. Tinderbeck used chili pepper graphics for sensitivity.

Saundra chose to start with the small black book that had four chili peppers. She settled at Mrs. Tinderbeck's desk and started reading.

"Bingo," she whispered, after only ten minutes. This was exactly what Jacob Styles had been searching for when he tried to hire Eden.

The "royal family" of Cadburn Township had indeed considered themselves royalty, with all the privileges that many despots in the Old Country took for themselves. Including taking any "peasant" girl they wanted and discarding her when she was no longer fun -- or, in the case of the genealogies recorded in the little black book, she produced a problem. The writer of the journal apologized to posterity for the arrogance of her predecessors who acted immorally and then got nasty when the scandals they generated wouldn't be hushed up easily. She wrote in the aftermath of the Civil War, when she and her brothers and cousins had agreed together to reform the Cadburn family, their reputation, and their guiding principles. The black book was being written to record the genealogies of the discarded offshoots of the Cadburn family as they were tracked down and woven back into the family history. The writer and her generation agreed that the income from specific properties in the Cadburn family estate would be assigned to these castoff children's descendants.

"Doing a little light research?"

Mrs. Tinderbeck's voice startled a yelp out of Saundra. She checked her watch before she turned to look at the office door. Twenty minutes until opening.

"Kai told me about the books they donated," she explained, and slid out of Mrs. Tinderbeck's chair. "He thought they might be what Stink -- what the man killed at their building wanted to hire Eden to find for him."

"It took them long enough to remember," Mrs. Tinderbeck said with a sigh. "Or maybe remembering wasn't the problem but deciding what to do about it. I'm surprised I haven't been served a subpoena to turn these books over to other interested parties."

"That might make things too messy. How do they explain when the evidence vanishes?" She picked up the book to slide back into the archival box.

"You still have quite a bit of research to do, don't you?"

"Barely got started."

"How to handle this and generate as few questions as possible ..." Mrs. Tinderbeck chewed her bottom lip for a moment. "My door stays open all day, but I'd rather no one saw you take that box out of the closet. Closing my door would immediately generate the wrong sort of questions. With my luck, the wrong person," she winked, "would look in at the wrong moment and see just how big that closet is. You'll have to take the box to your desk, tucked out of sight, and then do your reading in one of the conference rooms, on your lunch break. How does that sound?"

"Perfect. I hope this won't get you in any trouble." Saundra picked up the box.

"I can handle that kind of trouble. There's a certain element of respectful fear I've taken years to cultivate. Some of it will protect you for the time being, but you had better get started generating your own force field or whatever you want to call it."

"Yes, ma'am." Saundra locked the closet and exchanged smiles with Mrs. Tinderbeck, scooped up the box, and hurried across the library to her desk. All their precautions would be wasted if someone saw her coming out of the office with an archival box. In her experience, someone totally unconnected with a situation was always the weak point in any effort at secrecy. A chance remark always seemed to send words sailing through the air to land in exactly the worst set of ears to hear them.

At two minutes until the doors were to open for the day, Saundra had the archival box tucked away in the largest drawer of her desk, hidden under the puppets for the preschool story time and a bundle of flannelgraphs she intended to sort out and repair. She and the two kindergarten teachers had an idea of teaching the children to tell each other stories using the cutout figures.

Found genealogy book listing wrong side of blanket, she texted to Kai, and copied Eden and Troy. *More later.*

Twila scurried into the building at five minutes after opening time. Curious, Saundra got up and moved to where she could see the windows across the front of the library. Sure enough, a heavy-set figure in khaki sauntered past, heading for a patrol car in Cadburn Township green. So, a breakfast date with Officer Carruthers? Saundra didn't know if she should feel sorry for Twila, that she couldn't find someone better for romance. A snort escaped her. Maybe she should feel sorry for Carruthers?

Stop being so nasty. You're going to turn into her if you keep it up.

Then again, it might not have been a date at all, but a planning session. Whatever they had been doing, it was important enough to Twila that she was actually late for work. She was usually so punctual, Saundra felt tempted to set her watch by her.

The morning slid by with lots of laughter generated by the puppets, and little faces bright with fascination when Saundra and the kindergarten teachers introduced the flannelgraphs. She hoped some of the children equated the pictures with paper dolls. Did little girls play with paper dolls anymore? The effort was worth it when one child caught on and demonstrated for the others, and soon they were clamoring to have their own "dolly" and move him or her across the plywood board covered in flannel, to act out their stories.

A few times, Saundra looked up to see Mrs. Tinderbeck and a number of adults standing on the sidelines, enjoying the children's fun. She even caught a few thin smiles on Twila's face. That was a pleasant shock. Usually, Twila complained about the noise the children generated when they came for story time.

Later, Saundra wondered if she had grown careless because of those smiles and the unconscious assumption that Twila was relaxing a little. Or maybe it was Twila coming in late that made her think the other librarian was off her game and wouldn't pry into what everyone else was doing.

Saundra spent the first twenty minutes of her lunch break in the conference room just looking through the other books the cousins had donated, determining what they were. Some were printed by a local printing press and had notations that a limited number had been printed, at personal expense of the author. One book was full of maps, detailing the settling of Cadburn and the changes in the layout of the roads and plots of land through the years. It followed the transfer of titles as people settled in Cadburn or moved away, family lines died out, property was divided up among heirs, and other properties were consolidated through marriages and purchases. She made a note to herself to look up exactly how the old-fashioned printing presses of a century ago, or a century-and-a-half, had handled things like illustrations and maps. The journalism class at the high school might find that an interesting topic when their unit on the publication process came up, later in the year.

Another book was a log of marriages and births and deaths, and their causes. The first half was arranged by years, and the second half by family line. Saundra wished she could talk to whoever had put that book together to thank him for making it useful and cut down on the need to read through every single page.

At last, she could get back to the little black book of hushed Cadburn family scandal. Maybe that wasn't a nice way to think of it, but she couldn't think of something more accurate or kind. Saundra took a moment to pull out her phone, to snap pictures if and when she found the Bridgewaters.

"You're not supposed to be eating while dealing with archival materials," Twila snapped. "Didn't that two-bit university you went to teach you anything about proper procedure?"

Saundra carefully closed the book before turning around to face Twila. Why hadn't she heard the door open?

"For your information, I am not eating. My food is over there." She gestured at her insulated lunch bag, still sealed. "I assume there's some reason why you ignored the 'do not disturb' sign and you couldn't have the courtesy to knock before you came in?"

She reflected that the "do not disturb" sign had probably been like waving a matador's cape in front of a bull. If she had gone into the conference room and just got to work, no one would have noticed or cared what she was doing.

"One of these days, miss high-and-mighty, you're going to go too far. What are you doing?" Twila stepped up to the table and reached for the closest book.

Saundra slid it out of her reach and put it back in the box. "I'm studying some historical books to help me get ahead when the children come in looking for help for their papers."

Twila's nostrils flared. Saundra anticipated her next move and scooped up the other books to slide back into the archival box. Instead of spouting another lecture on rudeness or taking too much authority on herself, Twila hissed slightly as she inhaled and exhaled. Then she turned and stomped out of the conference room.

Saundra didn't find the pages she was looking for in the time left to her. She kept getting that prickling feeling up her neck, like ants were crawling. It took some effort not to turn around to see if anyone was spying on her through the small window in the door. Finally, with ten minutes left to her lunch hour, she put everything away, and managed to eat half her sandwich and drink most of her bottle of green tea before she had to go back to her desk.

Twila was watching, of course, and making a bad job of hiding the fact she was watching. There was nothing Saundra could do about it. Leaving the archival box sitting on top of her desk wasn't smart. She could get called away, and the moment her back was turned, someone could look inside or take the box. She wouldn't put it past Twila to steal the box, and then use it as proof that she didn't know how to handle valuable, fragile documents properly. If Twila figured out how valuable those books could be to Roger Cadburn, they might just vanish altogether.

Saundra figured the best thing to do was pretend that she didn't know Twila was watching and put the box away safely where it had been. Digging it out from the bottom of the drawer would take time. Twila could get caught digging where she had no right to be. She couldn't claim Saundra wasn't taking her responsibility seriously if it wasn't easy for someone to steal those books from her desk, could she?

An hour into the afternoon, Saundra remembered a trick she had used to protect her valuables when she was forced to spend a week at a time visiting Grandmother Mulcahy's house. Grandmother always insisted Bridget, Edmund and Saundra needed to spend as much time getting to know each other as possible, because the future of Mulcahy-Dresden Pharma would rest in their hands. Saundra had learned to jury-rig small locks on drawers. They didn't last long but did provide enough frustration that the sneak thief would either give up or would make the foolish mistake of complaining that "Saundra, that little pig, won't share with me!" Grandmother disapproved of name-calling and insisted that her grandchildren always ask and never, ever, on pain of spankings and loss of privileges, steal from each other.

"After all," she had scolded the twins constantly, "if you don't earn trust now, how can you be sure of trusting others, later, when you need it most?"

Saundra had always thought there was something slightly wrong with that principle, but she knew better than to question. At least her grandmother had defended her privacy, if nothing else. She had grown quite good at protecting her valuables.

She found what she needed with two rulers and several bulldog clips, a pompom caterpillar bookmark that was much sturdier than it looked, and a squeaky penguin toy confiscated from a first grader who had been irritating everyone around him. Saundra booby-trapped the three drawers on the right side of her desk. The hardest part was slowly squeezing the air out of the penguin so it wouldn't squeak and attract attention, giving away what she was doing and thereby ruining the trap. With that set up, she was free to use the bathroom.

When she came out again, Saundra was met with grins from a few patrons. Twila's movements were jerky as she took books to check out. Saundra wasn't surprised to return to her desk and find the boobytrap portion sprung, and two bulldog clips on the floor. The drawer hadn't been opened, however. Well, that taught her several important lessons. First, she wasn't paranoid. Second, the bathroom was soundproofed, so she hadn't heard the squeak of the penguin when Twila's efforts disturbed it and it popped loose and inflated. Loudly and squeakily.

The safest course of action was to put the archival box back in TPC and either stay late or come in early to read through the books without witnesses. When Twila took her regular bathroom break at 4, Saundra hurried the box back to Mrs. Tinderbeck's office. Her supervisor just smiled and took the box from her.

Saundra replaced the boobytrap on the handles of her drawers before she left for the day. She wished she could have a security camera trained on her desk to see how long it would take before Twila tried again, and if she didn't learn from the first attempt.

A short shopping detour to Green's Grocery filled her two square-bottom shopping bags with cereal and pasta boxes and a wide assortment of greens for salad. Saundra eyed the ice cream display, tempted by the caramel apple pie ice cream. However, she had walked to work, and her insulated lunch bag wasn't large enough to hold the carton. Her ice cream would be milkshake by the time she got home. She made a mental note to herself to drive tomorrow and get that ice cream. She deserved a treat after all the progress she had made on helping Eden. Wouldn't it be interesting if she determined that Curtis was indeed a descendant of the Cadburns, and he and his family had been denied their inheritance?

Her phone chimed with an incoming text before she got to the corner where she would need to turn left to get to Longview. She put her grocery bags down on the park bench in front of Green's and smiled as she pulled out her phone. Most likely, Kai was asking if she was coming to report what she found.

Nic asked her to get dinner for them. He would be waiting at the municipal parking lot at Longview and Ivy.

There was no denying him. He might have useful information. Besides, she could go back into Green's and get that ice cream, since she now had a ride home. She texted back, *Chinese?*

Nic didn't respond right away. She was waiting to cross Center, to get to the Celestial Dragon, when her phone pinged.

Careful. Shadow.

What was that supposed to mean?

Saundra turned and looked into the angry eyes of Officer Carruthers. Her heart skipped a beat.

"Hand them over." He held out his big hand.

"What?"

He snarled and lunged, reaching for her grocery bag with one hand, and the other hand shoving at her chest. Saundra yelped -- had that slimebag just groped her? She tightened her grip on both bags, spun on one foot, and brought her other knee up. Just like Nic had taught her.

Carruthers swore and leaped out of the way just in time to avoid singing soprano. Then his face got really ugly, and he swung, his hand closing into a fist as it approached her face.

"Stealing books, you filthy --"

A hand caught her collar and yanked her back, out of the way, so Carruthers' hand passed over her face and just brushed her nose. Saundra caught her breath as she landed hard on the sidewalk on her backside. Her tailbone was going to ache for weeks.

"Back off," Nic growled. He spread his feet so he stood over Saundra, at her calves. He was a good five inches shorter than Carruthers, yet with the fury in his eyes and his clenched jaw, he seemed a good foot taller, and about a hundred pounds heavier.

"You're interfering in police business," Carruthers snarled.

Saundra scooted back a foot or so and climbed to her feet. Francine Kenward hurried up and offered a hand to help her.

"Got a warrant? Got probable cause? I got witnesses. You spoke three words before you got physical, and none of them had anything to do with police business."

"She's a thief." He looked from side to side. "Stole valuable books."

Saundra looked around and saw a handful of people on the sidewalks. The faces closest to her were familiar. Funny, how she could get to know so many people in just two weeks. Most of them were smiling. Slightly nasty smiles that she hoped meant, "He's gonna get his," rather than condemning her.

"Did you steal anything?" Nic gestured at the grocery bags lying on the sidewalk. The little bag of salad toppings, with slivered almonds, cranberries, bacon bits, and sunflower seeds had slid out.

"No," Saundra said. A hand touched hers, and she yelped, then turned to see Allen Kenward holding out her purse, which she had also dropped. "I have receipts, if you have to have proof."

"Liar," Carruthers growled.

"Don't you call Miss Saundra a liar," Curtis called, stomping up and nudging other people aside. His hand trembled a little as he reached out to Saundra. "He didn't hurt you, did he?"

"Oh, shut up, Curtis," Carruthers said.

"What's in the bags?" Nic said.

"Groceries." Saundra bent and caught the side seams of both bags in either hand, stopping Carruthers with "liar" ready to burst from his lips again. "I didn't take any books from the library."

She tipped everything out on the sidewalk. The pasta hit with a loud thud and clatter. Two boxes of macaroni, one of angel hair, one of rotini, and one of choo choo wheels, for an art project she wanted to do with the preschoolers next week.

She stood up in time to see the shift from open-mouthed confusion back to anger on Carruthers' face. He looked ready to snarl something else at her, his face turning red. Instead, he pressed his lips flat together and turned to leave. Allen got in his way. His stern expression stopped Carruthers with his arm half-raised, elbow pivoting out to clearly shove him out of the way. Curtis let out a low, rumbling, wet-sounding chuckle.

"You owe the nice lady an apology," Allen said.

"Nice lady," Curtis echoed.

"Officer Carruthers," Captain Sunderson called from across the street. "Over here. Now."

"Ooh, mean old bully's in for it now," Nic murmured, as he bent down to help Saundra scoop her groceries back in her shopping bags. His eyes sparkled with malicious mischief, but he kept his face relatively somber. He did not watch Carruthers stomp across the street to answer to the captain.

"Lucky timing, but not all that lucky?" Saundra said just as quietly.

Nic didn't answer right away. Several people stepped up to ask if she was all right. Francine suggested she get home and sit on some ice. She had suffered enough falls in just that position, on the sidewalk, thanks to her rambunctious boys, she knew just how stiff and sore Saundra would be in the morning.

"I might have texted the police chief and told her one of Cadburn's finest was harassing you." He shrugged.

"Twila was sticking her nose into some research I was doing, some books from the special collection. I don't know why either one of them would think I would take those fragile books home with me. It's entirely against policy."

"Miss Saundra doesn't do things like that," Curtis insisted.

"Sorry about that," Allen said before he and Francine continued on their way. From the bags in their hands and the aromas of barbecue sauce and pork-and-beans, they had picked up dinner at Seevers' Cleaver. "The guy really is a good cop, or at least he used to be. Something messed him over a few years ago and ..." He shrugged, then held out a hand to Nic. "Thanks for stepping in. You new in town?"

"Visiting. I'm an associate of Saundra's aunt, and she asked me to check on her, make sure she was settling in all right." Nic cocked an eyebrow and looked across the street at the police station. "I guess you're settled in if you've been around long enough for someone to have a beef with you."

"Hank's a dumb bully," Curtis said, and turned and wandered off before they could respond.

"Just for that," Saundra said, "you're buying dinner."

"Of course." His smirk softened after Allen and Francine left them, and Saundra's testing rub of her backside earned a hiss. "Really, how are you?"

"I feel like I'm back on the playground in second grade and the jerk kids won't let me play tetherball."

"Do we need to pick up ice with our dinner?" He took both her grocery bags in one hand and looped his other arm through hers.

"No, I've got plenty. Let's just get to your car before Godzilla finishes getting his knuckles rapped and decides to punish me for that, too."

Nic snorted and gestured down to where Ivy met Center.

"Too?" he said, when they had left all the other pedestrians behind. "What books was he talking about?"

She told him, with as few details as possible, about the books the cousins had donated to the library and the defensive measures she had taken. The timing of the attack made her pretty sure Twila had got into her desk, discovered the archival box wasn't there, and called Carruthers. Most likely she believed Saundra had taken archival books out of the library, rather than putting them back where they belonged. Archival books were never to be removed, except to go to other libraries or to museums.

"Yeah, but what if she knew what those books were, and why you were looking at them, what you were looking for?" Nic asked.

By this time, they were in his car and heading to her apartment.

"You said this trustee knows the books exist, and he gave your friends a hard time about donating them, instead of turning them over to him, right? If Godzilla — good name, by the way — and his girlfriend are in his pocket, she could have been looking for those specific books. Especially since he seems to know what the dead man was looking for."

"Now my head hurts, too. And we didn't get any dinner." Saundra pressed hard at her temples.

Nic opened his mouth to say something, probably teasing. He was a great defender, but somewhat lacking when it came to skills in comforting and sympathy. Her phone rang. A jolt of adrenalin at seeing Kai's name on the screen eased her growing headache a little.

"Where are you? Are you all right?" Kai blurted when she answered.

"I'm on my way home --"

"Do you want me to come get you? I know you walked today. You always walk." A nervous-sounding chuckle cracked his voice.

"No, I got a ride from a friend. In fact, we're pulling into the parking lot right now."

"If he wants to come over," Nic said, voice soft, "I'll leave. You need to tell him what you found, anyway."

In moments, that was settled. Mrs. Tinderbeck called after Saundra reached her apartment. She confirmed Saundra's speculation that Carruthers had come after her on Twila's instigation. The penguin squeaky toy alarm went off before Saundra had crossed Longview. Before Mrs. Tinderbeck could get up from her desk and to see what Twila had been screaming about, the other woman rushed into her office, snarling her accusations that Saundra had stolen the books.

"I told her that of course you hadn't left them in your desk, you were very responsible, and you had returned them to the climate-controlled vault. I also told her that you had set the alarm on your desk on my orders, because there had been a rash of thefts from different librarians' stations, and we were trying to catch whoever was doing it." Mrs. Tinderbeck chuckled. "You really must teach me what you did."

"But Mrs. T ... we don't have a climate-controlled vault."

"True, but Twila doesn't know that. Since she called her guard dog, and he went after you, obviously, she didn't believe me. Hmm ... maybe she does know we don't have that vault after all."

Saundra was just frazzled enough, she asked Mrs. Tinderbeck the question that had been building from her first day of work: Why didn't they fire Twila, who required so much maneuvering around her prickly feelings, it added to everyone else's work?

"If it were anyone else, dear, any other situation ... Well," Mrs. Tinderbeck let out a sighing chuckle, "you know the old adage of keeping your friends close and enemies closer. I've grown quite adept over the years at interpreting Twila-speak. I usually have a good warning of what the opposing political party in town is about to pull at the next trustees meeting, and I can warn the friendly, sensible element of township government. Someone always wants to cut library funding or change the hierarchy of authority. I can normally circumvent such maneuvers with a little warning. If we fired her, we'd have to look for the new mole, so to speak. That's too much trouble for someone of my advanced years."

Saundra laughed at that, which she suspected was part of her boss's intentions.

"And despite what you've observed over the last few weeks, Twila really is a good librarian. She's quite efficient at what she does. She's simply been off her stride because yes, she did want your position. She didn't have the wits to simply apply. She wanted to be asked to take the job, and that just will not do. She mistakenly thinks she can be endearing and lovable to the children. I suspect because that sweet Daphne can find good and something to love in everyone. She's really the only small child Twila knows." A long sigh. "Anyway, she's quite useful simply because she knows

122

how to frighten people into turning books back in on time and keeps the rowdy elements quiet, or out of the library altogether."

Saundra thought she was developing a headache from repeating conversations, by the time Nic was caught up.

"This Twit-la may just realize you're on to her," he commented. That earned a snort of laughter from her, and he winked. "I need to look into her and Godzilla a little more closely. That might mean me staying around here a while longer than I expected." He grinned, cocking an eyebrow at her. "Maybe I really should settle down here. It's a nice neighborhood."

"You? Settle anywhere? You're more of a tumbleweed than Cleo." Saundra couldn't snipe at him. While she was on the phone, he had emptied her ice cubes into a zipper bag, wrapped a hand towel around it, and now she was sitting on it.

Kai buzzed to be let into the building as Nic was stepping out of the apartment. He winked and said he would take the stairs. Saundra decided to be amused rather than irritated. Nic seemed to enjoy playing sleuth and sneaking around, moving in the shadows. His sneaking and spying had certainly come in handy for her.

She shuddered a little at what might have happened if he hadn't been there. Yes, she was capable of defending herself, and there had been plenty of witnesses on the street. Allen and Curtis, at the very least, would have stepped in to pull Carruthers off her, if Nic hadn't gotten in the officer's way. But just how long would she have had to struggle with him before someone intervened? Something in his eyes had told her Carruthers wanted an excuse to use force. She could imagine him claiming she had resisted arrest, to justify any damage he did to her.

Kai brought dinner, enormous, drippy sub sandwiches from Deli-licious, and a murky yellowish potion of Troy's devising. He revealed that Curtis had come into Book & Mug, furious over what Carruthers had done to her. He had been especially upset that the officer had accused her of stealing special books. The potion was an herbal recipe Troy had come up with over years of tinkering. It was guaranteed to ease her aches and help erase bruises much faster.

The potion worked as promised, leaving her clear-headed, while easing the aches. They discussed what she had read while they ate dinner. He was intrigued by the photos she had snapped of sample pages in each of the books, and what she hoped to find after further reading.

"I feel like a real dummy, now. We should have held onto those books. Then we wouldn't have all the sneaking around and worrying about what the other side knows."

Saundra was glad to show him the email she had received from the friend who did the preservation and restoration work. It would take time and would be quite expensive, but he held out hope that the books Kai had brought her could indeed be cleaned and made legible. It would take time, months, before he could fit the books into his work schedule. She apologized to Kai for that. He laughed.

"This stuff has been sitting for years already. What's a few months more?"

She was drowsy enough, even if she could still think clearly, she agreed with Kai's advice that she get to bed and get a good night's sleep. They arranged to meet at the library two hours before it opened, so she could go through the books with him. Saundra wondered at her assessment of herself as clearheaded, when she realized that she hadn't cleared it with Mrs. Tinderbeck. Kai was still there when she made the call. The elderly head librarian chuckled when she gave permission, and threatened to join them in the treasure hunt.

Kai offered to pick her up in the morning. She was tempted, but she knew he had to open the coffee shop. It was enough for him to meet her at the library later and help her look through the books.

Chapter Thirteen

Saturday, September 3

Saundra drove on Saturday morning. There was something about the quiet and chill as the sun rose that made her feel like she wasn't alone. After first Styles, then Carruthers had come after her, that wasn't a good feeling. She went to Sugarbush for some donuts to fortify her and Kai. On second thought, just Kai, because she certainly couldn't handle the books and eat at the same time.

A police cruiser sat parked on the street, midway between the library entrance to the parking lot and the schools entrance. Saundra hesitated, stopping at the intersection of Apple and Longview to study the car. No one appeared to be in the driver's seat. Did that mean one of the foot patrol cops was here, parked while taking a long tour of the area, then moving to another part of town? She shuddered, imagining running into Carruthers or someone else who did "errands" for Cadburn, with no witnesses to what he said or tried to do, and no one to come to her assistance.

Maybe she would call Kai and find out how long until he showed up?

"I could call Nic," she murmured. Any other time, she might have found some amusement, anticipating a stream of smart remarks from him to confuse her attacker and distract him until more help came. Nic's wit sometimes made a more bruising defense than anything he could do with his fists. She had sometimes daydreamed about what school would have been like if Nic had been around, to sass and frustrate the "pretty people" who listened when her cousins said she was worthless and stupid.

There was no turning back time. Nic had taught her some basic, useful self-defense moves, verbal and physical, and she had more confidence now. She had done pretty good yesterday against Carruthers, hadn't she? The important thing was to get into the library to spend all the time she could looking through those books before the other librarians showed up.

She drove slowly past the patrol car. Why did the officer park on the street, and not in the parking lot? She looked closer.

The window on the passenger side was shattered.

Saundra looked around for some sign of movement, an indication that the officer assigned to this car was coming back.

No movement. Not even a hint of breeze moving the bushes sitting low around the foundation of the old library building. Nothing in the taller trees edging the playground on the other side of the lot, between the elementary and middle school buildings. How could this section of municipal property, this long block, be so empty of life at this time of morning, so full of shadows in broad daylight, perfect places for something or someone to hide?

She drove up the street and into the parking lot and pulled up to the front door of the library. She didn't care if she blocked the handicapped ramp and straddled the line of two parking spots. Taking a few deep breaths, she focused on slowing her heartbeats and steadying her hands before she pulled out her phone. Which was the smarter tactic? Call 911, or just call the front desk of the police department and let them decide if this was an emergency? What was more important: getting someone out here as soon as possible if there was a problem? Not looking like an alarmist? Or just outright silly?

Calling the front desk meant looking up the number on her smartphone. Maybe an extra ten seconds. She chose that. Brenda Dutton, who was in the choir, was on desk duty. Her friendly voice helped Saundra speak calmly, coherently, and even put a little chuckle in her voice.

"Hi, this is Saundra Bailey. I just pulled into the parking lot at the library, and there's a patrol car sitting on the street out front, with no officer in sight, and a broken window. I hope you already know about it, but if you don't --"

"No, we don't, as far as I know," Brenda said. "Thank you for letting us know. I'll send someone out there right away."

Saundra didn't hear what she said next. Nic texted.

Coming to the library? When? Call the police.

She assured Brenda everything looked quiet, and she would stay away from the patrol car. She finally got off the phone so she could text Nic.

I M here. Called cops. See car w broke window?

Not yet. Around back. Tell them we agreed to meet here.

She agreed, then got nothing more from him. No explanation why, even when she asked. Since he was there, it had to be safe to get out of the car. What was he doing out back?

Saundra got out slowly, looking in all directions. She tucked her phone in her pocket, her purse under her seat, and arranged her keys so they stuck out between her fingers. She learned that from Wolverine, not Nic. All the library keys were old-fashioned and long and stuck out far enough to make her feel a little more secure. She kept looking around as she walked around the library to the back, where the woods bordered the property.

No sign of Nic.

"Stupid," she whispered, when it occurred to her that maybe Nic hadn't answered her question because someone had knocked him out or did even worse to him.

The scent of blood came to her, thick on the warming morning air. The glisten of dew had long since faded from the grass, and wisps of steam were rising. It was going to be a scorcher of a day. The woods were close by --

126

maybe the smell of blood came from a rabbit? She had heard something on the news about the increasing number of coyotes in suburban areas.

That was no rabbit, lying partially in the ditch between the library property and the woods. At first, all she saw was a dark shape half-hidden by overgrown grass and green thistles, still with their dusting of grayish purple flowers. The rest of the grass was crushed by the shape. A long, heavy-looking shape. A few steps closer and her perspective changed, and she saw khaki. That was a long, thick leg, and a calf-high, muddy boot.

"Go back." Nic emerged from the woods, staying within the shadows from the trees, and gestured back around to the front of the library.

"You didn't --" She gestured at the officer on the ground.

"Do you think I should have?" No smirk. He shook his head. "He was that way when I got here. He's groaned a couple times, so he should wake up soon. Bring the Cavalry."

"Who?"

He bared his teeth. "Who do you think?"

A choked little laugh escaped her. She turned around and headed back to the front of the building. Whatever Nic was doing back there in the woods, he could just explain to the police himself.

Allen Kenward was pulling up next to her car when she reached the sidewalk that ran along the front of the library. The look he gave her clearly said she should have stayed in the car.

"Carruthers is out back in the ditch," she said. "I don't know how badly hurt he is. Do you need the first aid kit from inside?"

"Depends what I find." He offered a grim smile as he got out. "How about you go inside and lock the door, while I check on him. Just in case."

She thought about telling him Nic was somewhere near. By now, it made sense that Nic was probably looking for whoever had knocked out Carruthers -- if he hadn't. She still couldn't be sure he wasn't responsible. If Nic figured she was going to the library early, maybe Carruthers had expected the same? If the officer had been lying in wait for her, maybe Nic had argued with him?

"No, Carruthers is a creep, but he's not stupid. He wouldn't have been parked out front where I could see the car, if he was trying to trap me." She watched Allen as she walked up to the front door of the library. He stood at his open car door, talking on his radio, and looking around the parking lot.

The library door hung ajar, just an inch or two. Enough to see it when she got close, but not enough for someone standing on the sidewalk to notice. Saundra looked back at Allen. He was bending back into his car, probably putting the microphone away. She turned back to the door and bent over to cut the glare coming from the rising sun.

The display of books for the middle school reading list had been toppled and spread across the carpeting past the inner foyer doors. Saundra backed away. Only idiots in horror movies were stupid enough to go inside when there was clear evidence that someone had been inside and might still be inside.

"The door's open and someone knocked things over inside," she called as she headed back down the sidewalk to intersect Allen, who was on his way around the building to the back. "If you don't mind, I don't really want to sit in my car while you're checking on --" She gestured around the back of the building.

Allen nodded and waited for her to catch up with him. Nic was just coming around the far corner of the building when they came around the front corner. He nodded to Allen, stopped, and waited for them to come to him.

"I followed some footprints into the woods. I don't know if they're from the same person who clobbered Carruthers. They go down into a dry creek, all pebbles and twigs. No sign of which way the guy went from there." Nic shrugged. He didn't try to look sorry or worried.

He stayed with Saundra, a few yards away, while Allen helped Carruthers sit up and examined the broken skin on the back of his head. A siren beeped and popped from nearby. Allen looked around and seemed about to say something but hesitated.

"Want us to send them back here?" Nic said.

He barely waited for Allen to nod, before looping his arm around Saundra's back to lead her to the front of the library. She felt like commenting that she had gotten her steps in for the day already. Instead, she told him about the open door and scattered books.

"I wouldn't put it past that joker to do that," Nic said, once they had showed the EMTs where to go. "Go looking for those books, make it look like a robbery. But not clobber himself, or let an accomplice clobber him, to deflect suspicion."

"So we've got someone else interested in historical documents?"

"Maybe Styles' partner is getting active again."

Nic and Saundra settled on the bench in front of the library. She knew what she had to do, though she hated doing so. She pulled out her phone to call Mrs. Tinderbeck and report the break-in while they waited for the EMTs to come back with Carruthers.

"How odd," the elderly woman said once Saundra explained. "I should have gotten a call from the alarm company by now. First they notify the police, then they call me."

"So whoever broke in ... dismantled the alarm system?"

"It looks that way. Are you all right?"

"I'm fine. Just irritated that I won't get any work done before the day starts." Saundra tried to chuckle. She refused to even think that the intruder found what he was looking for -- and he had been looking for those books hidden in the archives.

Mrs. Tinderbeck promised she would meet them at the library, once she had made several required phone calls regarding the break-in. Starting with the alarm company to find out why they hadn't noticed that something was wrong. Everything had been upgraded just two years ago, so if power had gone out, or someone had messed with the computer system overseeing everything, the company should have gotten some kind of alert.

By then, the EMTs had taken care of Carruthers, and Saundra watched what looked like an intense but brief discussion between him and Allen. Several times they both looked over at her and Nic, and she was pretty sure some accusations were being thrown around. If she had been the one knocked out, and when she finally got her feet under herself again, she saw Carruthers standing on the sidelines, she would accuse him of being the attacker just because of the altercation yesterday. Finally, the EMTs took Carruthers away with them, and Saundra could breathe a little easier. Allen had a crooked smile when he sauntered over to join them, and he didn't look at them, but past them, at the door of the library.

"Well ... since you're an authority here, we can start the preliminary investigation, see what's been done inside," he said, and gestured at the building.

"Even though she's probably a suspect in the attack?" Nic said.

"You, yes, but not Saundra."

"Hate to break it to you, but I trained her, and she could take Godzilla down with no trouble." He shrugged and gave Saundra a smile that came nowhere near apologetic. "Hey, better to have full disclosure from the beginning."

Liar. She knew better than to ever think Nic West would give "full disclosure" or anything within a mile of it, when it came to events related to him. Or her, she had to admit a moment later.

"Trained her?" Allen cocked an eyebrow at them, but he didn't hesitate as he led the way to the library door.

"I have a background in intelligence work. I can give you my contacts, if you need to verify, but I'd rather not. Saundra's aunt, an associate of mine, is involved with an ongoing investigation -- not intelligence-related, however -- that takes her all over the world. We decided it was a wise precaution to teach Saundra some self-defense measures. In case someone Cleo irritated in the course of her investigations backtracked her and decided her small-town librarian niece was a good target for some retribution."

Saundra didn't think he was lying. Exactly. However, there was a lot of the story he had left out. She was proud of herself that she didn't react, as far as she could tell, when he admitted he had done intelligence work. It made sense, actually. Nic did have an attitude that matched a lot of movie and novel PIs and government agents. Not that she had any illusions about how close to the truth many of those books were. Even the ones written by former operatives. Lots of drama was added, and many characters who contributed to the story were combined into one, for the sake of speed and story flow.

Still, something had changed, a few pieces added to the background picture of what her aunt was doing and why Nic West was part of their lives.

"Okay, that kind of explains that interrupted move I saw yesterday. That wasn't an accident, you sidestepping him trying to clock you." Allen's smile widened and warmed. Just a little. He took a deep breath, and that smile faded as he studied the ajar door. He reached in his back pocket and pulled out some thin vinyl gloves, like examination gloves. "Not exactly procedure, but if you --"

"And a license to carry," Nic said, drawing a pistol from behind his back. Saundra hadn't caught the movement, so she didn't know if it was tucked into the waistband of his jeans, or he had a sleek holster under his polo shirt.

"You guys are scaring me a little," she said, as Allen reached for the handle of the big, heavy, brass-and-glass right-hand panel of the double doors of the library.

"Good. It'll keep you alive." He chuckled softly when she stuck her tongue out at him.

Saundra didn't mind admitting she was grateful that Allen took the lead and Nic walked slightly behind him and to the right, both of them providing something of a shield for her. She wished she had worn her sneakers instead of sandals this morning. Better for running for her life, if she had to.

Who would have thought she'd be afraid of getting shot at the library, of all places?

Other than the display of books in the entryway of the library, nothing else looked disturbed. At Allen's whispered questions, Saundra directed them to the security system panel inside the small room that held the after-hours book and DVD return slots and boxes. Nic stayed in the doorway, watching for movement in the library while Allen studied the panel.

"I'm not fully familiar with this system," Allen admitted, after several minutes.

"It's turned off. Nothing broken." She gestured at several lines of lights and code numbers beside them. "This gives an overview of the power leads and the phone connection, the wi-fi, backups, and redundancies. Whoever got in here probably has a key. The system has a timer, so anyone who enters with a key has two minutes to get in, unlock this door, and turn off the alarm."

"That narrows the list of suspects. A little."

"Why would someone who has a right to be in here knock over the books?"

"Maybe Carruthers did that, when he followed someone in here?" Nic said.

"Never got in. He saw someone moving around inside," Allen said as he stepped out of the book return room, "and got out of his car to investigate. Whoever it was ran, and he followed them around the back of the building and got clobbered."

"Nah." Nic's smile turned malicious. "He couldn't have seen movement inside from the street. The angle is wrong, and the shadows, and the distance. And if he came over to investigate, why'd he leave his car on the street, and not park by the door? He was sneaking around and saw somebody, and they got the drop on him."

"You know Carruthers says you did it?"

"Yeah, you said that before. Just because he says it doesn't make it so. Don't know how much good this will do, but it does pinpoint my activities and where I was about an hour ago."

He dug in his pocket as he spoke and pulled out a receipt. Saundra leaned closer and saw the logo for Bob Evans across the top, along with the date, time, and address. Nic had sausage gravy and biscuits and coffee for breakfast. She calculated it would have taken him half an hour to drive from the restaurant, where I-71 intersected Sackley Road, to Cadburn, if all the lights were in his favor. He had probably arrived at the library ten minutes before she saw the patrol car out front and noticed the broken window. Having seen his instincts in action, he had probably sensed trouble before he saw the broken window.

Nic looked around the library once more. "My gut says it's safe. Whoever came in got what they wanted, and they're long gone."

"But why would someone who has a right to be here -- Oh." Saundra felt incredibly stupid. Maybe she was still feeling some after-effects from that lovely all-natural potion Troy had sent over for her bruises. "Just because someone has keys doesn't mean they have the right to those keys."

"A building this old?" Allen gestured around. "I bet dozens of people over the years have been given keys and someone was sloppy about getting them back when they retired or quit or were fired. Or died. This building has served a lot of purposes, a lot of renovations and changes over the years. Those big old doors date back to the turn of the last century. There's even a plaque inside the foyer, telling how they survived a fire and tornado and a couple other disasters." He sighed. "Let's do a walk-around, just to check what might have been disturbed."

Saundra didn't know whether to blame instincts or just a guilty conscience. She headed for Mrs. Tinderbeck's office.

The door was open. It shouldn't have been. The head librarian locked her door every night because of all the records, the personnel information, the calendars for library activities, all sorts of information that needed protecting from people who had no right to see them. People who thought they were "helping" by rearranging the files and the office itself to be what they considered more efficient. People who thought they had the right to use a conference room that was already booked or attend a workshop or lecture that had no seats available. Saundra had heard some horror stories from the other librarians in the last two weeks. Even the ones who she didn't consider gossips.

The TPC closet wasn't hanging open, but the door stood out from the frame just enough to show it had been unlocked and opened. Saundra picked up Mrs. Tinderbeck's spare sweater and used it to grasp the knob. It didn't turn. That explained why the door hadn't closed entirely. The bolt wouldn't move. Whoever had unlocked that closet didn't know the trick of making sure the lock didn't reset itself when the key was taken out.

Did that help narrow down the suspect list? She didn't mention it to Allen, but she made a mental note to ask Mrs. Tinderbeck when she arrived.

Still protecting her hands, and avoiding leaving fingerprints, she found the light switch and turned it on.

"They're gone." She pointed at the empty spot on the shelf where the archival box had sat. Even the notation label on the shelf had been peeled off. Who would do something like that?

"What is?" Allen asked.

"Some historical books that tie into what Stink -- what the man who was killed at Book & Mug tried to hire Eden to find. I'm sure that's what Carruthers wanted to take from me yesterday."

"Why? No, don't tell me. Forget I asked. This is something you should probably explain to the Captain."

They were nearly finished with the walk-through of the library by the time Mrs. Tinderbeck and Captain Sunderson arrived, along with the man who was the alarm company shift supervisor. He agreed with Saundra's assessment, that someone with a key, who knew the alarm system, had gotten in and turned off the system.

Rather than make everyone move over to the police station, they set up the investigation in the large conference room. Saundra was stunned and felt a little sick with guilt, when she learned Kai had been outside the library for more than half an hour by this time. Another officer had arrived as backup and to help secure the scene right after Allen, Saundra and Nic went inside, and wouldn't let anyone into the building. She stepped out to apologize to him and explain. Kai was more concerned about her and asked her four times if she was all right, Carruthers hadn't hurt her or threatened her, or whoever had clobbered him hadn't done anything. That warm glow from his concern stayed with her through the hour of questioning and discussing and putting together a timeline of events. She was a little proud that they got through the process so the library could open on time. Other than those involved in the investigation, no one was the wiser that something had happened.

But the historical books that Jacob Styles was looking for, had probably died trying to find at Book & Mug, were missing. Someone who had keys to the library had taken those books. Someone who knew how to get into places, get around alarm systems, and knew people's schedules. Someone who knew how important those books were. Maybe the same person Kai had heard arguing with Styles, who had kept him from shooting Kai, and then had fought until they fell from the second-floor fire escape. The man who landed on Styles, killing him, and was strong enough, unharmed enough, to get away.

Who had that kind of access and knowledge and ability to get around the township without anyone noticing or wondering what he was doing there? It had to be a "he," because Kai felt sure he heard two male voices. Did the list of details she had compiled help to narrow the list of suspects at all?

Maybe she didn't feel all that safe anymore. Was she paranoid, or had those instincts Nic praised and the self-defense skills he had trained into her kicked in because they were needed?

On a bright note, Carruthers was on medical leave. Saundra overheard Captain Sunderson arguing with him on the phone, threatening him with suspension if he kept insisting that Nic had ambushed him. All the evidence spoke against it. Carruthers was just a bully and a liar. Saundra would have liked to accuse him of being the thief, but while he could have gotten keys to the library from Twila, he didn't get the key to the TPC closet because Twila didn't have it.

So who did?

Chapter Fourteen

Sunday, September 4

Saundra had breakfast with Pastor Roy and Patty, Sunday morning. They had planned it, sort of a "look back and assess how things are going so far" kind of meeting and celebration of her new life. They had heard about the break-in and attack at the library, on top of all the other exciting and unpleasant events Saundra somehow found herself involved in over the last week, and they were understandably concerned. She was relieved they didn't ask her outright if she was keeping Cleo updated on what was going on, but she knew they would hint and nudge until they were sure. That was just the way they were, always concerned and looking out for her. How could she resent it, when they were responsible for all the good new things in her life now? So, she told them about the letters she had sent to Cleo so far. No answers yet from her aunt, but that just meant she was somewhere without Internet access or maybe limited electricity to charge. It happened regularly.

She suffered a few recurring twinges of guilt when Pastor Roy prayed for Saundra's safety and for God to guide the people doing the investigation, to give them resolution. How much praying had she done lately? Panic prayers weren't as meaningful and useful as the ones where she had conversations with God.

Maybe the troubles she kept tripping over were the result of not including God in her routine? Maybe she wasn't spending enough time in her morning devotions and prayer? As Cleo had put it multiple times, the enemy was taking advantage of the sloppy gaps in her armor.

Sharing her new insight with her friends and praying with them helped in ways she couldn't quite describe. She just knew she felt better as she helped Patty clean up the breakfast dishes, and the three of them walked down the street to the Chapel for Sunday school and then the service.

Until an idea struck her that nearly made her trip on a nonexistent crack in the sidewalk. What if this insight was a gift from God this morning specifically, to prepare her for even more trying and strange times ahead of her?

Okay, Lord, help me trust You. Help me relax into Your strength and listen better and ... Lord, Kai, and Eden, and Troy don't go to my church, and I guess I need to find out if they go anywhere, and where they stand with You. If they're going to be the really great friends I feel they can be, I owe it to them. I should be concerned about them. So ... help?

~~~~~

"There he is," Mrs. Tinderbeck said glancing past Saundra's right shoulder.

They stood on the steps of the Chapel, greeting other members of the congregation as everyone dispersed for the afternoon, and headed out for Labor Day weekend activities. Saundra had three invitations to join other single girls on different outings. One group was piling into a car on the far side of the parking lot for an overnight trip to Sandusky and Cedar Point amusement park. Another group wanted her to come canoeing in Loudonville on Monday. She already had plans with Eden, Troy, and Kai, just relaxing, and hopefully talking greenhouse management, on the patio on the roof of the Mug Building. A quiet day of relaxing sounded wonderful, after all the excitement of the last few weeks.

"There who is?" Saundra turned, and her gaze connected with Nic's.

"That young man giving Kai Shane a run for his money." She chuckled when Saundra turned back and frowned at her.

"I don't think so."

"Oh, so Kai is making headway?"

"He isn't running, and Nic is a friend of my aunt, and is checking up on me."

"He seems to be conveniently close when you need him. He was your knight in shining armor Friday and yesterday."

Saundra stopped herself just short of telling Mrs. Tinderbeck to hush. It wasn't respectful, and she liked the woman too much. Besides, Nic was within earshot now and she just did not want to get him started on teasing her. He always seemed to know when someone was interested in her before she saw any evidence. If she could depend on his judgment, six young men in the last five years had been interested. Two had been sidetracked by Bridget, who actively pursued a reputation as a man-eater. One fell under her spell and was tossed aside within the span of a week. The other ran for his life. Two others had left the area after Saundra had seen them talking with Nic. She wasn't sure if she should blame him for driving away potential boyfriends, or maybe thank him. The other two had been nice, but that was as far as it went, and two dates each was as far as they went. She hadn't really wanted to get to know anyone, hadn't felt like she had made a connection with anyone until Kai. Could she really trust this sense of connection? Maybe all that linked them was the stress of Styles' activities, his threats, the mystery he presented, and the complications of him being murdered on Book & Mug property.

"Mrs. Tinderbeck, how nice to see you again. Under nicer circumstances." Nic waggled his eyebrows at Saundra.

She wanted to deck him. Why did he delight in giving the impression he was a truant officer checking up on an accident-prone, innocent bookworm who preferred research to reality?

He went on to apologize for the "excitement" surrounding the library, as if his presence somehow made it his fault.

Maybe it was? Just the fact that he intervened on Friday had given Carruthers reason to go snooping around the library. Maybe Twila had been planning to meet him and they were going to ransack the place to find out what was in the archival boxes Saundra hadn't removed from the library after all. She couldn't remember if anyone had mentioned Twila, or even if anyone had seen her since Friday. Not that she could ever imagine Twila having the strength to knock Carruthers out -- though yes, she had the temper, and the sneaky skills to creep up behind someone and ambush them.

"I have permission from Captain Sunderson to let you know, before the official report is filed and given to the trustees," Nic went on. His mouth twisted in a brief smile. "Since I have a personal interest and the credentials, I was allowed to be present while they were debriefing Officer Carruthers at the hospital." He shook his head, eyes sparkling. That earned a snort from Mrs. Tinderbeck. "He was such a difficult patient, they put him under partial sedation. Funny, how some people get very sentimental, and others just get sloppy. Furious and whining like a snot-nose five-year-old is not becoming in a man of his size and age. And in a uniform, on top of it." The sparkle in his eyes turned downright gleefully malicious. Saundra knew it well from other unpleasant incidents in her life when he had intervened.

"He confessed?" she guessed.

"Confessed to what?"

"Harassing Saundra on someone's orders," Mrs. Tinderbeck said, squeezing Saundra's hand to quiet her, "or trying to break into the library?"

"Ma'am, you should work for the Bureau. All it would take is one word with a few low friends in high places, and you'd have a brilliant career as an interrogator." Nic snorted. "Seems Trustee Cadburn assigned Carruthers the job of keeping an eye on Saundra and making sure she didn't give anything useful to our friends at the coffee shop. He's of the opinion -- the trustee, not his hound dog -- that you've been led astray, and your loyalty should be to him and not to a bunch of troublesome newcomers."

"I'm more a newcomer than they are," Saundra said. Yes, that was the attitude she had come to expect from Trustee Cadburn. And his wife.

"Loyalty has to be earned," Mrs. Tinderbeck said. "What damage his arrogant father did to the family reputation, Roger just finished the job." She sighed. "Let me guess. When confronted with the confession, the poor, misunderstood, maligned head of the trustees insisted Carruthers was deluded and lying?"

"A demented idiot who should have been put out to pasture, or sent to the glue factory, years ago," Nic said with a straight face. "Not exactly his words. Cleaned up because you are ladies, and this is church property."

Saundra laughed. More a snort than a chuckle. She was tired, suddenly, as if all the excitement and tension of the last two weeks had been compressed and tied to her shoulders, draining her, and weighing her down.

Someone called her name from across the parking lot. She turned around, fighting the whine building up in her throat. More than anything, she wanted to just go home and sleep the day away. Maybe not go out tomorrow, though she really did want to spend the afternoon with Kai and Eden and Troy. The thought of her lunch plans with Charli --

That was Charli calling and hurrying across the parking lot. How weird was that, to think of her and immediately see her?

"Oh, hey, I'm sorry to barge in, but ..." Charli shrugged and waved her cell phone at them, as if that was explanation. Then she gave Nic a little frown. "I know you, don't I?"

"I just have a face that blends into the crowd," Nic said, his expression perfectly straight.

Saundra expected to see mischief in his eyes, but that glint was wariness. What didn't he like about Charli Hall, of all people? Sometimes his paranoid streak was useful, like on Friday and yesterday, but to find something suspicious about Charli? Maybe he needed a good kick in the head. Or other parts of his anatomy that would give Saundra a little satisfaction.

"Yeah, right," Charli said, her grin coming back. "Honey, you'd be great on the cover of my ... well, I'm working on this suspense novel, and you'd be the stereotyped Mafioso boss."

"Just the boss?" Nic grinned back at her. "I'd rather be the hit man. You know, lurking in the shadows."

"Yes," Mrs. Tinderbeck said. "That seems entirely appropriate and suited to your character."

"Mrs. T, I am wounded." He pressed one hand over his heart and pretended to stagger. "We've only just met, and you're already -- Saundra, you've been telling tales out of school."

"Me!" Saundra slapped his arm. Everyone laughed. "I haven't talked about you to anyone. Mrs. Tinderbeck is an insightful person who has an incredible talent for reading minds."

"Well, this is fun, but I'm in a crunch." Charli waved her phone at them again. "I'm sorry, Saundra, I have to cancel lunch. Carson and I have to run up to the islands to check on something with my cousin and ..." She shrugged. "Last-minute stuff, but this is something Leo has been working on for a few years and too many clues have slipped through our fingers."

"Are you an investigator?" Nic asked.

"Considering it. A lot less stressful than being a writer." She rolled her eyes. "I'm sorry for ditching you. Especially when the girls came up with some theories for what's been happening." She took a few steps back. "Can we talk later? I'll probably be back in town by Tuesday. Is that okay?"

138

"That's fine." Saundra fought not to let out a long sigh of relief.

"Carson Fletcher?" Nic murmured, once Charli had jumped into her car. "That's the investigator she works with and uses as a source, right?"

Saundra nodded. She wished she had never mentioned anything about Charli to Nic. Or to Aunt Cleo. There was the tie to Charlie's glass heart, after all. Saundra hated the certainty he was investigating all her new friends. Even without the mystery of the Venetian glass heart lockets. Did they tie Aunt Cleo to Eden to Charli? How?

While Nic's protective investigative tendencies might be helpful when it came to figuring out what Styles wanted, and what had gotten him killed, and who his murdering partner might be, she squirmed a little at the thought of all the extra digging Nic was probably doing. Just because he was the kind of guy who wanted to know everything about everyone, and displayed an occasional obsession with defending her.

"Who else is an investigator here?" Mrs. Tinderbeck said. Nic flashed her one of his cheesy smiles. At least he was smart enough to try to charm the woman, rather than fluster her into forgetting to be curious or suspicious.

He looped his arm through Saundra's and announced that since her lunch plans were cancelled, he was shanghaiing her. Aunt Cleo would insist. Mrs. Tinderbeck laughed, bade them farewell, commented that she trusted Saundra not to fall for "this sly charmer," and ordered her to enjoy the holiday. The last week had been just a warmup for the fall crush at the library.

To Saundra's relief, Nic didn't take her out to eat in public. Despite trying to focus on something else, anything else, Mrs. Tinderbeck's comment about Nic giving Kai a run for his money kept popping up to the front of her conscious thoughts. That relief turned to a mix of dismay and chagrin. He took her east down the highway closer to Cleveland proper, where they picked up gyros, baklava, and almost enough Greek olive salad to satisfy her, and ate in the car. They had to eat in the car, because Nic drove from one open house to another, looking at homes for sale. Saundra refused to give him the satisfaction of asking who he was buying for. He had mentioned considering settling in the area, but she hadn't really believed him. What were the chances he was looking for a house for Aunt Cleo? Nic wasn't going to insist Saundra would be safer in a house and had to move, was he?

At least he didn't take advantage of the situation and tease her when a few of the realtors hosting the open houses made comments implying the two of them were a couple. Such as, "What do the two of you have in mind?" or "Where are you two moving from?" or worst of all, "Are you looking for a bigger home, expanding family?" with that bright expression just primed to congratulate them on expecting a baby. Nic always deflected the conversation in another direction, asking about details of the houses and never asking her opinion in front of anyone. Though he did ask her what she thought of some of the places when they were in the car, Saundra couldn't decide why he wanted her around. The only explanation she could come up with was that Nic was tired of being alone, of not having someone around who knew his name and had a little shared history. That was totally ridiculous, she was sure. Nic West, feeling lonely and wanting some security? Hah!

Unless ... maybe he was providing *her* some security? Keeping watch over her because of some threat he hadn't told her about?

That sounded more like the Nic who had been lurking in the shadows all her life.

"So what else did Carruthers say while he was sloppy drugged and spilling his guts?" she asked.

The sun was starting to slide down the sky. She figured it was maybe going on 6 in the evening. Could that really be considered evening when the day was still bright and there was plenty of daylight to enjoy the warm weather and lazy atmosphere for at least three more hours? Saundra supposed that just being able to detect the slow dying of the day was evidence enough that fall was approaching.

Maybe she should be grateful that Nic had kept her busy this afternoon so she wouldn't sit at home and brood? Not that she would ever express that thought to him. The less he thought she owed him, the more comfortable her life would be. Besides, she had been longing to spend the day napping or just lying on the couch and reading, drowsing the day away. Maybe sit on her balcony and take one final opportunity to get a hint of a tan. Nic was always showing up and interfering and changing her plans. Why did she think she could ever feel grateful to him?

Kai would never shanghai me.

Why had she let herself think about Kai, and what Mrs. Tinderbeck had said?

"What made you think Carruthers said something else?" Nic returned slowly.

"All right, what did his royal lowness say that you considered a threat to me?"

That got a snort and a grin from Nic. He glanced at her, then focused on getting back on the highway. He asked, so she explained where she got the nickname for Roger Cadburn.

"Appropriate. And you're right. He mentioned that while he didn't approve of what Carruthers did -- I'm thinking he meant messing up the job of keeping an eye on you, not attacking you -- while he didn't approve, he thought you had brought some of the trouble on yourself. Sticking your nose where it doesn't belong and helping troublemakers just makes things worse. He said something along the lines of, if you want to be a member of the community, you should devote yourself to helping fix the messes others have made, refusing to deliver lost property back to the rightful owners."

"Edited to protect the delicate ears of present ladies?"

"More like untangled and a lot of guesses to fill in when he was snarling under his breath." Nic took his hand off the steering wheel long enough to pat hers, resting on the console between them.

"Hmm ..." Despite feeling drowsy from all the walking, and a little headachy from the odors of cleaning solution, scented candles, and that chemical aroma of new carpet and fresh paint that she had been breathing all day, Saundra's brain shifted into gear.

"What?" Nic glanced at her before flipping the turn signal and moving over, aiming toward the highway exit that would put them on a straight shot for Cadburn.

"It just occurred to me that ... well, I guess I had this idea, even if it was only subconscious, that someone else working for Cadburn took the books. Maybe I just assumed they were covering their tracks, and when Carruthers caught them, they had to clobber him."

"Or he was helping them, and the henchmen argued about who got to bring the prize to the boss, and the other guy clobbered him. No honor among thieves. Good idea."

"Not good enough. From the way you said he was grumbling, whoever took the books didn't turn them over to him."

"So there's someone else out there interested in those books. Maybe the same guy who landed on Styles clobbered Carruthers." He snorted. "I don't know if I want to shake his hand or clobber him myself."

"So you got me out of the house because you think someone would come after me? Threaten me?"

"Maybe I like spending time with you. Maybe I want to give Mr. Designer Coffee a run for his money?" He gave her a sidelong look that threatened to turn into his trademark smirk.

Saundra chose not to answer and tried not to respond with any change in expression or posture. Leave it to Nic to hear the one thing she didn't want him to and to ruin what had been a relatively pleasant afternoon. She much preferred to see him as her irritating, interfering big brother. She needed a big brother at times.

Nic's phone rang through the Bluetooth connection in the car. The number displayed on the screen in the dash. Saundra had a moment of shock, realizing this had to be Nic's own car, and not a rental, as she had assumed. Somehow, that changed his comments about settling in the area from a joke to something like a threat.

Then she recognized the area code and the exchange. That was someone calling from Cadburn. She glanced at Nic and caught him giving her that narrow-eyed, assessing look before he gave the verbal command to answer the call. At least he didn't signal her to be quiet.

"Kenward here. Just wanted you to know your theory was correct. We caught him. Don't know how he's going to explain this. That's the Captain's problem, not mine. Thanks for your help."

"No, I'm thanking you. Saundra's aunt is a good friend and I owe her a few. Taking care of Saundra is important to me." Nic didn't look at her.

Saundra shuddered, but she was pretty sure she was more angry than afraid. She could put the pieces together. Probably Carruthers had come after her, either to redeem himself or punish her because Cadburn had disavowed him and the job he had bungled. Would it have been so hard for Allen or Nic or both to just tell her their suspicions and ask her to cooperate in setting up a trap? Why all the subterfuge? Why did Nic treat her like she had to be protected, emotionally as well as physically? It kind of put a lie to his praise of her self-defense skills and common sense and mental toughness.

"Carruthers tried to break into my place, or the library again?" she said, when Nic finished with Allen. He promised to come by the police station as soon as he finished up an errand. She assumed dropping her off at home was the errand.

"Yours." By this time, they were passing Center Avenue, heading for Longview. "You should know that he insisted first you, then me, then both of us ambushed him at the library. He couldn't keep his story straight about what he saw or even where he parked and what he did. But it was pretty clear to me that he thought you had taken the books. I found out last night that his father was a locksmith, on call for the township. Sunderson was very interested in learning whether Carruthers senior turned in all the patterns and master keys he used for getting into all the township buildings. She found it just as interesting, as I did, that he was also on call to reset locks on all the buildings the Cadburn family owned."

"Re-set locks?" Saundra shivered. "Like, during renovations?"

Nic turned right on Longview, a straight shot to her apartment building, taking them past the municipal buildings, schools and library and town hall.

"Maybe. Still digging into dates to determine when he got let go, and how long he worked for them. Most of what I've found so far is all sorts of complaints and legal claims, filed against the Cadburns as landlords. Seems that whenever they wanted to sell a piece of property, they'd conveniently lose rent checks. Then after two months, they would evict tenants for being consistently late with payments. It was kind of hard to blame the post office or the tenants themselves, when everyone in the building was going through the same problem at the same time."

"Greed makes crooks stupid," she muttered. Something Aunt Cleo had said long ago, many times. Saundra had always suspected she was talking about the Mulcahy side of the family.

"You got it." Nic winked. "Toward the end, they stopped giving warnings, or a chance to fix problems their tenants hadn't made in the first place. The first anyone knew they were in trouble was when the locks were changed, and they couldn't get into their offices or homes to remove their own property. When a pattern builds up like that, the really intelligent officers and legal beagles figure out what's going on, and it's all dirty business. Wouldn't put it past Cadburn or his father to punish their minions, rather than accept the fact of their own stupidity."

"So ... you expected him to get keys to my building and my apartment and try to break in today. That's why you got me away, so you and Allen could set a trap?"

"With the good captain's full knowledge and blessings." Nic chuckled. "Leave it to you to see the important details, through that whole convoluted story."

Saundra was not flattered by his thin praise. The irritation lingered after Nic dropped her off. He only nodded when she asked him to call back and tell her what else he found out when he checked with Allen.

Saundra didn't expect him to call. And he didn't. Maybe he was just too busy, and whatever he learned had sent him down another path of investigation. Or maybe he just didn't want to tell her. Nic was always playing things close to the vest.

So when Charli sent her an email that evening, telling her the theories the writing gang had come up with, Saundra decided not to tell Nic.

She did intend to tell Kai, and Eden, and Troy the next day when she went over to Book & Mug for the afternoon and evening. After all, it was their business more than anyone's.

Chapter Fifteen

Monday, September 5
Labor Day

Saundra had never had a picnic on a roof before. The Mug Building was just one big cube, slightly sloped on top to facilitate drainage, but not enough to notice or inconvenience anyone who spent time up there. Kai demonstrated by putting a can of ginger ale on the surface of the area set up as the patio. The can didn't move until he gave it a nudge. It rolled grudgingly in one direction, but did pick up a little speed when he pushed it the other direction, showing the angle of drainage for rainwater and melting snow. There were regular gaps, four inches square, about two feet apart, in the three-foot-high wall that ran around the perimeter of the roof. Those gaps were covered with coarse screening, to catch debris and let water through.

Two-thirds of the roof contained the greenhouse where Troy grew the plants he used in his health food and medicine-through-nutrition research. There was still plenty of room for the patio where the cousins had lounge chairs and an umbrella table. A little shed sat on the west side, past the shelter for the stairwell door. It had enough awning to shelter the gas grill and a small refrigerator for provisions and stored the furniture in bad weather. Kai made her laugh, with stories of patio furniture being blown off the roof the first year after they moved into the building, until they learned to set up wind breaks and tie down their furniture. Then they realized they would have to carry all the furniture downstairs in the fall, and store it somewhere, so they bought the pre-fab shed and anchored it securely. He claimed the building would fall apart before the shed blew off the roof.

The various clubs and civic groups in Cadburn had a Labor Day parade starting at noon. Saundra made sure she was at Book & Mug by 11:30 to help carry provisions up to the roof. She was surprised, and pleased, that Kai had given all his employees the afternoon and evening off. He claimed he couldn't in all good conscience deprive the caffeine addicts of Cadburn their morning jolt, but his employees had a right to some time off at the end of a long, hot summer. Saundra was just pleased, and relieved for him, that he wouldn't get called away by any coffee shop business. Not that she had any claim on him, other than as a friend and guest for the holiday.

Mrs. Tinderbeck's comment about Kai's supposed interest in her kept invading her thoughts at the most inconvenient times.

The four settled on the roof soon after she arrived, and had the best seats in town to watch the parade. The same barricades for the street festivals had gone up early that morning, blocking off Center. The participants gathered in the big Metroparks parking lot by the river's edge at Sackley Road, where people could leave their cars to go hiking, or rent roller skates or bikes or cross country skis, depending on the season. The parade would go up Center to the township park. Game booths and concession stands waited to entertain and feed residents. Several summer sports leagues were having their championship tournaments in the baseball diamond, basketball court, and soccer field. The day would conclude with a concert by the township musical society in the gazebo at dusk, and then fireworks. Eden assured Saundra they could hear the music from the roof, and they would be free of all the trees that would block portions of the fireworks display for anyone on the ground. It was already shaping up to be a perfect holiday, relaxing with her friends, even before the trumpets and banging of snare drums down by the river announced the start of the parade.

They stood at the wall at the front of the building and watched and commented on the different groups represented. The high school marching band, which had been practicing for two weeks before school started. The Cadburn Barnstormers, the saddle club. The Four Corners square dancing club. Saundra cheered with the people down on the street as the club performed a few simple dance moves without making the small parade stop in the middle of the street. The fire department had firefighters and EMTs marching and tossing candy to the children. A few clowns tossing more candy to the children capered alongside the cars with the township officials. Saundra found that quite appropriate but held her tongue. Later, she found out the three trustees rode in Cadburn's convertible. He sat up on the back of the open compartment, while the other two trustees sat down in the back seat, where they weren't as visible. Then there were a few off-duty police officers, a team of Civil War re-enactors on foot and horseback, members of the Rotary, and schoolteachers. When she commented on three women in Union Army uniforms, Kai told her Cadburn had a local legend of several girls who disguised themselves as boys and fought in the war. One legend said the ghost of one, a Cadburn daughter, haunted the town. She vanished somewhere on her way home from the war and was said to show up at unpredictable intervals. She supposedly would do so until her remains were found and she was properly laid to rest in the family cemetery.

The parade ended with a man on horseback, in Revolutionary War era costume, representing Hiram Cadburn, who had surveyed the territory back when it belonged to the Western Reserve. He had written down his impressions of the rivers and meadows and forests and urged his sons and grandsons to come out to the Ohio Territory to settle. One grandson, Silas, had come west to fulfill Hiram's dream.

That reference to history sort of took some of the gloss off the day for Saundra. She had hoped to forget about the whole dispute and question of heirs and inheritance and stolen books and the threats and complaints from Roger Cadburn. And Ashley, come to think of it. What were the chances of putting all that out of her head for any length of time, until the books had been found and investigated and the man who had perhaps unintentionally killed Jacob Styles was identified and caught? That reminded her of the email from Charli. Even though it was helpful, she hesitated to mention it today, simply because she didn't want to ruin the relaxed, fun atmosphere with unpleasant business. She would tell the cousins eventually, but she figured she had all day.

She and Kai teamed up against Eden and Troy in a few card games and then Trivial Pursuit. While the question cards had been put together when they were babies or hadn't been born yet, that didn't mean they were clueless when it came to the pop culture references. Eden had an advantage, because of all the research she did in her investigative work. Troy was constantly following what he called rabbit trails. Saundra and Kai were voracious readers, so that made them pretty even with the other team.

They played and argued over interpretation of questions and phrasing and teased each other and laughed. The best part of the day, Saundra decided later, was that the three cousins made her feel like she had been their friend for a long time. Only a few slips occurred, when someone made reference to people or events in a past she didn't share with them. In some ways, she was relieved by the slips, because it meant the cousins weren't making some effort to censor their words and include her. Everything felt natural.

The day grew long, and shadows slowly stretched across the roof. Kai and Troy adjusted the tilt of the umbrella to ward off the sun as it crept a little lower in the sky. Saundra helped Eden bring up the prepared custard and chopped fruit and nuts and bits of chocolate that had been waiting and chilling in her refrigerator. Troy and Kai were in charge of fetching the ice cream freezer and the bags of ice and rock salt. They teased each other that they had beaten last summer's record for making ice cream -- five times, as opposed to only three the summer before, when Troy bought the ice cream freezer. They had a pleasant half hour or so, discussing recipes Troy had altered into decadent, creamy desserts. Saundra wasn't surprised to learn that Kai had been playing with the idea of adding homemade ice cream to Book & Mug's menu. The lack of time to decide on recipes and calculate the supplies they would need, and then find someone to put in charge of producing it on a regular basis, had all added up to delay initiating the project.

Eden suggested that since Saundra actually had experience making ice cream at home when she was a child, Kai should hire her. Saundra thought her chest felt so full and yet so light, it might crack open. Especially when

Kai eagerly grabbed hold of the idea. She wouldn't even need to leave the library to devote time to making ice cream, because how much would they need each day? The thought of working with Kai was tempting, though. For another half hour or so, the conversation drifted toward business ideas, how they would facilitate expanding Book & Mug's operations, if they needed to set up an annex to the kitchen, or rent a storefront, and if they were wasting their time even considering competing with Goody Two Scoops.

The whole thing crumbled, with some laughter thrown in, when Troy pointed out that this was September, and by the time they got the ice cream division going full speed, they would be in the dead of winter. Who would want ice cream then? Even if they produced all sorts of holiday flavors, such as pumpkin pie or mincemeat or eggnog or peppermint stick, was it enough to be worth the extra effort? They agreed the timing was off, and then agreed to play with the idea during the winter.

Saundra was almost relieved when Eden declared it was time for the semi-annual bocci tournament and sent Troy downstairs to fetch the bocci set. That ended the topic on a high note. Kai excused himself to take care of the containers that had held the ingredients for assembling the ice cream, and bring up the scoop and dishes. He didn't care about the instructions that the ice cream needed to sit and harden for a few hours after it had been churned thick. He liked soft-serve ice cream, anyway.

"They can be overwhelming, can't they?" Eden said, when it was just her and Saundra on the roof. She opened the door of the refrigerator and lifted out two peach teas, asking with a gesture. Saundra nodded, and Eden tossed one of the plastic bottles to her. "I've been meaning to ask you about your friend, Charli. How long have you known her?"

"Oh ... a few years. My previous library ran a yearly writers conference. Charli and her friends attended, and we clicked. We look for each other at the conference every year. Or at least, we used to." Saundra laughed. "I didn't even know she lived in the area until I ran into her at church."

"She's interesting. Is she published? Or maybe I should say, does she publish under a pen name? I got the feeling from things she said that she has some books out there."

"Yes, she does. But ... well, she has a pen name to protect herself. And now she's having trouble from some real wacko fans, so it's really good she has the pen name, so they can't find her."

"And since you're her friend, you're not going to tell me, because you've known her a lot longer than you've known me." Eden nodded slowly, her smile thoughtful. "I'm kind of glad you're that way. A good friend. And okay, I won't ask, but I'm curious. That heart she was wearing when you guys came in the week before. Do you know where she got it?"

"It's her grandmother's. She loans it to Charli. Kind of a good luck piece." Saundra shrugged. "You should see the huge collection she has, all sorts of glass hearts. Someday, Charli hopes to find one just like her grandmother's."

"Any … oh, I don't know, does it have any significance?"

"I don't really know." That was the truth, and yet it tasted like a lie in her mouth all the same. She tried to focus on the opening Eden had given her, to get past the discomfort. Thanks to the work Aunt Cleo had her assist with from time to time, there were things she would have to keep secret from these friends who were starting to feel like the family she had always hungered for.

"Oh, hey, speaking of Charli, I got an email from her. From her writing group, actually. They were playing with theories about who could be the murderer. That's the kind of books they write. Occupational hazard, I guess." Saundra dug in her pocket and brought out her phone. "It's kind of cool. They made up a chart, to kind of divide people up into how they'd have access to this building and my building and other historic buildings, and who would know about the books you found. Who would know about the ones you donated to the library, and if anyone would know about the other books you found and didn't donate."

"Nobody knows about those. Except maybe the crew coming in after we did the tear-down, if they heard us talking. We might have let things slip while we were asking questions, learning township history, and who was who. Until politics made things so nasty." Eden put down her bottle of tea and moved over into the seat next to Saundra's at the table. "Thanks," she murmured, when Saundra handed her the phone to see the chart on her screen, instead of Eden having to lean over to see it.

Kai and Troy joined them while Eden was still looking at the chart. The phone screen was too small for more than a cursory study of it. Kai trotted downstairs to his apartment to get his laptop, and asked Saundra to forward the email to him. He put the chart on his laptop, and they filled in more names, added several rows and columns, ruling out some names, adding others, changing as they remembered bits of township history and gossip, and dividing up the population into friendly, neutral, and unfriendly. Then after a while, they further refined the list to people they had only heard about but never met, people they only saw on the street but didn't converse with, business relationships, political, and antagonistic.

Somewhere the task turned into a kind of game, a challenge, or perhaps more accurately a puzzle they needed to solve. Troy brought up maps he had made of the area, and maps that had been created by the historical society -- specifically the ones designating land that had belonged to the Cadburn family and the other families who were, sometimes grudgingly, acknowledged as the founding families of the township. Saundra remembered what Nic had told her about Carruthers' father and being a locksmith. Eden made a note to contact Captain Sunderson in the morning to ask what she had found out about the lock patterns, records, keys, and other tools of the locksmith trade that had or hadn't been turned in when the man retired. And perhaps why Carruthers' father had retired, if there were negative reasons, or just old age.

"I wonder if Carruthers is finally going to get his walking papers," Troy murmured. He snorted. "I wonder how long it'll take for this information to get leaked by folks who have a grudge against the royal family, just to use him to embarrass them."

"I wonder how long it'll take before people start connecting access to township keys to things going missing without any signs of break-ins and ..." Eden sighed and leaned back in her chair, to scrub her face with her palms for a moment. "Sometimes I really hate this line of work I'm in. You have to think about the negative options and the positive ones, from every piece of information you dig up, every lead, every weird, inexplicable piece of data that might or might not have any impact. And then there's the whole factor of whether we can trust what people tell us."

"Such as, if the records are lying when they record that Carruthers the locksmith turned in all that information on the locks he set and fixed and changed out?" Saundra offered.

"I wouldn't be surprised to have him claim everything was destroyed," Kai said. "No way of proving it wasn't. Without a search warrant, at least." He tipped his head to the left, and his eyes lost a little of their sparkle. "So, this guy who gave you the information ... is that the same guy who got between you and Carruthers the other night?"

"Nic. Yeah." Saundra tried not to read anything into the shift of his expression -- mostly because she couldn't read it. For good or bad? Maybe she had watched too many mystery shows and police procedurals growing up, but her brain seemed to freeze up, unable to decide how much information to offer. What was enough? What was too much? What would make Kai suspicious?

Suspicious of what, exactly?

Yeah, she wanted Kai to be interested in her. She was too tired to think of a word other than jealousy. There were such negative connotations to the word, thanks to self-righteous social gurus. The original meaning of the word was more protective than possessive. What was the right kind of jealousy? If a guy wasn't interested enough to be jealous enough to protect a relationship, to keep working at it, then what was the use? If someone broke a promise, the other person had a right to be angry. Saying someone was wrong to be jealous in any way basically absolved people of the crime of breaking promises.

Her parents, for all their obliviousness and inability to break free of the domination of the Mulcahy clan, had loved each other devotedly, and loved her. They kept their promises. They didn't take the easy way out. Saundra hoped to find a love like theirs someday. Her chest felt hollow for a moment when epiphany struck: possibly for the first time in her life, she truly was free to look for and hope for and pursue that kind of relationship.

Thanks, God. You always answer prayers, no matter how long it takes or how impatient I get.

"You okay?" Kai reached over and rested a hand on her shoulder. A grin crooked up one side of his mouth. "You kind of zoned out there."

"I am tired ... of this whole stupid mess getting in the way of us relaxing and enjoying the holiday. Tired of people sneaking around and playing games and accusing people and spying and stealing and keeping secrets. I'm really sick of secrets." Her breath caught as an image and idea leaped to the front of her brain. "That's what we need." She gestured at the screen with the chart, which Kai had started to color code.

"What?" Eden looked back and forth between her and the chart.

"It's not a table, but the color coding helps. We need one of those diagrams where circles overlap, and the colors indicate how many places each one overlaps."

"Doesn't guarantee that the people who have the most overlaps, the most in common, are the guilty party, but yeah ..." Troy's tired face lit up as he nodded. "The more access people have to information that nobody else has, the more access they have to buildings, the higher on the list of suspects they go."

"We're gonna need a bigger sheet of paper." Kai grinned and made the *da-dum, da-dum* sound from the *Jaws* soundtrack. That got snorts and grins from the others.

"We need a bigger surface to work on if we're going to do that. And probably a few preliminary charts, weed out most of the people we have on the suspects list." Eden raised her arms over her head and arched her back a little. "I vote we close up here, move things downstairs, and push some tables together in the shop. If you don't mind, Saundra? We've had some instances like this before, where we just can't stop until we get an answer. Besides, I don't think I could go to bed any time soon."

"Why would I mind? I feel like I'm to blame. If you guys are staying up late, staying up until dawn if that's what it takes, I'm with you." Saundra slid her chair back from the table. "What should I take down, and where should it go?"

"The ice cream freezer goes down first," Troy announced. "Somehow, we managed to obey the instructions this time, and it's nearly ready to eat."

"It's a ploy. Eden's just running away from the bugs," Kai retorted. "I keep telling you, the mosquitos don't fly this high."

"Yeah, yeah." Eden stuck her tongue out at him and bent over to get one of the serving trays leaning against the leg of the table.

Eden and Kai took the clean dishes and computer to his apartment and went to get the necessary office supplies for creating the colored chart. Since the dumbwaiter was full of the ice cream freezer, Saundra and Troy took the last of the dishes and trash downstairs to the coffee shop. She loaded their mugs and utensils in the dishwasher while he took the trash out. The dumpster sat in the alley between the Mug Building and the building that backed up to it. Saundra finished the job and stepped out into the back hallway to ask him what she should do next. He was standing by the security panel next to the door into the alley. The bag of trash sat on the floor at his feet.

"Troy?"

"You don't happen to have your phone on -- never mind."

The sound of rapid footsteps came from the stairwell. He tapped the security panel, making the red numbers and letters change and scroll across the narrow display like a marquee, then headed down the hall to the stairs. Eden and Kai were just coming down from the landing between first and second floor.

"Someone's been in our places," Eden said.

"Someone turned off the alarm system. Didn't find it until I tried to turn it off to take the trash out." Troy hooked his thumb over his shoulder down the hall to the alley door.

Saundra held out her cell phone. Eden thanked her with a nod and made the call to the police while Troy and Kai went back down the hall and tapped more buttons on the security panel.

"Was anything taken?" she asked, as Eden gave the phone back to her.

"Not that we can tell yet. A few things were out of place. Cushions, pictures. I've got a cupboard that doesn't want to close all the way unless I lift up on the edge of the door. It was hanging open a few inches. Someone was searching. I don't know if I should be grateful they didn't make a mess or not."

"Maybe they just got started when we came downstairs," Kai said as he and Troy came down the hall to rejoin them. "They could still be here, hiding until we're out of the way."

"Oh, thanks very much. Just creep me out." She stuck her tongue out at him.

"They were looking for the other historical books you found, you think?" Saundra said.

"That means people know about the books who shouldn't know."

"I had a friend in college who had a theory about mystery TV shows. Depending on how old they were, the guilty party was always either the most famous guest star, or someone everybody trusted. Someone who was invisible because they were always there." She shrugged. "I don't know if that helps, but maybe you should look at the least likely person in town?"

"That'd be the kids in your preschool reading group, then," Troy said.

"She does have a point, though," Eden murmured.

"Uh oh." Kai grinned. "Check your watches. Is it ten minutes until the end of the episode? Time for Castle and Becket to have a brainstorm that solves the crime?"

"Oh, great, a *Castle* fan." Saundra grinned back at him. "My writing friends hate that show, just because this guy is a famous writer, but you never *see* him writing."

Kai proposed a Castle marathon some weekend. Before Saundra could respond, a banging came from the front door. Eden and Troy went to let the police in. Kai tapped Saundra to help him make coffee for everyone. They would be up late, just as Eden guessed, but Saundra wondered when they would have a chance to get back to assembling the chart and narrowing down the list of possible suspects.

The problem with considering everyone in the township who might have reason to be looking for the historical books, who might have wanted to help Styles find his proof or stop him, was that chances were just as good the murderer was someone from outside the township. Saundra stepped away for a moment and texted Nic. She asked if he had any leads on Styles' true identity. He didn't respond right away. When he did, she was having her turn with the responding officers, giving her perception of the break-in and how it had been discovered. She didn't read his text until she was sitting in her car, parked across the street from the side door of Book & Mug, ready to go home. Kai was standing in the doorway, backlit by the stairwell light, watching to make sure she got away safely.

Saundra didn't want to get into a phone call at that time of the night. Maybe it wasn't late, barely 10 by the time the police wrapped up the search of the building and finished talking with them, but the day certainly felt a week long by then. She drove home and waited until she was safely inside her apartment. She turned on all the lights and looked in all the rooms to make sure nothing was disturbed before she texted Nic.

Book/Mug broke into. Alarm trnd off. Apts searched.

She sent the text and went into the kitchen to put away the takeout box full of tiramisu that Kai insisted she had to take home with her. They had been so busy with the chart and playing their sleuth game, they hadn't eaten the second dessert he had ordered special. Maybe she was tired, but the fact Kai had learned how much she liked tiramisu made her feel a little teary.

Maybe she should have some? Just a little. To soothe her before she went to bed. The sugar, mascarpone, cocoa, and espresso wouldn't keep her awake. If anything, they would help calm her.

Her phone rang. Sighing, she stepped over to the table where she had dropped her purse. Of course, her phone had slid to the bottom of her purse. Of course, it was Nic calling. Didn't he get the telepathic message that she didn't want to *talk*? Shouldn't he have figured out that if she texted him, it really wasn't an emergency?

Maybe he had information on Styles? If he did, maybe she would offer him some of her tiramisu.

"Please tell me you drove and didn't walk over there," he said, before she finished saying hello.

"Yes, I drove, and I'm home already, so ..." She sighed and bit back some angry words she would feel guilty about in the morning. She should be grateful Nic was watching out for her, but if he was worried, then he had to have good reason. That meant she wasn't as safe as she thought, which raised her tension levels, and she had just started to finally relax.

Her gaze landed on a square white box sitting on top of two gray boxes just a little wider and higher than the white one, stacked on the end of her kitchen counter. The gray boxes belonged there, but the white one didn't.

It looked familiar, though.

How had she missed that when she came in and looked around? Maybe because she was looking for things that were messed up and out of place?

"Saundra? I'm ten minutes away, but I swear, if you don't answer --"

"I'm okay, but somebody was in my apartment."

"That doesn't equal okay in my book. Get out."

"Unless there's a bomb in the box, I think I'm fine. They didn't take anything." She took a deep breath. "They left me something."

"I'm on my way. Meet me downstairs." Nic hung up before she could think of a response.

Saundra knew what she would find because she recognized the box. That gave her the courage to pick up the box and move it to the living room and put it on her coffee table. She opened it and looked inside, nodded -- just what she had expected -- and went to wait by the speaker grid next to her door. Nothing could persuade her to leave the box alone and go downstairs to wait for Nic. If this was a suspense movie or novel, when she had her back turned, someone would re-enter her apartment and take the box again. Just to play with her mind. Kind of like an updated version of *Gaslight.* She wasn't taking her gaze off that box until someone else verified it was there, and its contents.

When Nic buzzed to be let in, she pressed the button that would open the inner door of the lobby, then opened her apartment door, and walked back to her sofa.

Nic didn't sound like a herd of angry elephants when he came down the hall, like other men did when they were being overly protective cavemen. Saundra felt the disturbance in the air and almost called out a teasing comment she had wanted to use for years: he had superhero powers of flight and telepathy, or at the very least really strong breath that could burn holes in walls. She didn't turn, but she held up the black book with the Cadburn family tree, so Nic saw it as he came in the door.

He shut the door and sighed with very clear exasperation as he crossed the room to settle on the couch next to her.

"If these were the books stolen on Saturday ... I think we can safely say whoever clobbered Carruthers is a friend of yours." He offered a crooked smile. "Maybe an admirer?"

"Kai wouldn't --"

"Not saying it's your caffeinated Romeo." A glitter touched his eyes and softened his smile, warming it from cold and brittle and concerned. "Someone who thinks you're pretty special."

"Someone who knows about the books and what Styles was looking for. Who can get into my apartment and Kai's building. Who can turn off the alarms there and at the library. Did you find out about the locksmith yet?"

"Our friendly neighborhood police captain is working on it. She's asked me to step back and let her weave through all the political tangles. A frustrating thing about small-town politics and grudges and history and feuds and all that fun crap. Someone who's ready to take your head off over one issue will have your back on another issue. It's not smart to bruise feelings and burn bridges. You might need those bridges for a strategic retreat later. She needs to move slowly and test the water as she goes. Test for boobytraps with each step. Asking questions of one person who wants to help could warn the wrong person, who then has time to destroy evidence. Half the historical society and people protecting the township archives are dead set against my lead suspect, the Clown Prince, at any one time. The problem --"

"The problem is that the people who are in that half keep changing places?" Saundra sighed and started to knuckle her eyes. She caught herself before she touched her face. She had touched the crumbly, dusty pages of the genealogy book. Now was not the time to get dust and who knew what ancient dirt in her eyes.

Nic left half an hour later, after they agreed on what to do. He took the books with him to have an expert look them over. If they were going to dust for fingerprints, they had to be careful not to damage the old, delicate books. One fingerprint from someone who didn't have the right to touch the books could untangle the whole mess.

Saundra wished she had offered him some of that tiramisu. Bottom line, no matter how arrogant a know-it-all Nic might be, he was looking out for her. He knew what he was doing when it came to stealth and digging out information no one wanted to relinquish.

For now, she would keep the return of the books secret. In the morning, which was much closer than her body cared to admit, she would go to work and start the work week as if it were perfectly normal, no change in her routine. Other than a Monday holiday. The question was if she could do that convincingly. If she didn't go to Book & Mug for an iced coffee on the way to work, would Kai worry and wonder? If she did go in, could she carry on a conversation with him without signaling she was hiding information?

"Oh what a tangled web," she whispered, and decided Shakespeare had only the faintest idea what he was talking about.

Okay, Lord, help me depend on You? I don't pray nearly enough. If this whole mess is intended to teach me to keep in touch more regularly ... I'm sorry, and I really hope I'm suffering exhausted brain syndrome, because that feels kind of arrogant. Just please, keep everybody else safe? And help us figure out who this mysterious friend is before someone else dies?

Chapter Sixteen

Thursday, September 8

Twila was late for work Tuesday morning. She stayed at the front desk and didn't go wandering around when no one needed to check out books. She fixed everyone with a glare and refused to speak, effectively discouraging anyone else from speaking to her, even if they were in need of help. Saundra thought she saw Twila's lips twitch a few times, and a few other times caught her wiping at her eyes. She felt sorry for Twila, until she heard the woman snarling to someone on the phone on her lunch break. Everyone was being nasty to her. Everybody who came into the library was laughing at her and making comments about her bad taste in boyfriends.

Saundra could not make herself apply the word "boyfriend" to Twila's relationship with Carruthers. It implied something young, hopeful, and positive. Besides, with the twenty feet of silence that circled the front desk, how could anyone be accused of laughing at Twila and saying things about her? At least, not in her hearing.

Saundra didn't hear from Nic about the books, or Styles' identity, or what Captain Sunderson had found out about the locksmith's records. When Kai called on Thursday to remind her of the Guzzlers meeting after work, she almost told him she couldn't make it. She didn't, though. How could she explain or excuse why she hadn't been in to visit Book & Mug since Tuesday?

Ashley Cadburn was among the mothers helping to chaperone the kindergarteners for story time that morning. Saundra felt the burn of the evil eye the woman gave her from the other side of the story circle. It totally escaped her how Daphne could be such a sweet thing, so obedient and cheerful, with such sour, critical, judgmental parents. Had something happened to drastically change and embitter Roger Cadburn when his first wife, Deirdre, died? From everything Saundra had heard about Daphne's birthmother, she had been a wonderful, sweet, giving woman. Daphne certainly took after her mother. It couldn't be all genetic, could it? Maybe Ashley had initiated the change in Roger? Maybe there were pods in the basement of the Cadburn home, and Daphne was the only human member of the family?

By the time story time ended, Saundra decided she would rather throw a few stones at the hornet's nest than keep ducking and hiding. At the very least, the nest would be down on the ground where she could throw something over it to contain the hornets, even if she did get stung.

Not a good analogy, she told herself, as she headed across the room to intercept Ashley. By this time, she didn't much care. Too bad hornets didn't die when they stung someone. However, honey worked as an antibiotic as well as healing and sealing wounds. It could soothe rashes, and in a pinch, it could trap irritating insects that needed to be smothered. Maybe that was a mixed metaphor or whatever, but hornets and bees were neighbors in the entomological charts, weren't they?

The Cadburns might have their own cache of historical documents nobody else knew about. It wouldn't be the first time founding families and community leaders had skeletons they wanted to keep firmly locked in the closets.

The woman Ashley was talking to gave Saundra what had to be a look of gratitude, maybe relief, when she approached them. Not a good sign of Ashley's mood, perhaps? Saundra had lots of practice dealing with people who thought they were "all that." She had developed a small repertoire of phrases and expressions for when she needed to defuse unpleasant situations, soothing bruised feelings without giving someone the validation they wanted.

"Ashley, I'm so glad I caught you," she began.

Not really.

"I've been involved in some research into the township's history."

"Yes, so we've heard." The corner of Ashley's mouth twisted.

Didn't she know that sneering like that brought on wrinkles five times faster than smiles? Would knowing that make her at least visibly more pleasant to be around?

"I was hoping, as the leading family -- I've heard the Cadburns referred to as the royal family, actually -- I was hoping you would have access to historical documents and records and inside information that nobody else has. The historical society," she caught a dangerous glint in Ashley's eyes, "quite frankly isn't much help. They mean well, but ... well, what can you do?" Saundra shrugged helplessly. "I think it would be a great service if we put together a detailed and accurate history of the township, giving names and little-known events. The Cadburn family was in the center of it all, so you would know better than anyone what really happened. The children would benefit tremendously from an accurate sense of their history, don't you agree?"

A little bit of the sneer relaxed. "What makes you think I would ..."

Ashley glanced around. From the corner of her eye, Saundra saw the kindergarten teacher and her aide, and other mothers, were all looking their way and seemed interested. The kindergarteners' giggles and shuffling in and out of the bathroom didn't seem to have muffled any of the confrontation. Whether or not Ashley really cared about history, she was the wife of the head trustee. From the gossip Saundra had overheard,

Ashley Cadburn was as much a political animal as her husband.

"... that I would have ready access to that kind of information?" Ashley continued. "Especially the really old records?" She sniffed and took a step back.

"Well, the Cadburns have been the leaders of the community since before the township was chartered, weren't they?" Saundra thought about using the "royal family" line again and decided against it. She hated flatterers and toadies, and certainly didn't want to sound like one.

"We have." She sniffed. "Not that I'd trust you with family records. I heard you have a nasty habit of losing important documents. Taking them out of the library without permission, then misplacing them."

"You heard wrong. If you'll tell me who is making these false accusations --"

"You have to prove they're false, first."

"Just how do you propose that? It's always harder to prove a negative."

"That's not my problem. If you want to keep your cushy job, Miss Saundra." Her voice rose half an octave, turning into a sugary sneer. "You'd better get your act together and figure out which side you need to be on." Her voice turned into a squeaky parody of a little girl. "Miss Saundra knows everything in the whole world." A snort. "Not the important things."

Ashley turned and stomped away, straight to the front desk, where Twila was waiting. Miss Tucker, the kindergarten teacher, met Saundra's gaze and shook her head, rolled her eyes, and offered what had to be an encouraging smile. Then she turned to the children gathered in the open area in front of the bathroom and spread her arms, preparing to herd everyone out of the building and back across the parking lot to the school.

Mrs. Tinderbeck came up behind Saundra and waited until the kindergarteners and their chaperones had left the library before speaking.

"Jealousy is an ugly thing. I think I should feel sorry for Ashley, who is so unsure of herself, she thinks her stepdaughter loves you more than her." With a chuckle, she patted Saundra's shoulder.

"How do two people like them end up with such a sweet little girl?" Saundra murmured.

"People wear different faces in public and in private. You know the old saying that the best defense is a good offense? Maybe Roger Cadburn feels so strongly he has to be on the *defensive* all the time, he finds it necessary to be highly *offensive* in public?"

That gave Saundra something to chew on for the rest of the day.

At 5pm, Cilla and Melba Tweed came in and asked Saundra if she was going to the Guzzlers meeting. Did she want to meet them for dinner before going? Did she need a ride home afterward? Saundra caught Twila watching the exchange. Something about the woman's sharp gaze, after three days of being caught in her own private world of self-pity, made her shudder. Maybe she was being paranoid, but Saundra wouldn't have been surprised if Ashley had asked Twila to spy on her after that little exchange about history books and township records.

Well, better to stay in the company of others, she reasoned. She accepted the invitation to dinner, and they arranged to come back in an hour to pick her up. There was a new seafood restaurant they wanted to try. They would have plenty of time to get there, eat, and come back for the Guzzlers meeting.

Nic texted her at ten minutes until 6, quitting time. He asked what she had done to upset the queen and king. Saundra muffled a chuckle and stepped into Mrs. Tinderbeck's office, which was empty, so she could text back the lengthy response without stirring up Twila's suspicions. Or worse, generate a lecture from her about tending to personal business when she was off the clock.

You're going to have car problems. Don't be afraid.

Of course, that immediately sent a prickly chill down her back.

R U the problem?

He responded with a smiley.

Saundra swallowed down a need to scream. She was half-afraid the scream would turn into laughter. Nic was planning something. Obviously. If he had sabotaged her car so she couldn't drive it, or had seen someone else sabotage it, he was still setting up a trap and using her as bait. Without asking if she had plans.

Three minutes until 6. The Tweeds struck her as extremely punctual.

Dinner plans. Back to Mug 4 meeting at 8. Spring your trap 18r.

She came out of Mrs. Tinderbeck's office in time to see Twila heading for her desk. Saundra just didn't have time for games. She cleared her throat, loudly. Twila changed course so abruptly, she nearly tripped over her own feet. Just a few moments to shut down her computer. She reassembled the makeshift lock with the rulers and bulldog clips, but left out the squeaky toy. What mattered was making Twila think something had been hidden in the desk again. Then she snatched up her purse and headed out for the night. A detour to Mrs. Tinderbeck's office to say farewell and comment she was going to the Guzzlers meeting, then she was out the door. Two minutes after 6, and the Tweeds were just pulling up.

Her phone pinged a text coming in. A winking smiley face. Saundra scolded herself to relax and enjoy the evening.

The Tweed were, in a word, adorable. Clever and full of mischief and plans for the future. They were excited about a storefront opening on the south side of the river and the possibility of opening up the candle store they had been dreaming about for what felt like years now. They admitted they had ulterior motives for asking her out to dinner. They wanted to pick her brain, as someone not entrenched in township attitudes and traditions. Did she think there was a market for candles, custom-made and specialized, large enough to make it a profitable venture?

For all their flutter and laughter and teasing, Cilla and Melba had sharp minds when it came to analyzing their needs and the pros and cons of what they wanted to do. They had done piles of research, and admitted they feared they might have gone overboard. Their heads, they claimed, were crammed so full of facts and figures and statistics, they weren't sure what to do next. That was why they wanted her input. Saundra thought about introducing the two dear, elderly, but still very lively and adventurous ladies to Aunt Cleo. She thought the three of them would get along so well, they might just strike fear into the stuck-in-the-mud population of Cadburn.

The candle talk continued through dinner and the drive back to Cadburn, and carried them until everyone had assembled in the back of Book & Mug for the meeting. Saundra decided Kai was her hero when he commented that candles would be a nice addition to the bookstore. Maybe the ladies could come up with candles that smelled like some of his specialty coffee drinks?

Most of the meeting turned into a discussion of how to capture the scent and taste of hot and cold drinks in the aroma of candles, and whether the reverse could be done. If Kai could come up with coffee and tea drinks that tasted like the scent of candles. The meeting took on a silly turn, with friendly arguments about perfume and how scent never translated into taste properly, and what kind of syrups and herbs and other flavorings to use to achieve the desired results. Saundra thought she was the only one who noticed Curtis didn't even try to participate. She was content to sit back and sip her frozen white chocolate raspberry whip and just watch and listen. She had a chance to notice.

"Are you all right?" she asked Curtis, when the meeting started to break up and the members trickled out of the coffee shop after 10. "Sorry." She reached to steady his arm, when her question seemed to startle him, and he nearly dropped the handful of mugs he was trying to take to the bus pan on the counter.

That was one thing she liked about Curtis. He was always willing to help out and look after people.

"Do you like books?" His eyes looked so big with concern, as if it were the most important question in the world. Saundra didn't know whether to hug him or laugh -- or maybe be worried.

Most of the time, Curtis just struck her as quiet and thoughtful. She didn't see him as the town dummy, as some people referred to him. She didn't think he was dimwitted or useless or a nuisance, as some people treated him. Even members of the community whom she considered good people, kind people, displayed a little bit of an unconscious attitude toward Curtis that indicated they expected him to be rather dense, slow -- stupid. A big, clumsy child to be ignored.

Fortunately, Kai, his cousins, and a handful of other people in Cadburn didn't treat Curtis that way. Saundra had seen the difference, and it put a little ache in her chest, to see how he responded to their respect and concern. She had heard several people say that Curtis would do anything for the people he considered his friends, and she believed it.

"I love books. So do you. I see you in the library all the time." She held out her hands, and Curtis thought for a moment before giving her some of his load of dirty cups and saucers and spoons. "I think you're always learning from all the things you read, and you've gone to places around the world that most of the people in this town will never see. You know things they'll never know."

"Things they'll never know." The words came out slow and low, as if he were tasting them before he said them. "Daddy told me to take good care of the books. He had to hide them. Uncle Jerome gave them to Daddy to protect, because they almost got thrown out." He sighed. "Daddy hid them good. He told me to protect them, but I couldn't. I tried."

"It's okay." She gestured with a tip of her head for him to follow her. Saundra had an image in her head of Curtis getting upset and dropping the mugs and cups and saucers without meaning to. "You tried. You did the best you could, didn't you?"

"Always."

"Then your father couldn't be disappointed in you."

Kai met her gaze as the two of them stepped up to the counter to put the dirty dishes in the bus pan. He cocked an eyebrow and tipped his head toward Curtis, questioning the frown and the trembling in the big man's bottom lip.

"They took away my keys. They didn't get all of them, but I couldn't go back and guard the books like I was supposed to. But I got the keys back. But then the books were gone." Curtis shrugged and looked back and forth between Saundra and Kai. He tried to smile. "I like you. You're good. You're smart. Daddy would have liked you. You take care of the books. Right?"

"Curtis." Kai stepped up to the counter and leaned on it, braced on his elbows. "Your father hid books ... in the walls?" He gestured around the coffee shop.

The big man's face brightened in a grin. He nodded.

"Here?" Saundra said.

Again, a nod.

"Who is Uncle Jerome? Why did he give the books to your father?"

"Oh, heck," Kai whispered. "You're talking about Jerome Cadburn?" He glanced around. The last few customers were on the other side of the coffee shop, talking in two booths, or heading out the door right then. "The prince's grandfather," he said, his voice just above a whisper.

It took Saundra a moment. She blamed the really long, stressful week and the late hour.

"Why did you call him uncle?" she asked, and rested her hand on Curtis' forearm, where it rested on the counter.

"Always did," he said with a shrug.

"Why did he give the books to your father?"

"Protect them." Another shrug.

"Probably because they held family history the next generation didn't want people to know," Kai said.

"Daddy said we had to hide the books because they proved we're family. Uncle Jerome always said we were family. He was the only one."

Saundra met Kai's gaze and the words clogged in her throat. Was Curtis saying what she thought? That his family were indeed Cadburn descendants, a line that had been discarded because they were illegitimate? If that was true, then the rumors she had been picking up, the bits and pieces she had read, were true too. Considering her few unpleasant encounters with Roger Cadburn, she found it entirely believable that he and his father had tried to destroy the books that proved who else had claims on the Cadburn estate. Claims that had been violated when the economic crash occurred and the Cadburns lost so much property. If the claims were legitimate, they had sold property they didn't have legal rights to control, to pay off their debts and avoid bankruptcy.

Money and power, she reflected, were always considered legitimate reasons for committing unspeakable crimes.

"You know we found the books your father hid, right?" Kai said.

Curtis nodded. His smile relaxed and looked a little wet. He really was just a big, overgrown kid in a lot of ways.

"You take care of them. Daddy would be glad. I wish you could have met Daddy. And Uncle Jerome. He liked coffee and books." Curtis sighed and looked around the coffee shop. "He would like this place a lot." Another sigh, and he stepped away from the counter.

"Hey, where you going, big guy?" Kai reached out as if he would stop him.

"Bathroom." He grinned and trundled around the counter, to the back hallway.

"I just had a really ... I don't want to say scary thought," Saundra said, speaking slowly and testing each word before she let it out. "Did I hear right, before? Curtis did the maintenance for the Cadburn property, and still does a lot of handyman work?"

"Yeah. He has no retirement savings, so he has to keep working. The guy is good, though. People trust him for that kind of stuff, when they don't think he has the sense to come in out of the rain."

"He helps with a lot of maintenance work in town, right? He helped with all the renovations? All the buildings that got bought up during the crash and changed over?"

"Yeah. The guy is like a genius -- what do you call them? Idiot savants? When it comes to electronics and things like that. It's all instinctive. He can't get a license or join the union because the tests and paperwork and all that is just beyond him, but I've seen him work. Sherman and the other guys who do renovations and upgrades and things, and Eden's tech guy, Rufus, they all hire him, fudge the paperwork and regulations, to let the guy make a living."

"Like ... the alarm system at the library?" Saundra gripped the front of the counter to keep her hands from trembling, and the trembling to get into her voice.

"I don't know about the library, but he -- " Kai's mouth dropped open. He took a step back and muttered a few harsh-sounding words in a language that was vaguely familiar, though Saundra couldn't place the words. She just sensed they were really angry, scorching, maybe with an element of surprise. "He helped Sherman install our basic alarm system."

"So he would know how to turn it off?"

"Why would he need to break in here?"

"To look for the books? To make sure they're safe?"

"And if he had keys for here ..." Kai shook his head. His eyes flicked from side to side, and she imagined his brain was spinning as he analyzed what they had just learned and theorized.

"Would he still have the keys to my apartment building?" she had to ask.

"He was the one they turned to for everything, over there. Even after Cadburns had to sell it. The new owners are good folks, and they know who to trust. Why?"

"I'm sorry. Nic said to keep it quiet for now -- I should have told you -- the books that got stolen from the library? Someone, I'm thinking Curtis now ..." Saundra softened her voice to a whisper. "Put the archival box in my apartment while I was here Monday."

Kai whistled low and soft. He thumped the counter with both fists, then reached under the counter and brought out a key on an oversized ring. He handed it to her and dug in his pocket for his keyring. "Go upstairs and get Eden and Troy. I think they're both home now. Tell them what we've been talking about. I'm going to wait for Curtis to get out of the bathroom and bring him up to have a long talk." He looked around. "After I lock up."

~~~~~

Saundra barely finished walking through the sequence of events for Eden and Troy, and the path of reasoning as she and Kai came to their conclusions. Kai's feet pounded on the stairs, and she had a bad feeling, just from the loudness, the frantic pace. She wasn't surprised when he came into the office, a little out of breath -- and alone.

"I was busy locking up, processing the dishwasher, but I kept an eye on the hallway. He just slipped out." He thumped the edge of the conference table where Eden, Troy and Saundra had been sitting. "The big guy probably wasn't even running away, he just gets distracted sometimes. Maybe he figured he didn't have anything else to say, so he just left."

"He does have free run of the place," Eden offered. "We've told him to consider himself family."

"We can't just let him run off, though," Troy said. "How much of a head start does he have?"

"Can't we just go to his house and talk to him?" Saundra asked.

"No guarantee he'll go home. People spot him at all hours, all over. Shrieve says they ought to make him an auxiliary cop. He notices everything. Sometimes he gets to places on foot, when there's an emergency, faster than somebody in a fire truck or a patrol car."

"Curtis likes to help everybody," she murmured.

"He protects his friends," Eden said, enunciating carefully.

For some odd reason, that sent another chill up Saundra's spine.

"Are you thinking ..." Troy gestured upstairs.

"Heck, heck, heck." Kai finally dropped into the nearest chair with a loud crash, and muttered more of those vaguely familiar, harsh words. "You think he's the voice I heard arguing with Styles?"

"He wouldn't think about the danger to himself," Eden said. "He'd just see someone pointing a gun at his friend -- someone who treats him like family -- and jump in to defend him."

Saundra shuddered, envisioning that night Kai had described to her. The two dark forms struggling, falling down the fire escape, then going over the edge, to hit the sidewalk. One big, dark shape getting up off Styles, whose body had cushioned his fall, and staggering away. Did Curtis even know that he had, perhaps unintentionally, killed Styles that night?

"We need to find him," Kai said.

"Should we bring in the police?" Troy's face crinkled as he said it, very clearly not wanting to do just that.

"I'll call Nic," Saundra said. "He's ... he's good at this kind of stuff. Then maybe we should go out, look around? For all we know, he's up on the roof, enjoying the weather."

"We have to keep her," Eden said with a smile.

Curtis wasn't on the roof. Troy ran up quickly to check. He spent a few minutes walking around the roof, looking over the sides, trying to spot Curtis on the streets around the building. Saundra reflected that it was a good thing the Mug Building was one of the tallest buildings in town, and the downtown area was relatively small.

She called Nic before they headed out to look around on foot. Naturally, he didn't answer. Saundra was actually grateful to have to leave a message. She outlined what they had theorized and why it was important to find Curtis and talk to him before getting the authorities involved. The last thing she wanted was to have Kai and Eden and Troy listening while Nic questioned her and dug more details out of her.

The cousins split up, going different directions, heading for the three most likely places for Curtis to hang out after dark. To the Metroparks building down by the river shallows. He liked to wade in the water. To the town park, to sit in the gazebo or lie in the grass to look up at the stars. To the woods beyond the library. He had been known to spend a lot of time in those places. Hearing that detail now made Saundra shudder. It made so much sense that Curtis had clobbered Carruthers, maybe just because he had gone after Saundra the day before. Curtis was loyal to his friends. His brain worked along simple lines, making everything black and white. The question was what he considered black, and what he considered white, and how he would react when so very many things were turning gray.

Saundra went to get her car, to drive around the perimeter of the downtown area, and then drive to the apartment building where Curtis lived. It was the second apartment complex the Cadburns had lost, overlooking the river on the south bank. She hated to acknowledge the shiver of relief that Curtis didn't live in her apartment complex. Bad enough knowing he still had keys to get in many places in town.

"Oh, come on," she muttered, as she got within sight of the library parking lot and saw her car sitting there all by itself, just on the edge of the puddle of light. Of course, she forgot about the trap Nic had set up until just now.

Had he set up a trap, or was he taking advantage of the trap someone else had set for her? No way in the world was she going a single step closer to that car until she had talked to Nic. He hadn't called her back yet. Dilemma: make the call here, safe in the circle of light on the street corner, or walk back to Book & Mug and hope she ran into one of the cousins? Saundra knew better than to venture anywhere alone. That was what idiots with targets painted on their foreheads, wearing "please kill me" signs in horror movies did. She wasn't one of them. She knew all the rules for surviving horror movies or slasher films.

Saundra dug her phone out of her purse and called up Nic's number in her address book as she turned around.

Roger Cadburn stepped out of the shadows with a gun pointed at her, and a genial, smug sort of smile lighting his face. The kind of smile she imagined he wore when he won another argument or pushed through some legislation or measure in a trustees meeting, and overpowered everyone who stood against him.

The arrogant creep just stood there, smiling. Probably waiting for her to burst out in tears or shriek in fear, or maybe go to her knees and beg for her life?

No way was she giving that jerk the satisfaction.

"Put it away," he said. His smile faded a little. Probably because she didn't scream or faint or pee her pants in terror.

"Put what away?" Yes, she was a little scared, focused more on that gun than anything else.

Wait a minute. That gun didn't look right.

Not that she was an expert, but --

"The phone." He waved the gun closer to her. The light gleamed softly on the black surface. The muzzle seemed wrong.

Saundra looked down at her hand. She still held the phone. Her finger was next to the circle to press to dial Nic.

"Put it away," Cadburn repeated.

"What do you want?" She slowly lowered her hand and turned it enough to hide the movement as she slid her finger over the spot to dial Nic's number.

"Besides keeping your nose out of my business? Can't have that, but I'll settle for those books you stole." He waved the gun at her again as he stepped closer.

"I didn't steal any." She choked as one detail leaped out at her. The muzzle of that short, black gun was closed.

No wonder the light didn't look right -- that was a black plastic squirt gun he was waving at her!

"Don't lie to --"

Horns blared through the night quiet, the musical signature for *The Avengers*. Cadburn cursed and turned around, waving the gun. Saundra choked back a giggle that was half-hysterical and turned to run. Nic was going to show up any second now. That was the ringtone he had assigned to her on his phone. He had taken great delight in letting her know.

A dark shape let out a muffled roar of fury and dropped from the fire escape directly overhead to smash Cadburn into the sidewalk. Curtis knelt on the man's backside and raised his big hands in fists and smashed them down on his back. Cadburn yelped, the sound cut off with the air knocked out of him.

"Curtis!" Allen Kenward dashed out of the shadows across the street, followed by Nic. "It's okay, we got him. Hey, big guy, it's okay!"

"He was gonna hurt Miss Saundra!" Curtis wailed.

"Calm him down." Nic gestured to Saundra.

For a moment, she gaped, while Allen and Nic struggled to get Curtis off Cadburn's back. Curtis kept pounding, and Cadburn let out gasps and yelps, and then begged for someone to save him.

She wasn't sure how she did it. Everything happened in a blur, but she caught hold of Curtis' arm and nearly got knocked off her feet as she shouted his name. Allen told Curtis he was going to hurt her. Somehow that got through to him. Saundra tugged and kept saying his name, until Curtis slumped and rolled off Cadburn's back. He sounded so pitiful as he pleaded for her to be okay. Saundra nearly teared up as she assured him, over and over, that yes, she was all right. He had stopped the bad man.

Someone needed to stop the bad man's ugly mouth. Cadburn glibly ignored the fact that he had threatened her with a gun in front of witnesses. Forget the fact the loser had used a squirt gun. One of those witnesses was a police officer. He shouted insults at her, at Nic, at Curtis, at Allen, threatening his job, when he found himself hauled to his feet, his arms were pulled back, and handcuffs slapped on his wrists behind his back. He continued shouting threats as the four marched him up the street, heading for the police station. Allen and Nic took tight grips on Cadburn's arms. Saundra led Curtis by the hand, continuing to assure him she was all right. He blubbered and promised he would take care of her because she was a nice lady and she loved books and she was friends with Kai, and Kai liked her more than anybody.

~~~~~

The force of Curtis landing on Cadburn resulted in twelve stitches in his face and two broken ribs. He denied that he had threatened Saundra, or that he had stuck roofing nails in three of her tires, or that he had lain in wait for her to come back from dinner. He had complained to Carruthers and several supporters, by phone, leaving messages the police were able to retrieve later, about how unreliable Saundra was. She was the rude one, making him wait so long to ambush her and take her somewhere to threaten her until she turned over the books and kept her mouth shut. Saundra wondered later, when she heard the details, if he had left those messages because the people he called didn't want to talk to him, and let his calls go to voicemail. Even his wife. She could understand Carruthers refusing to answer Cadburn's call, after the way the trustee had treated him, essentially throwing him under the bus. The others? That was cold.

Allen and Nic recorded the entire confrontation with the squirt gun on their smartphones. They had been lying in wait the whole time, watching from the roof of the building, directly over Cadburn's realty office, which gave a convenient view of the library parking lot. He had left the windows open as he kept watch on Saundra's car. They had heard all his phone calls, and got to work ahead of time, requesting access to those call records. Obviously, he had no idea how clearly sound carried on warm night air.

Dealing with Curtis was a far stickier problem than maneuvering around the political fallout from arresting the head township trustee. Saundra cried a little, when Captain Sunderson and Allen finally made the big, gentle man understand that he had done a bad thing, even if he didn't mean to. He and Jacob Styles had gone where they had no business being, even if he did have keys. Curtis looked so sad when he explained that he wanted to ask Kai about the books, but Styles wouldn't let him. The other man had insisted they had to look when nobody knew they were there. Curtis wept and insisted he had to go to jail, when he finally understood that Styles wasn't angry with him and ignoring his phone calls, but he was dead, and it was Curtis' fault. When Nic escorted Saundra out of the police station at nearly 1am, Curtis was sitting in a jail cell, the door unlocked, rocking on his cot and insisting he didn't mean to, but he was a bad man, and Daddy would be so sad.

Friday, September 9

Saundra overslept Friday morning. She wasn't sure how that happened. She had showered and climbed into bed, positive she wouldn't sleep at all, settled in to do a lot of praying, thanking God for all the close calls and answers, then she opened her eyes to broad daylight. She was late for work, even though she drove and all the traffic was in her favor. More than anything, she wanted to stop in at Book & Mug, not for a double espresso with cream and three shots of chocolate and two of caramel, but to check on Kai and Eden and Troy. She barely noticed that Twila wasn't waiting like a vulture at the front desk as she dashed into the library. Saundra hurried to Mrs. Tinderbeck's office, to apologize. She found Kai there, sitting in the visitor's chair, as she skidded to a halt in the doorway.

"There you are, dear." Mrs. Tinderbeck shook her head. "Kai just now finished explaining all the excitement you had last night. I suppose it's too late to call, but you deserve the day off."

"I do?" She laughed a little, realizing how stupid that sounded.

"Will this help?" Kai leaned over and picked up a takeout tray from the floor on the other side of the chair. He held out an extra-tall plastic takeout cup with a dome for frozen whipped cream drizzled with chocolate syrup. Saundra nearly scratched him as she snatched it. She had skipped breakfast and her stomach pinched at the thought of all the sugar and fat in the decadent drink.

After her first ecstatic suck on the straw, she saw the half-emptied cup in front of Mrs. Tinderbeck, and a matching one in front of Kai. "My hero." Her throat ached slightly from the frozen, creamy indulgence. "Always prepared."

"Eh, I try." He shrugged and got out of his seat. "I think you need this, and I need to get back to work."

"How are all of you?" She clutched her cup, when she wanted to grab him by his shoulders and look into his big, dark eyes until she could be sure everything was all right. Last night had been more painful surprises for him and his cousins than it had been danger for her. Someone they trusted, someone they loved, was a murderer. It didn't matter that Curtis had done what he did to protect them or that Styles' death was, in the final analysis, accidental. Curtis was so torn up over what he had done. How could anybody win in a situation like that? Where was the justice?

"Sometimes justice is impossible," Mrs. Tinderbeck said a short time later, when Saundra shared her thoughts with her.

Out in the library, Twila sounded especially nasal as she scolded someone for being a day late returning their books. The tenth graders were due for book discussion time in twenty minutes. The world was starting to settle back into the Friday routine. Fortunately.

"All we can do is be happy with having the truth revealed and some mysteries cleared up. And a few solutions to several uncomfortable problems." She leaned back in her chair. "What do you say to giving all those troublesome documents to people better suited to handle them?"

"The FBI?"

"No, dear." The elderly woman chuckled. "The preservation specialists at the Western Reserve Historical Society. Let them determine if there are any descendants of Silas Cadburn remaining. If Jacob Styles is ever identified, and his real name found, then others with more authority and legal understanding can determine if his family has a legal claim. Let's just get rid of those books and wash our hands of the mess, once and for all. What do you say?"

"Mrs. T, you are a genius."

END

ABOUT THE AUTHOR

On the road to publication, Michelle fell into fandom in college and has 40+ stories in various SF and fantasy universes. She has a bunch of useless degrees in theater, English, film/communication, and writing. Even worse, she has over 100 books and novellas with multiple small presses, in science fiction and fantasy, YA, suspense, women's fiction, and sub-genres of romance.

Her official launch into publishing came with winning first place in the Writers of the Future contest in 1990. She was a finalist in the EPIC Awards competition multiple times, winning with *Lorien* in 2006 and *The Meruk Episodes, I-V,* in 2010, and was a finalist in the Realm Awards competition, in conjunction with the Realm Makers convention.

Her training includes the Institute for Children's Literature; proofreading at an advertising agency; and working at a community newspaper. She is a tea snob and freelance edits for a living (MichelleLevigne@gmail.com for info/rates), but only enough to give her time to write. Her newest crime against the literary world is to be co-managing editor at Mt. Zion Ridge Press and launching the publishing co-op, Ye Olde Dragon Books. Be afraid … be very afraid.

www.Mlevigne.com
www.MichelleLevigne.blogspot.com
www.YeOldeDragonBooks.com
www.MtZionRidgePress.com
@MichelleLevigne

Look for Michelle's Goodreads groups:
Guardians of Neighborlee
Voyages of the AFV Defender
Neighborlee Streets

NEWSLETTER:
Want to learn about upcoming books, book launch parties, inside
information, and cover reveals?
Go to Michelle's website or blog to sign up.

Also by Michelle L. Levigne

Guardians of the Time Stream: 4-book Steampunk series
The Match Girls: Humorous inspirational romance series starting
    with **A Match (Not) Made in Heaven**
Sarai's Journey: A 2-book biblical fiction series
Tabor Heights: 20-book inspirational small town romance series.
Quarry Hall: 11-book women's fiction/suspense series
For Sale: Wedding Dress. Never Used: inspirational romance
Crooked Creek: Fun Fables About Critters and Kids: Children's
    short stories.
Do Yourself a Favor: Tips and Quips on the Writing Life. A book of
    writing advice.
To Eternity (and beyond): *Writing Spec Fic Good for Your Soul.* A
    book defending speculative fiction.
Killing His Alter-Ego: contemporary romance/suspense, taking
    place in fandom.
The Commonwealth Universe: SF series, 25 books and growing
The Hunt: 5-book YA fantasy series
Faxinor: Fantasy series, 4 books and growing
Wildvine: Fantasy series, 14 books when all released
Neighborlee: Humorous fantasy series
Zygradon: 5-book Arthurian fantasy series
AFV Defender: SF adventure series
Young Defenders: Middle Grade SF series, spin-off of *AFV Defender*
Magic to Spare: Fantasy series
Book & Mug Mysteries: cozy mystery series
Quest for the Crescent Moon: fantasy series starting in 2022

CPSIA information can be obtained
at www.ICGtesting.com
Printed in the USA
LVHW041755230322
714085LV00008B/1085